KURT RUSSELL • WILLIAM BALDWIN • SCOTT GLENN
JENNIFER JASON LEIGH • REBECCA DeMORNAY
DONALD SUTHERLAND AND ROBERT DE NIRO

Silently behind
a door, it waits.

One breath of oxygen
and it explodes
in a deadly rage.

In that instant
it can create a hero...
or cover a secret.

A RON HOWARD FILM

B A C K D R A F T

IMAGINE ENTERTAINMENT PRESENTS
A TRILOGY ENTERTAINMENT GROUP/BRIAN GRAZER PRODUCTION
"BACKDRAFT"

MUSIC BY HANS ZIMMER ASSOCIATE PRODUCER TODD HALLOWELL CO-PRODUCER LARRY DeWAAY
EXECUTIVE PRODUCERS BRIAN GRAZER AND RAFFAELLA DeLAURENTIIS
FILM EDITORS DANIEL HANLEY MICHAEL HILL PRODUCTION DESIGNER ALBERT BRENNER
DIRECTOR OF PHOTOGRAPHY MIKAEL SALOMON, A.S.C. WRITTEN BY GREGORY WIDEN
PRODUCED BY RICHARD LEWIS PEN DENSHAM JOHN WATSON
DIRECTED BY RON HOWARD

 DOLBY STEREO A UNIVERSAL RELEASE UNIVERSAL
©1990 UNIVERSAL CITY STUDIOS, INC.

COMING THIS SUMMER

BACKDRAFT

a novel by Kirk Mitchell
based on a screenplay by Gregory Widen

BERKLEY BOOKS, NEW YORK

BACKDRAFT

A Berkley Book / published by arrangement with
MCA Publishing Rights, a Division of MCA, Inc.

PRINTING HISTORY
Berkley edition / May 1991

ISBN: 0-425-12879-2

A BERKLEY BOOK® TM 757.375
Berkley Books are published by The Berkley Publishing Group,
200 Madison Avenue, New York, New York 10016.
The name ''Berkley'' and the ''B'' logo
are trademarks belonging to Berkley Publishing Corporation.

PRINTED IN THE UNITED STATES OF AMERICA

10 9 8 7 6 5 4 3 2 1

BACKDRAFT

· 1 ·

It always begins with his brother Stephen saying, "You're doing it wrong." Stephen holds the flashlight. Bigger, stronger, infinitely more competent, he always holds the flashlight.

He sweeps the beam around the cramped darkness that smells of stale perspiration and the smoke of fires long dead. White reflective stripes leap out from black turnout coats. A dozen helmets painted an anxious yellow. [Like huge Amazonian beetles that had crawled up the walls to hibernate.] "You're doing it—"

"Shut up," Brian hears his child voice say. The resentment is strong. Even back then, it was strong.

"Wrong, wrong, wrong." Stephen's fingers start to close the snap fasteners, but Brian brushes them away. He will do it himself. Eventually.

"It doesn't go like that," Stephen goes on.

"Yes, it does."

"No, it doesn't. *Honest*."

The word pricks Brian, makes him glance up from the coat-front. He struggles to bring Stephen's twelve-year-old face into focus. But he can't, of course. The past fogs over everything except the disastrous.

Only deaths are recalled perfectly.

"Who asked you?" Brian hears himself ask. A soprano snarl. He is seven years old again. Three feet eleven inches. Sixty pounds. But another part of him realizes that the side of his face is pressed against cold auto glass in the far future. Through it comes the rumble of a diesel tractor, other sounds of a busy highway. But behind his closed eyes he is seven again and Stephen is saying, "If you do it like that it'll open in the fire."

"It'll not."

"Yes, it will—and you'll get burned. You'll die. Just like . . ." Stephen names a name. It seems familiar, but Brian can't quite make it out. He won't remember it when he opens his eyes. No matter. The best part is coming. Warm anticipation washes over him.

"You'll die," Stephen insists again, trying to crush that kernel of good feeling.

A door slowly opens. A dazzle of light leaks around the edges.

Brian turns, smiling already.

A fire fighter stands in the doorway, backlit by something more blinding, more eerie than daylight. He is improbably tall. He has a well-defined face, but it is black and white and glossy like the face in a photograph.

"Who's going to die?" the fireman asks.

"Brian, Dad," Stephen says. "He's not doing it right. He never does."

Brian is transfixed by the image of his father stooping before him. He starts to throw his arms around the muscular neck, but then stops.

Trying the impossible will only awaken him.

The sounds of another tractor-trailer outside. Should he go ahead and wake up? No, not yet. Best to see it through. The sadness will fade more quickly that way.

"Let's have a look here," his father says.

Brian steps forward, trailing half the coat behind him like a bridal gown. The tops of the fireboots he wears come six inches higher than his knees. He hates his own galoshes, but these are wonderful and brave boots. Giants walk in these boots.

His father releases the fasteners one by one, straightens the skewed coat-front, then begins closing the snaps again.

He closes his eyes, feeling his father's fingers at work. The realness of his touch is overwhelming. An anguished murmur from deep inside his throat.

"What's that?" his father asks.

"Nothing." Adult voice.

"Your brother's got a point."

Brian winces, but says nothing.

"If you don't fasten these right," his father goes on, "they could pop open and you'd get burned."

Stephen butts in. "And die!"

What comes next is not true. It was never said that day. Yet, it seems as true as all the rest, especially the ending.

Brian asks, "You wouldn't leave us, would you, Dad? Mom and us?"

A look of concern. "What's this about?"

Brian aches to say, but can't—not without messing up the chronology. The sacroscant chronology. He has a duty toward it, even though he is powerless to reverse anything.

"McCaffreys are smarter than fire." His father rises. "How about lunch, fellas?"

"Fireman shit?" Stephen asks.

"What's with the mouth?"

"Sorry, Dad."

"Where'd you grow up, a pool hall?"

"Firehouse."

"Cute."

Brian stiffens, and his face squirms against the clammy glass. He knows exactly what is coming next. The alarm Klaxon. He wants to awaken, but then it is too late: the Klaxon begins barking, echoing against the brick walls of the station house.

"Never fails," his father sighs.

Adcox appears out of the misty fringes, waving the dispatch card like a winning lottery ticket. A young Adcox.

3

The same hard, angular face but with fewer lines etched in it. The lines that would start sprouting soon. From loss. Sadness.

"Big deal?" his father.

"Medium deal," Adcox says, tousling Stephen's hair.

Brian freezes as his father slowly turns toward him.

The moment of decision is coming.

The universe grinds to a halt.

"Want to come along, Brian? Watch the old man earn his keep?"

He murmurs a no, but it is drowned out by his own seven-year-old voice, overjoyed, unknowing, more eager than he will be about anything again, and then by Stephen complaining that this is the greatest injustice the world has ever known.

"You've come along lots of times, Stephen. Give your little brother a chance."

"No," Brian whispers, but then his father scoops him up and tosses him headfirst inside the cab of Engine Seventeen.

He rights himself on the bench seat, sits, begins rolling up the cuffs to the turnout coat he still has on. The boots dropped off when his father picked him up. He does not feel complete.

He will never feel complete again.

The engineer gets in behind the wheel, and the diesel coughs to life. A crunch of gears. The engineer turns and asks, grinning, "How many damn McCaffreys does Chicago got on the payroll?"

His father jumps in next, and then Adcox. The engine is already rolling through the door and out onto the apron. "Hit the button, Brian," his father says.

He reaches out with the toe of his sneaker and presses the chrome knob on the floorboard. The siren moans up to speed. Red spangles play across the front of the station.

The engine pulls out onto the street.

Brian looks back. Stephen is standing at the open door, forlorn.

"Be grateful," Brian murmurs.

4

"What's that, Bri?" Adcox asks.

"Nothing, Axe."

"You loving this?"

"No," Brian says in his adult voice. "I want to go back. We can still turn around and go back. Have lunch and be together always instead of—"

"You bet you do," Adcox says brightly. "It's in your blood."

They come to the first intersection. The signal is against them. His father holds him back, protectively, until the engineer has stitched through the maze of stopped cars.

Brian watches the reflection of the engine skitter across the department store windows, its emergency lights and colors dimmer than usual, the truck looking like the ghost of a truck. Pedestrians gape. Children do something he would never do: cup their hands over their ears.

"Dad . . . ?" Again Brian tries to warn him. Impossible, but he must try. "Dad, I don't think we should go on."

But his father doesn't hear. He is joking about something with Adcox.

A haze of smoke is visible down the block.

Brian sits back. Too late.

The engineer radios in the arrival. Brian peers up through the windshield at the thin streams of gray smoke sifting from the second story of the commercial block, a level of apartments above the storefronts.

"Medium deal," Adcox repeats, getting out.

"Stay near the truck," his father warns Brian as he starts to bail out of the cab. But then he winks. "Keep an eye out for us, okay? We're shorthanded today."

"As fucking usual," Adcox says.

Brian's father kids him for having built up twenty years of vinegar after only eighteen months on the job. "Why all this goddamn anger, Axe?" Then, together, they drag a hoseline up the front steps and through a doorway. They vanish into the gloom beyond. The hose continues to snake in after them.

Brian climbs down from the cab.

"Don't stray too far, little man," the engineer says from his panel of gauges.

The smoke has darkened and thickened. It is now like black cotton gushing from the roof vents. It hisses as it unravels above Brian's head.

He stands with his hands thrust into the pockets of the turnout coat, staring open-mouthed up at the second story. As he watches, a window glides opens, and his father steps out onto the fire escape. Adcox is right behind him. They pause, side by side, and gaze across a thirty-foot drop-off at the next window balcony as if its rusted iron bars were a mile away. They study the window itself; lazy smoke is seeping from the cracks between the panes and the frame, as if the fire were crouched behind the darkly stained glass, waiting for them.

Adcox shrugs. Natural caution.

But Brian's father climbs up onto the fire escape railing. He rests the head of his axe against the wall for balance, then leaps.

His coat spreads against the sky like a cape.

"Jesus, Dennis!" the engineer says.

Brian says nothing.

His father lands on his knees, hard, but bounds up again, unhurt. He is beyond injury at this point. He smashes in the window with his axe, reams the glass splinters out of the sash, then dives into the smoke.

"Somebody ladder that balcony!" Adcox cries from the fire escape. "And hit another alarm!"

A ground ladder rises to the window, and a fireman scurries up just in time to take a choking, soot-covered little girl from Brian's father. A flashbulb ignites. Brian turns. The photographer from the *Tribune*. In another few seconds he and this man in a fedora will be linked together forever: Pulitzer Prize winner and subject.

"Go away," Brian murmurs.

The photographer doesn't hear. The shot of the rescue is not enough. He wants more. Spent flashbulbs shatter on the sidewalk.

Brian looks up again.

6

His father is grinning down at him. Triumphant. His second son has witnessed his finest moment. What else in life could possibly top this? Does he wish that Stephen were here instead? No, his wink says otherwise.

Brian is filled with desperate love. Yet, that love makes him feel all the more helpless.

And the ending begins.

A crack appears in the awning twenty feet down the roofline from his father. A sickly, malevolent tongue of flame slinks out. It brightens, moves along the roof, pausing here and there as if to gather strength for the last few feet of its stealthy advance. It is beautiful.

No one but Brian notices. The engineer is watching his gauges. Two laddermen are helping the little girl into the back of an ambulance. A ventilation crew is cutting a hole in the roof. A chain saw whines.

Brian can see his father inside the apartment once again. He and Adcox are probing the ceiling with pike poles, searching for the flame that is slowly working toward them, unseen.

Brian tries to shout. Nothing comes out of his mouth.

He stirs slightly. Time to wake up. His head rocks sorely on his neck, but then his chin comes to rest against his breastbone.

Must see it through. Less sadness that way.

His father finally sees the flame. Too late to do anything except throw a flying tackle at Adcox, drive him out into the hallway. His helmet comes off, and Brian has a final glimpse of the back of his father's head. Exactly like Stephen's. Same shape. Same thick hair.

He feels the explosion pass through his body before he hears it. A clap that leaves his ears hurting. Shards of glass and bits of plaster dance around him, but before they stop falling he finds himself wrapped tightly in the engineer's arms.

A helmet has come to rest on the sidewalk. It rocks like a tortoise struggling to right itself. Lt. McCaffrey, the printing on the neck guard reads.

"Jesus," the engineer says, trying to cover Brian's eyes with his glove.

7

But Brian breaks free of him and goes for the helmet. His father will want it back. He holds it as he stares up at the blasted-out window. No fire. Not even much smoke now.

He waits for his father to show himself again, to wink down at him.

After a few moments, he tires of holding the heavy helmet and puts it on.

A flash.

The photographer has taken his picture. *The* picture. It will make the cover of *Life*. It will make him a symbol of bereavement to the entire world. Yet, in the split second as the shutter clicks, he does not know that he is bereaved.

That comes now as Adcox bursts from the door, sobbing. Terrifying—to see a grown man cry. He kneels clumsily and kisses Brian again and again.

The kisses feel like pinpricks.

Brian awoke.

"Ouch." He had a monstrously stiff neck.

The windows to his BMW were fogged over but shone grayly with first light. He rubbed a circle in the windshield with his palm and looked out in mild surprise on a picnic table covered with an inch of wet snow. It hadn't been snowing last night when he had finally pulled over, exhausted, immune to caffeine, twelve hundred almost continuous miles of driving behind him since Fort Lauderdale. It had almost seemed balmy late last night.

He stepped outside. Cold. Trucks were coming and going from the rest stop, their rear duals leaving black swaths in the slush. Mostly Illinois plates. He gazed down the interstate to a snow-dusted sign:

Champaign   13
Chicago   151

Leave, the child voice warned him. Turn around and leave before it is too late. One hundred and fifty-one miles more, and it will be too late.

He stood in the cold, listening.

8

• 2 •

Interstate 57 cut north over frosted prairie. The sky was like oil smoke. Brian kept to the right lane. He slumped over the wheel, half-dozing, trying to save something for his three o'clock appointment. Trucks passed at seventy and sprayed his windshield with salty slush, but he used his wipers sparingly. Looking through the glazed windshield was a little like wearing an ash-coated facemask in a smoky corridor. Get back in the groove, he coached himself. Find the goal again. Cling to it. Visualize the confrontation and slash through it. Win.

Kankakee came ever closer, according to the mileage signs.

"What d'you think?" he asked the plastic hula girl affixed to the dashboard.

She rocked out a no. At least what he took to be a no. He frowned. "That's what I think too. They'll understand. Not today."

The tires thumped over a tarred crack in the pavement, and the hula girl spun around, showing him the logo on her back:

He drove past the first Kankakee exit.

No use putting the day in a tailspin. He had worlds to conquer. Promises to keep.

Yet, two miles later, he jerked the wheel to the right and took the second exit. He went through town, then continued north along the old state highway, out into fallow, tan-and-white farmland again. A patch of black ice gave him a floating sensation.

He glanced in his rearview mirror.

An Illinois trooper had sneaked up on his rear bumper. The cop was visibly mulling the situation over. Was the rattly 1974 BMW smoking too much? Was the driver with two-days growth seedy looking enough to roust and run for warrants? But then he overtook Brian—without using his turn signal like a good scout—and cruised on after bigger prey.

Brian relaxed, leaned over the wheel again. Whistled an Irish folk tune.

He could sense Chicago ahead: big, grimy, too much humanity in one place. He would have to find a studio apartment. First and last month's rent. References. Get a new driver's license. Would those Florida parking warrants show up on the Illinois computer?

Then he saw it a mile ahead: a crop of granite and marble dark against last night's dusting of snow. He began to slow, reconstructing those two days long ago. The first had been in summer, with uniforms and fire engines everywhere. The second had been in November, with the grass brown and threadbare. No uniforms, except for Adcox in dress blues and white gloves.

"Come back some other day," he told himself as he neared the big wrought-iron gates. He hoped that they would be locked.

But they weren't.

He started to turn, but then swerved back into his lane

10

again. "This ain't the day." He drove on, tight-lipped. How could they ever know?

But he wasn't sure.

Suddenly he braked and pulled over to the soft white side of the highway. He growled, checked his Timex, then got out and crossed the pavement to the stone wall that enclosed the cemetery. He vaulted over, then stood looking out across the thin, unbroken layer of snow.

Problem. Their graves were marked by bronze plaques flush with the ground. Insurmountable problem today.

Relieved, he went back over the wall and jogged to his car.

His hand gripped the door handle, squeezed hard. "Shit." He let go, turned and gazed out across the graveyard again. "I don't even have any flowers."

And he wasn't about to swipe any of the plastic ones he saw sprinkled here and there against the snow. She wouldn't want stolen flowers over her; she'd thrown a fit when Stephen and he had taken an old water heater from Flaherty's Junkyard, planning to make their own fire pumper go-cart. He began going through the boxes piled across the backseat. Nothing even close to flowers. He popped the trunk lid—and saw a possibility. He realized that he would find nothing closer to a bouquet. He took it in his hand, and the Pacific coast south of Los Angeles sprang to mind, condo-encrusted bluffs, date palms. He had thought that living within earshot of the surf would be a comfort, but he had been no less restless in Laguna than in Laramie, Wyoming.

He began blowing, stopped to spit the sour taste of vinyl out of his mouth, then went on inflating.

A small palm tree crinkled and mushroomed into shape, and with it another logo, another milepost of futility, struck his eye:

Laguna Palms Jamming
Custom Surfboards

Back over the wall he went. Section E. That was all he remembered, and he didn't want to trudge all the way to the register at the gate.

He kept to the rows like a fire fighter on a ventilation team keeping to the tracings of beams showing through the tar paper of a smoldering roof. Use everything to get ready for this afternoon. Desire. They will have to see some desire this time. *This time*—the recollection of last time brought up an aftertaste of bile. It wasn't even ten o'clock, and already failure was worming up his throat.

He came into Section E and stopped. Not a trace of their markers, anywhere. He closed his eyes. He listened.

After a while, her voice welled up out of the whitened ground, mingled with the wind. She was murmuring the everyday things that had shepherded him most of the way to adulthood: put on your galoshes, go to confession, feet off the coffee table, dinner's getting cold, stop hitting.

She was here.

But he couldn't sense his father's presence.

He listened again, but heard only the stiff prairie wind being sliced by the telephone lines strung along the highway.

No, Dennis McCaffrey wasn't here. He was airborne, soaring between balconies with his coat spreading behind him like a cape.

Brian began scraping off plaques with the side of his shoe. Other names. Italian. Polish. Lithuanian. But at last:

MARY ELIZABETH McCAFFREY
1936–1975

That's right, he realized with a mild start: she had gone four years after his father, when Stephen was seventeen and he was twelve. Memory had somehow compressed those years between the deaths into six months of sickness and fear and sudden trips to the hospital in the middle of the night.

He put the little palm tree over her, propped it up with handfuls of snow.

His father's plaque was left covered. No use. He wasn't here. Soaring through the smoke.

Brian stared down. Into the ground. But then he laughed, helplessly.

"I'm sorry, Mama," he said, staring off, "but I've just put a vinyl palm tree on your grave . . . and I don't have a clue why." His eyes darkened. "I guess I'm just trying to give you something back. For fighting so hard to hang on. For Stephen and me. I'm sure it'd have been easier, a lot less pain, to slip away sooner." Tired. He realized that he was exhausted. "I was just twelve, Mama. I didn't know what pain is. I didn't . . ."

He pinched his lower lip between his teeth, then flapped his arms. Why do I insist on fucking myself over with sorrow right before a challenge? A tough afternoon is coming. I don't have to settle all scores today. I just have to clear one hurdle.

"I'm gonna try again, Mama," he concluded, scooping up the little palm tree. "Next time I'll bring you something decent. Real flowers."

He started back for his BMW.

Drizzle darkened the fluted columns fronting the Chicago Fire Department Training Academy.

Brian hesitated at the entrance, suffocating in gloom. It was no good. He was wasting his time. Making a fool of himself. But he took a breath, tried to smooth his wrinkled paisley tie, and then strode into the foyer. A drill master was barking somewhere down a waxed corridor. Blue-suited candidates were rushing to make classes. No one met his eye. Only a uniform earned you a face here. Civilians were invisible spirits from an alien and inferior world. This is where it began: the separation from that world, the gelling under intense pressure of that holy distinction between *them* and *us*.

Stop it. Don't be critical. Cost me dearly the first time here.

The gold letters on the pebbled glass read, E. J. FITZGERALD, Academy Chief.

He offered a forced grin to the secretary, hoping that she wouldn't recall his face. She looked up from her tidy desk and frowned. She remembered. "Please take a seat, Mr. McCaffrey. Chief Fitzgerald will be with you soon."

An hour passed before Brian was ushered into the inner sanctum. American, Illinois and city flags. Warm rosewood paneling. Plush burgundy-colored carpet. Framed photographs of Fitzgerald in brotherly poses with Richard Daley the elder and his paunchy minions. The Old Guard. His father had thought of them as practical men who would never cross the Fire Department.

The chief stood at the window, smoking, watching it rain. Fitzgerald was a dumpy, balding southside mick with the hunted eyes of a ward boss under federal indictment. Brian's father had disliked him, and Fitzgerald had probably heard about it. Discretion had not been one of Dennis McCaffrey's virtues.

Fitzgerald finally turned and looked Brian over. He didn't offer his hand. "This some kind of joke?" he asked, stubbing out his cigarette in an ashtray stand.

Brian focused on the man's eyes. Was Fitzgerald expecting a show of contrition—or some balls? Brian decided to bank on balls. They liked spunk, even if it was then the aim of their regimen to destroy it. "If it was a joke, sir, you'd be laughing."

Fitzgerald harrumphed, then motioned for Brian to take the leather-upholstered hot seat set in front of the desk.

Brian sat. He sensed that he was on the right track with Fitzgerald. Balls.

"You think I'm feebleminded, McCaffrey?"

Best to let that one slide. But yes, he had it on good authority that Old Eamon had been pushed upstairs to the academy for possessing less than stellar critical faculties under pressure. Fought fires with a textbook under each arm. Brian just stared back, expressionless.

"You expect I forgot you walked out of this academy six years ago? Is that it?"

"No, sir."

"Two days to go, wasn't it?"

"Yes, sir. Two days."

Fitzgerald chuckled in disbelief. "You finished your last final, changed into your civvies and just floated out of this building like a helium balloon."

Brian glanced away. Actually, he had bolted like a rabbit before a brushfire. But no arguments now. The taste of bile was seeping into his mouth. He swallowed hard. Don't make it sound like begging. "I want another chance, sir."

Silence.

He half-expected to be dismissed, but Fitzgerald lit another cigarette. A good sign. "Just one more chance?"

"Yes, sir."

"Look, everybody remembers your old man. He and I went way back together." A flat lie, but another good sign, nevertheless. "Being Dennis McCaffrey's kid, all you had to do was breathe to graduate here. Dead Hero Father Rule. But you blew us off. Me, your dad's friends, everybody. Why?" But before Brian could answer, the chief went on. "You got mental problems?"

"No, sir."

"You light in the loafers?"

"Sir?"

"Were the showers too much temptation for you?"

"No, sir. I like girls."

"You carrying too much family luggage?"

"I don't—"

"Trying to live up to your old man, and your brother now?"

Brian paused, then said carefully, "I don't think so."

"Then what happened six years ago?"

"I wasn't ready. I was just twenty-one. Didn't know what I really wanted to do."

"And now you do?"

Brian nodded. Not too much conviction. Just enough to show sincerity.

Fitzgerald leaned back in his swivel chair. "Why should I take you back?"

"If you recall, sir, my test scores were in the top—"

"I don't give a crap about your test scores. So you know the wet stuff goes on the red stuff. That doesn't tell me what kind of fireman you'll make. Maybe you could've been a good one, but you had your shot, McCaffrey. You blew it." Fitzgerald took his eyeglasses off the edge of his blotter, put them on and began going through his department traffic.

"I need another shot, sir."

"Sorry," Fitzgerald muttered, reading.

"I'm serious."

"It's out of my hands. Try again next year."

"No, it isn't out of your hands."

Fitzgerald glared at him, then pointed at the door, but Brian went on in the same dogged tone. "You would've brushed me off when I called if it was out of your hands. And if I push, you got to let me back in."

"Says who?"

"The Dead Hero Father Rule. Sir."

· 3 ·

Everything had been familiar, mechanical even, until this afternoon. Lineups, physical training, combustion and extinguishment theory, protective equipment and safety drills, knots and hitches practice, nozzles and fittings, hose loads, ladders, rescue, ventilation, overhaul, property conservation, fire protection systems, hazardous materials, communications, vehicle extrication and emergency care. He had breezed through with the highest scores in Class 322.

But now, sitting in an auditorium warmed by a crush of bodies pushing the fire code limit, sweating in blues too heavy for mid-July, he realized that he had come to the end of his own faded footprints. From this point he was staring down a fresh trail. The way seemed darker than he had expected. Full of twists. Blind alleys. Box canyons. The future was waiting to undermine any determination he showed, leave him with even less self-confidence than before; he had regarded this threat too casually. What now? He felt no eagerness to get out to his station. He didn't even feel any relief that the academy was behind him.

Leave, the child voice kept urging him. Pick out a green exit sign and start walking toward it.

He began listening to Fitzgerald, if only to shut out the inner voice. The chief had been at the podium thirteen-and-a-half minutes now, his face and bald pate bleached by the stage lights. He looked like a cadaver. "Though the world changes every day," he was saying, "some things are truly forever . . ." Diamonds, Michelin tires, an evening with an insurance salesman—Brian worked at a mental list to keep from checking his wristwatch once again. ". . . Courage. Devotion. Honor in what we do." Fitzgerald paused. "This class is a special one, for we dedicate it to the three fire fighters who have fallen this year . . ." Then he named the names. Brian had known none of them. But he knew what it was like for their families, sitting behind the mayor and the chief of chiefs on the stage in dark clothes, trying not to look self-conscious in front of the dead eyes that had been conjured by the naming of the names in public. Curiously, he felt little for them. He had the sense that this was all fading away from him, like a spent wave flowing around his ankles on its rush back into the ocean. He didn't belong here. They were asking him to make allegiances for a lifetime. Too much was being asked. Of him. Of the families of the dead.

Where was Stephen? He scanned the crowd again. Absent.

"Ladies and Gentlemen . . . ," Fitzgerald went on, and the candidates, sensing the end at long last, sat up, ". . . it is with pleasure that I certify that Candidate Class Number Three Hundred and Twenty-two, having successfully completed all academy requirements, are hereby graduated to the Chicago City Fire Department."

Welcome to nine months of probation.

The candidates rose around him, cheering.

Brian got up a moment later. He reached for his cap under the chair, but somebody seized his hand and began pumping it. "Can you believe it, man! We made it!"

"Yeah, great," Brian said. He tried to smile, but couldn't. The cold wave was still tugging at his ankles.

Leave.

The portly man standing across the darkened street from the renovated brownstone had just come to the conclusion that he was a torch. It had not been easy for him, coming face-to-face with this truth. A *frigging* torch. Scum of the earth. It left a burning sensation in his chest, a bad taste in his mouth. But he blunted the self-disgust by telling himself that he was doing this for his family. They would perish, one fiery ambush at a time, unless he did something.

Headlights slowly turned the corner and started toward him. A black-and-white, cruising. He started walking toward the patrol car, not away from it. He didn't carry a tool bag. Cops looked for people carrying things. The patrolman in the shotgun seat idly glanced at him, but the torch trusted that his face was hidden by shadow. He waved. The cop waved back, and the cruiser moved on.

The torch kept walking. He sized up the evening. Muggy and windless. Good. He wanted heavy, static air.

He made the corner, then turned back for the brownstone again, this time along the alley.

Even the back side of the place was trendy: French Quarter–style ironwork, copper flower boxes, royal-blue window awnings. A tenement rescued from urban blight by Lake Forest money homing in on a juicy tax break. The place didn't fit the neighborhood. It stood out like an orchid feeding off a dying tree. The tree was southside Chicago. His home. Dying.

He stepped up onto the gas meter to inspect a window.

The original double-hung windows had been replaced by aluminum sliders—for greater security, no doubt. He took his pen-sized flashlight from his rear trouser pocket and ran the beam over the glazing. No metal foil strips or other contact sensing alarms, as far as he could tell. A length of doweling had been lodged in the track in the hope that it would keep an intruder out.

19

He put away the flashlight, slipped on a pair of surgical gloves, then pressed the flats of his hands against the glass. He pushed upward, and the sliding panel popped out at the bottom. He set it aside.

Another inspection of the frame convinced him that it wasn't wired.

Crawling through gave him no difficulty. He was graceful for so heavy a man. A photocopying machine stood below the window, and he crouched atop its lid. Something made him pause. He reached for his flashlight again. A vinyl mat had been placed in front of the photocopier, and in the few inches between it and the machine he could see a gray wire.

He smiled to himself in the darkness.

Beneath the mat was a touch pad, a pressure-sensitive alarm. One step on it, and a couple minutes later a potbellied security guard would be shining his Kel-Lite through the windows.

Nothing on the windows, but a pad—that told him something about this evening's mark. This guy relied on his second line of defense; he preferred to confront his enemies on his own turf. "Just like a damn pencil pusher," the torch whispered.

He eased down off the copier without touching the pad and turned for a row of six file cabinets. All were locked, as expected.

He hiked up his loose-fitting denim shirt, unbuckled his belt and dropped his size forty-four trousers. Inside them was a thirty-five-inch waist and a pair of booster drawers, bulging with his fire-setting gear. Overhearing a chance remark by a cop in a doughnut shop had given him the idea of using a shoplifter's getup; it left his hands free and, unlike a toolbag, drew no attention from the beat cruisers.

He examined the lock to the first cabinet. The warded type. Piece of cake.

From the drawers he took a battery-driven drill. Lock picks were out of the question. They were burglary tools, and mere possession could land him in Cook County Jail.

In his world he could hide nothing. Trust no one but family. The bit dug into the key hole, shearing off the pins.

He yanked on the top drawer—twice, before it opened. Nothing of interest there. Tax stuff.

The second drawer held even less interest for him. IRS forms.

But his eyes widened as he ran his beam over the contents of the bottom file. Familiar acronyms. Maps of city blocks. Spreadsheets. Graphs. *Eureka*. He grunted in satisfaction. He would drill the other locks just for show. But he had what he needed.

It was time to get to the heart of his work.

After reaming the last lock, he left the photocopying cubicle and carefully threaded his way through two well-appointed offices—no more pressure pads—to the reception room. Exactly what he had hoped for: no more than a thousand cubic feet, stout masonry walls and one opening—the front door. He took a slab of putty from his booster drawers, tore off a chunk with his gloved fingers and began slapping it into the crack around the door.

Cheer up, Brian told himself, you're finally being let in on your own ticket.

He had first come down through this door into the cigarette smoke and warm gloom as a kid with his father on his days off—or Kelly Days, as they were known in fire parlance—and later at Stephen's invitation. But academy candidates, as a lesser form of life, were not allowed inside Willie's Engine House. Now the place was thronged with new probies and their dates. The double doors at the back were propped open on a small courtyard. It was ringed by high walls that were wet from the charged hose-line Willie kept for the amusement of his patrons. The preferred targets were neighborhood cats mincing along the top of the wall, but brother fire fighters were fair game as well.

The hose was being used at the moment to pin a probie against the wall.

21

Brian elbowed his way through his classmates to the bar. Willie noticed him, and his fat face broke into a hectoring grin. "I'll be damned."

"Long time no see."

"That's my line." A clubfoot had kept Willie from becoming a fireman himself, but he had consoled himself by becoming the most devoted buff in department history. In fact, he loved to explain to anyone who would listen that the term "buff" came from the buff-colored turnout coats worn by New York volunteers in the last century. He was a world-class authority on fire fighting, all of this knowledge gained secondhand. Most "wanna be's" were scorned. Hangers-on with pathetic self-esteem. Kooks who might even be good for a little arson now and again, just for the glory of pulling the box alarm. Yet, long association with firemen had given Willie the idea that he was on equal footing with them, and he felt free to dispense advice along with his drinks. His advice was usually sound, and that only irked his customers. He was a swift and accurate judge of character. But so were hookers and panhandlers.

He set a double shot of Bushmill's Irish and a Harp beer in front of Brian. He had not forgotten. Brian was touched, but not overly.

Willie began rubbing his eyes.

"What's wrong?" Brian asked, realizing as soon as he had said it that he'd been taken in.

"I don't know. Something's with the bastards. I keep seeing you in fire department blue."

"What can I say that sounds sincere?"

"You can say that it's in your blood."

"It's in my blood."

Willie had stopped grinning. "You sure this time?"

Brian stared down into his shot glass. His mind stopped tossing out words.

A lieutenant from headquarters marched in, carrying a box full of envelopes, and announced that he had the station assignments. The bar cleared as everyone jostled toward him—everyone except Brian, who remained hunched over his drinks, sipping and chasing while Willie took an index-card box off the top of the cash register.

With a knowing smile, he banged it down in front of Brian, who asked, "What's that?"

"Freebie File."

Brian shrugged that he didn't understand.

"Somebody retires or quits, goes into another line—I file his card. Your brother gave me yours. That ways, if a fireman needs something, we got a contact who might pop for a freebie, or at least give him a good deal. One hand takes care of the other, you know?"

Brian nodded. "I know." Chicago. Retail is for bumpkins. Downstaters.

Willie moistened his forefinger on his wipe rag and began flipping through the M category. He removed a total of four business cards.

Brian recognized them at once. He looked away, shook his head. The petty humiliations of coming home.

"Let's see what else was in your blood." Willie then read: "Assistant Director, Sales, Aspen Snowmobile Tours." He glanced up for an explanation.

"Aspen wasn't my kind of town," Brian said. "Nothing but gourmet grocers, espresso vendors and stuck-up movie stars trying to look Western. Only place in the country you can shoot somebody in cold blood and be forced to do a couple hundred hours of community service. While I was there, the chief of police asked for public support while he wrestled with his cocaine addiction."

"No shit?"

"No shit. I was the biggest square in town."

"That's saying something."

"Yeah."

"Did you like Laramie, Wyoming, any better?"

Brian reached over and helped himself to a handful of cocktail onions. "What's it matter?"

"Well, see, one of the guys actually wanted to vacation in Colorado with all them cokeheads and murderers, but he found out you'd quit Aspen Snowmobile Tours after only two months. Moved on.'' Willie picked up another card. ''Pioneer Pride Mobile Log Cabins.''

''Yeah, yeah.'' Brian polished off his Bushmill's in a gulp.

''A truckie from Company Forty-six was dumb enough to see merit in owning a mobile log cabin. Me myself I don't get the concept. But maybe he figured he could use it as an ice-fishing shack in winter and take it down to the Gulf Coast in winter. I don't know. But by the time he phoned, you was . . . ,'' he paused to consult another card, ''. . . assistant manager at Laguna Palms Jamming.'' He had to grin again over this one. ''Nobody here gave a fuck about surfboards, but what happened out there?''

''Sharks in that big blue pond, Willie. They must've smelled me bleeding.''

''Sharks everywhere,'' he said thoughtfully. ''And seems to me you're still bleeding.'' He regarded the last one. ''Says you were owner-manager of Brian's Sound Spectrum down in Fort Lauderdale. Your own company, even. Big step. Go under?''

''Went under,'' Brian said evenly. ''I was ahead of my time.'' Then he picked up his beer and moved out among the tables.

Tim Krizminski, the candidate he knew best, was passing out the last of the station assignment envelopes. A big-footed kid fizzing over with the joy of wearing blue Nomex, he just loved to help out. He would do fine as a firehouse maid. ''McCaff,'' he said, ''got yours here, buddy.''

They were not buddies. Brian had had an academy buddy the first go around, and no one had been more hostile toward him for quitting. ''Keep it.''

Tim was stupefied. ''Aren't you even curious?''

''Engine One-fifteen, right?''

A lithe black probie turned around in his chair. ''Who the hell you think Krizminski is? Karnak the Magician?''

Hodge or Hodgkins—Brian had already half-forgotten his name. He wanted to put the academy behind him now. Forget these people. They all knew that he had gone

24

through twice, and although his cumulative score was only two points higher this time, they felt that his success came from his being a repeater.

"Open it," Brian told Tim.

Krizminski did so. "Jesus . . . he got the One-fifteen all right. Aren't these things supposed to be sealed?"

"Hermetically," somebody offered.

"Say what!" Hodge-or-Hodgkins exclaimed. "My ass got shipped to Engine Ten. Up in Vanillaland. So quiet they roll everything they got on cigar smoke in the card room at the Elks Lodge. But Engine One-fifteen—that's a slum. Cookers every goddamn day. Who'd you bribe to get that engine, McCaffrey?"

Brian looked at him straight-on. "The captain in station assignments." He could feel the silence set up around him like concrete.

"You shitting us?"

"No," he went on matter-of-factly, "I gave him a case of Cutty Sark." This isn't being taken well. Back off.

"That's just not fair, McCaff," Tim said in a slow voice that belonged on "The Prairie Home Companion."

"There's nothing fair about drawing a slow station. You won't learn as much. Won't be promoted as fast. I just play the odds."

"What odds?" Hodge-or-Hodgkins asked.

"I studied the last lieutenant's list. Half the guys on it came from that battalion. What's that tell you?"

Hodge-or-Hodgkins didn't smile as he said, "Tells me you looking through us peons at some silver trumpets on your shirt collars."

"Nothing wrong with trumpets."

"Especially when you know how to blow your own," a voice said behind Brian.

"I got the Seventeen," Tim said. "You know anything about it?"

Brian just stared at him.

"Sure he does," somebody said after a moment. "That's his brother's engine, isn't it?"

"Good outfit," Brian said quietly, then worked his way back toward the bar.

Alan Seagrave sped toward his office in his magenta-colored Porsche. 9:17. Meigs Field by ten o'clock. Pick up the Sappington account file, try to go over it this weekend, if he could take a peek on Mackinac Island without angering Cindy. She had complained that, like other men in their fifties she had dated, he worked too much. He had no answer to that, other than the wry observation that only Herculean labor could feed her appetite for the five-star life. Yet, she was reasonably intelligent—Bryn Mawr or some debutante factory like that—and wore well enough in public for him not to have to introduce her as his niece.

It had finally dawned on poor Felix Sappington that he was under IRS surveillance. Seagrave's orders had been strict. Stay away from the Arlington Park Racetrack. Don't phone your bookie. Don't even play the lotto. No transactions over ten grand, lest they be reported to the feds. He had not told his client that he would most assuredly spend some time in federal minimum security for not having reported gambling winnings in excess of three hundred thousand dollars over the last five years. The truth would only stampede Felix to O'Hare and exile abroad.

Clients in exile tended not to settle their accounts.

Seagrave parked diagonally in front of his brownstone. Nice building. Crappy neighborhood. But he had gotten a substantial tax credit for restoring it, plus a generous grant from the National Trust. Briefly the Chicago apartment of Senator Stephen A. Douglas, or so the bronze placard next to the door attested. A local historian thought otherwise, but a paltry thousand had shut him up. So much for academic integrity.

He turned off the engine, and the purr died away.

He just sat for a few minutes.

He *was* working too much. Yet, to earn any less was to court disaster, it seemed. Always the good life, but always on the edge. Mackinac Island would restore him. The long, breeze-swept veranda of the Grand Hotel. Making love to Cindy tomorrow afternoon. After dinner, he intended to collapse, sleep at least ten hours.

Heavily now, for he had spoiled his last reserve of nervous energy with thoughts of rest, he got out of the car and trudged up the steps. He turned the key in the lock, but the door seemed to stick a little. No rain in days. Why? He pulled hard, and a faint scent of smoke tickled his nostrils just as a searing dazzle reached out for him. He felt as if he were lying flat on his back, scorched and winded, watching a rocket launch away from him.

· 4 ·

Brian sat alone at the bar, flanked by two middle-aged captains. They had dropped in for a quiet drink and been disappointed to find Willie's crawling with probies five hours out of the academy. They talked back and forth across Brian as if he weren't there, ignoring even his offer to trade stools with one of them. He didn't offer twice, and after a while he was glad to be invisible.

Dr. Willie was busy counseling an engineer whose wife was suffering from vaginal dryness following her recent hysterectomy. Old Willie had no more been a gynecologist than a fireman, but that didn't put a dent in his commanding tone as he droned on about sexual lubricants and the anatomical fundamentals of female arousal.

Maybe that's what I need, Brian thought as he guzzled Bushmill's and got progressively wasted. A sense of my own authority. Stephen had it. In spades. Their father had exuded it. Brian came close to it in bursts, but then self-doubt barked his confidence back into its hole. His sense of his own absurdity never failed him.

A distant explosion. At least five blocks away. A couple

of probies took their beers out to the sidewalk to investigate but came back inside moments later, announcing that it was nothing.

He wanted to kick himself for spouting off to Tim and Hodge-or-Hodgkins and all the others about how he had finagled an assignment to the One-fifteen. Stupid. He should have kept his mouth shut, just as he had all through the academy. The booze had been talking.

Somebody whistled lasciviously.

Then someone else shushed the whistler. Brian realized without turning that a woman—other than a female probie—had come into the place.

He waited a moment, then swung around on his stool.

She was of medium height, thin. Her slight overbite was masked by her full lips until she smiled to say hello to Willie. Frizzed blonde hair. It had once been lank, and he had preferred it that way. But more than her hair was different. Her entire bearing had changed. Solidified. She no longer projected tentativeness.

She noticed him, and he felt the color leave his face. He slumped for an instant, as if old pressures were molding him into a shape he had outgrown, then got up and went to her.

"Jennifer Marie." He didn't touch her. Taking her hand would be too little, kissing her too much.

"Brian."

"You look great." And she did.

"So you're back." She sounded a bit surprised, and then her gaze slid past his shoulder and began working the room. She had not come looking for him.

"Yeah, I'm back. Graduated from the academy today." No reaction.

"Can I buy you a drink?"

"Well, actually," she said hesitantly, "I'm looking for somebody."

He struggled to keep a blank face, although he instinctively took a step back from her. "Understood."

"What's understood?" When he didn't answer, she

smiled. "I'm working tonight, Brian. I'm supposed to meet someone from your union for my boss."

"Sounds like a pretty good job. Hitting the pubs on overtime."

"I'm on salary," she snapped. "I work for city hall now. I meet people whenever and wherever I have to."

His tone softened. "I'm sorry. Truth is—I wasn't quite ready for this."

"Me neither." A less cursory smile. "I don't see my contact. Buy me that drink?"

"Sure."

Distant sirens, and more probies filed outside to have a look. Brian led Jennifer to a table near the open back doors. It was cooler, less smoky there.

"Bicardi cocktail," he automatically told Willie, but she said she wanted a white wine with a twist this evening.

"So," he said, forging ahead, "what department you working for?"

"I'm Martin Swayzak's assistant."

His eyes widened. "The alderman?"

She nodded, then smiled at Willie, who was setting down their drinks. A politicking smile. She had developed a full arsenal of varying smiles.

His first suspicion had been ludicrous. She wasn't sleeping with a fire fighter. A smoke-eater wasn't good enough. She had hitched her wagon to the hottest candidate for mayor. The champion of fiscal responsibility who was leading the crusade to cut firehouses. But Brian tried to look pleased. "That's great, Jenny."

"It's a living."

"You still live in the neighborhood?"

"No, Lincoln Park." She didn't ask where he lived.

He sat there, stupidly hurt, afraid to say something else that she could snip off like a wilted rosebud. She was no longer even remotely interested. He was not even a closed book to her. A closed chapter. He had expected anything but this.

She took a sip of wine.

"I'm keeping you from your work," he said. A stung voice.

She frowned. "Why'd you say that?"

"I can see you've got other things on your mind."

"Yes." She held his eyes. "Like—why'd you leave the way you did?"

He was vaguely reassured by her anger. But, in a blink, they were right back where they had been six years before. It felt as if every word had irreversible consequences, as if every look could spark a bitter fight. He had said hurtful things to her, and had regretted each of them over the past years—until this moment. All at once, those things made emotional sense once again.

"It wasn't just the leaving," she pressed. "That was hard enough. It was the way. No call. No letter. Nothing. I had to find out from your brother, who didn't know himself for two weeks."

For a split second, he thought of describing the relief he had felt as he sped across Iowa toward the Rockies, eighty miles an hour and no more anxiety over losing her. He had beaten fate, the same wicked flame that had borne away his father and then his mother, to the punch. He had ended that gnawing expectation of disaster. But he could never hope to explain that to Jennifer, not without cutting her. And he was all too skillful at that.

"You were too good for me, Jennifer Marie," he said at last.

She looked away, dissatisfied.

And suddenly he was flat on his back, drenched, as if a comber had broken over him and was shoving him up the beach. Water rushed up his nose, and he gagged.

The stream died away, and Willie was ranting that he'd had enough: all the probies were kicked out until further notice. A chorus of protest.

Tim Krizminski put away the fire hose. "Jesus, Willie, I was just making sure McCaff didn't overheat on us."

Brian stared up at Jennifer. She was on her feet, clutching her purse, one sleeve soaked. He had seen the look aimed down at him before. She had worn a plaid skirt

31

and white blouse then, way back then on the hot asphalt playground at Sacred Heart. "Quit fighting, Brian McCaffrey, or I'll tell Sister Beatrice. Why're you always picking fights?"

He wiped his face with his hands, and when he glanced up again she was gone.

For six years, in Colorado snows, Wyoming wind, California surf and Florida sun, he had rehearsed a reconciliation. He had refined it so exquisitely that he had begun to fear the actual performance, and had put it off, not phoning her as soon as he got back in town. Now, in less than six minutes, it was blown forever.

But again, he felt that shameful sense of relief. And guilt.

"You all right, McCaffrey?" Willie asked.

"Yeah, sure."

"Then get out."

Willie limped off, and Tim helped Brian up. "I'm sorry as hell, McCaff. Was the little lady pissed off?"

"A long time ago."

They joined the other disgruntled probies and started for the front door. "I didn't mean to hose her." Then Tim giggled idiotically. "Not that I *hosed* her. Know what I mean?"

"I know what you mean."

"Will you apologize for me?"

"I doubt I'll get the chance."

They staggered outside. Tim looked crestfallen under the jaundicing glow of a streetlight. "That bad?"

"That bad."

"Jesus, I'm sorry as hell, McCaff."

"It wasn't you."

"You sure?"

"I'm sure."

"Because I'll go to the little lady myself and—" Tim shut his mouth.

Sirens were coming.

An engine rounded the corner, emergency lights tossing blue-and-red confetti against the storefronts. It was followed by a ladder truck, and then a rescue unit. Tim whooped and toasted the passing vehicles with his bottle of Bud. "Why, that's my cousin's company, McCaff! Come on!" He started loping down the sidewalk, but then shambled to a halt and gaped about: he had obviously forgotten where he had parked his car.

Brian grinned. "We can hop in mine."

"That's great, McCaff!"

Brian got behind the wheel of his BMW and gunned the engine while Tim scooped an empty pizza carton and several used napkins onto the floor. "My cousin's crazy," Tim said, slamming the door.

"Gregor Mendel would no doubt agree."

"What station's he with, McCaff?"

The tires chittered as Brian sped away from the curb. Far ahead, the cavalcade of engines made a right turn.

"I love this job," Tim said. Enormous conviction.

"You haven't started yet."

Tim paused, his expression thoughtful. "I mean Monday, when I start." Then he shook off any abstractions and slapped Brian's knee. "Come on, man—don't you just love it too!"

"Shut up a minute." Brian cranked down his side window and listened for the sirens. "They've turned again." He took the next right, and then a left against the light. The window he kept down; the breeeze was whispering coolly through his soaked clothes.

"Can I ask you something?" Tim said, solemn-faced all of a sudden. "Something personal?"

"I guess."

"You think a lot about your dad dying like he did? In the line and all?"

"No," Brian lied, "not anymore."

"There they are!" Tim cried, pointing down a side street at a glint of emergency lights. Brian nearly stood on the brake pedal and brought the front of the BMW around to the opposite direction in a four-wheel skid.

"Awesome," Tim said, rubbing his nose. His face had bounced off the dash. No blood. And he forgot any pain

33

he might have felt as Brian pulled alongside the cab of the aerial ladder truck. Tim rolled down his window and hung halfway out, capping his beer bottle with his thumb and shaking it. He let go a stream of fizz, catching the driver in the face.

"Dammit, Tim!" the engineer asked. "You drunk?"

"Kinda." Tim ducked back inside, and told Brian that the man was his cousin, then leaned outside again and hollered, "What you got, Duane?"

"Box alarm. Walton Avenue."

"Meet you there."

"My ass!"

"No, it's mine!" Tim plopped back down onto the front seat and said cheerfully, "This is great. First night out of the academy, and I'm going to get canned. I said we'd meet him there."

"We're there," Brian said, turning the corner onto Walton.

Embers were wafting up into the night sky. Brian followed their sparkling trail down to a brownstone, where a textbook fire attack was being mounted. The crew of the first truck company on the scene had already laddered the two front corners from the ground and was lugging a rotary saw to the roof to cut a ventilation hole. An engine company had beaten the flames back from the doorway and was getting ready to drag a line inside as soon as the building was ventilated. Dirty steam was roiling out of the doorway.

Brian parked with the windshield toward the fire.

"Just like a drive-in movie," Tim said, taking a swig of beer. "What's that, McCaff?"

"What's what?"

Tim pointed, and Brian tracked his finger to the scorched hulk of a sports car across the street. A late model Porsche, maybe. Something was lodged in the windshield. "I don't know. Let's have a look."

They got out and picked their way over a latticework of hoses to the still-smoldering car.

"Jesus Christ," Tim said, staring, sickened, "is that a kid?"

"No," Brian said, holding himself in his arms, chilled. Visual horror. Unexpected. Yet, seeing Tim so shaken steadied him a little. "They shrink when they crisp like that," Brian said as if he had come upon dozens. Then he needed an excuse to look away. Any excuse. He glanced across the street; some of the facing windows had been shattered. An explosion had driven this man through the windshield of what was probably his own car—no others were parked along this stretch of Walton.

"Pretty, ain't it?" a passing fireman said as he jogged toward the door, carrying a pike pole.

Tim couldn't answer. Brian gave out with a soft croak. "Lovely."

The corpse was in the pugilistic attitude, arms drawn up like a contender who, after the first few punches thud against him, realizes that the best he can hope for is to hang on until the bell. The fingers had been fused to the palms. Brian's mind took refuge in the theoretical. He doubted that the fire accompanying the blast had lasted long enough to contract the muscles like that. The blast had ignited the Porsche, and that intense secondary burn, fed by gasoline and molten plastics, had reduced the victim to a charred, faceless featherweight boxer.

Brian gripped Tim's upper arm, although his own hand was shaking. "You sick?"

"A little."

"Go back to my car, but don't puke inside."

"I won't." Tim walked slowly across the street, and Brian faced the brownstone again.

An engine company lieutenant was standing motionless on the sidewalk, watching him. Brian couldn't see the officer's eyes; he was in his breathing apparatus, and the facemask was coated with ash. The company number on his helmet was obscured by the same dusting. But then the man started moving toward him, and the deliberate swing of the long arms, the square set of the chest, ended all doubt.

Stephen McCaffrey took off his helmet and then his mask. Brian had a jolt: six years had left his brother's face even more like their father's. The same deep squint lines. The same laughingly critical eyes.

"Nice costume," Stephen said. "Rent it for the evening?"

Brian decided not to parry. "Naw, Fitzgerald was passing them out to any bum who could blow out a match."

A flicker of a smile. Their father's. It gave Brian an ache.

"No more baby fat in your face," Stephen went on.

"All work and no play'll do that."

"Sounded like lots of different work. How'd you get wet?"

"The hose at Willie's."

"Right." Stephen turned and said to a fireman hovering behind him, "Pull another pre-connect and take it through the back door. There's still some fire in that soffit. I'll be along in a sec." Then he eyed Brian again, hard. "So you're really gonna do it this time, huh?"

The *really* tightened Brian's jaws. "I'll make it."

"We'll see. All probies figure they're going to make it, just like all salmon figure they'll make it upstream. Lots of bears along the way think otherwise."

"Should I be taking notes?"

"Wouldn't hurt." That infuriating smile. You couldn't punch it off Stephen's face. Brian had tried once and wound up with bloody teeth.

"Thanks for coming to my graduation," Brian said. "Nice to have somebody from the family there."

"I showed for the last one. But the guest of honor didn't." Stephen started toward the breezeway that led to the rear of the brownstone. "See you around."

"Not likely."

Stephen stopped and strolled back, touched his sooty glove to Brian's cheek. "Well, you're wrong already. Where d'you think you're headed?"

"What station, you mean?"

"Yeah."

"The One-fifteen."

"Wrong."

"Bullshit." Brian took the sopping envelope from his

36

rear trouser pocket and shoved it under Stephen's nose. "Read it and weep."

Stephen ripped up the station assignment, scattered the limp pieces over the sidewalk. "Null and void."

"Fine, you ripped up my notification. Congratulations, you arrogant dick. The original still says I'm on my way to the One-fifteen."

"A new order's been cut. A copy is probably already in your P.O. box."

"Sure." Yet, Brian knew it was true. Stephen would never stoop to bluff.

"I had a long talk with Chief Fitzgerald, and we decided in the interests of brother love that maybe you shouldn't be way over on the other side of town. Fitzgerald had a talk with Captain Belt. Know him? He's in Assignments. Reasonable guy. So starting tomorrow, you're stuck with me and Engine Seventeen." He started to leave, but then turned once more. "By the way, Belt doesn't drink Cutty. He's strictly a Johnny Walker man. But his parish priest'll drink anything. He thanks you for the good father."

Brian kicked at the tatters of his assignment. "I'm doing it on my own!" he shouted after him. "You hear me!"

"You did it on your own for six years—and fell flat on your face. See you Monday morning."

Stephen rounded the back side of the brownstone and leaned against the wall. The masonry was still warm from the fire. He hadn't looked forward to seeing Brian again, and now everything he had dreaded might be true about his brother was realized. Brian was a loser. He had the lusterless eyes of a loser, and his face was full of self-ridicule. He was looking to hit bottom, not win. Stephen was surprised that Fitzgerald had let him in again, and even more surprised that academy pressures had not loosened a few bolts, opened some fissures in his faked calm.

You took care of your own in this business. Now it had fallen upon him, as family, to put Brian through another cooker, probation, and see if he rattled apart. Stephen

37

didn't want to hear from some other company that Brian had cracked and taken some good firemen down with him. The issue here was survival, not log cabins or surfboards or CD players. Failure was always total, and it couldn't be hidden behind affability, a self-conscious chuckle. Yet, Brian *was* affable, and Stephen had missed him these past years, particularly these past months.

But it was no time to reveal that. And he would have to risk Brian hating him when all was said and done.

Shoes scraped the alley pavement behind him.

Stephen stood away from the wall and watched as Don Rimgale came trudging toward him out of the darkness, a small-waisted giant carrying two large investigation cases. They looked like shaving kits at the ends of his long, hairy arms. "Had to park in Joliet for all the apparatus out front, Stevie. You guys roll everything on the southside to justify more manpower or something?"

"Evening, Don."

The arson investigator set down his cases. A broad, homely face, gentle-looking but for the slightly cunning eyes. "I saw you—holding up the goddamn building on L.T.'s pay. How's that go on the stats sheet?"

"Community support."

"Where's your fatal?"

"Out front."

"Coroner called so he can do his usual magic show—and turn evidence into dogshit?"

"Not yet."

"Good boy." Rimgale fished inside one of his cases for a flashlight, then sidled past Stephen and up the steps. "You're a damn good boy, Stevie."

Stephen followed him into the steamy darkness, sloshing through two inches of standing water. The charred walls were still hissing and crackling.

"What's this?" Rimgale asked, running his beam over a volcano of molten plastic. "Computer?"

"Xerox machine."

Rimgale grunted and inspected the exposed beams. The wood had been turned into alligator skin.

"Got a cause?" Stephen asked.

"What's the rush here?"

"No rush. Only asking."

"I just take off my socks, and you ask if I'm coming already." Rimgale took a penknife from his pocket and scratched the char on the baseboard. "Investigation is like sex, Stevie. The slower you go, the more you get out of it. You fuck like a rabbit or something?"

"I forget. It's been a while."

"Sorry I asked."

Stephen knew, from the arson module he had crammed for the captain's exam he'd just taken, that Rimgale could tell how long the wood had been exposed to flame by the depth of char. What was that formula again? Lumber ignites at 660 degrees Fahrenheit, and then at a fully involved temperature of 1400 degrees chars at the rate of an inch per forty-five minutes. Rimgale had exposed about a quarter inch of char. Eleven minutes of burn. That approximated the time between the tap-in and when Stephen's company had knocked down the flames in this room.

Rimgale lumbered on, shining his light into smoldering nooks and crannies, over the studs and joists, the whalelike skelton of a building that been bared by searing heat. He paused inside the first office. "Who we got doing business here? An accountant?"

"Right."

"Then he'd know the many financial advantages of bankruptcy arson."

"How's that work?" Stephen asked. The criminal aspects of fire had never really interested him. A sideshow.

"Usually with the help of somebody like my distant cousin Eddie." Rimgale moved into the larger office, tested the char there. Shallower. "Say a guy like this accountant has a bad habit of betting on the Cubs. Gets behind to Eddie, who tells him no problem, we'll arrange a little loan. Turns out to be a big loan. Balloon payments like the *Hindenberg*. Our accountant gets so far behind he finds himself with a new partner—Eddie's boss. Accounting ain't as profitable as it used to be, especially if you put

39

all the profits on the Cubs, so the boss suggests they sell the building to the insurance company and split the proceeds."

Stephen said, "What if the fatal out front is our accountant?"

"Well," Rimgale said, "then I'd say he didn't intend to split the proceeds." He went into the reception room.

Stephen followed again. Through the doorless, smoking entryway he could see the corpse.

But Rimgale gave it only a quick glance before giving his full attention to the room. "Now this is interesting," he said, turning completely around, surveying the walls. "Masonry. No openings except the two doors."

"So?"

"This room is a big rifle barrel, Stevie."

"Explosives, then?"

"I didn't say that."

"But arson, at least?"

"Didn't say that either." Rimgale inspected the bricks. Even at a distance of five feet Stephen could see that the spalling was limited to discoloration instead of the pitting or pockmarking caused by lingering heat.

Rimgale stooped, knee joints cracking, and scratched the wooden baseboard. Almost no charring. A flash fire in this room, and then nothing more as the flames spread through the rest of the structure. He glanced over his shoulder at Stephen and said, "Bizarre."

"*How*?" Stephen asked sharply. A twinge of irritation that the investigtator was waltzing around the obvious. It was arson.

"I don't know . . . just bizarre." Rimgale used the tip of his knife to unscrew the electrical outlet cover. He gave the inside of the plate a once-over, then examined the encrusted receptacle.

"What makes this different, Don?"

Rimgale sighed. "If we got a torch on our hands—and that's still an *if*—he's got some kind of imagination. Most firebugs got the imagination of a toaster."

Stephen looked through the doorway at the corpse.

· 5 ·

Saturday morning. Not too hot yet. Brian decided to walk. During the sleepless night, between fragments of the dream, he had made up his mind to confront Stephen at home, catch him without his silver trumpets on.

He cut across Marquette Park, dallied a few minutes to watch the blue-collar golfers chop divots in the greens and make the sand fly. "Frigging A," one of them groused, hooking a drive into an Impala carelessly parked on Seventy-first Street. Both Stephen and he had caddied here long ago. For varicosed matrons in white shorts and their bald, ill-tempered husbands. Stephen had been accused of stealing money from a locker—and fired. He had nearly gone off the deep end, having his honor impugned like that. Stephen McCaffrey did not steal. A year later, somebody drove most of the golf carts off a footbridge into a pond during the night. Brian had always suspected Stephen. His brother simply could not accept an injustice without getting his own licks in.

And I always let it slide, figuring it's my fault somehow, Brian mused.

He came into a neighborhood of shoulder-to-shoulder houses. Names of Donnelly, Croghan and Muldoon on the door-side mailboxes. The navel of the civilized world. All around were hordes of barbarians only pretending to be true Chicagoans: Germans to the north, Poles to the north-west, Italians and Jews to the west, Bohemians and Lithu-anians to the south.

McCaffrey.

Brian didn't quite believe the name on the mailbox. Stephen would never live under a roof in such need of new shingles. He checked the number. "But this is it," he whispered, turning up the walkway.

A five-year-old boy was sitting behind the porch pillar. He startled as Brian came up the steps.

"Hello there."

Nothing. But he was definitely Stephen's. That certainty raised a new and somewhat comforting possibility: his brother's censuring eyes might be genetic, not behavioral.

"You must be Sean Dennis."

The child finally blinked.

"Is that a yes?" Brian prattled on. "You don't know me because you were born when I was out West, but I'm your Uncle Brian." Another blink. Was he slow? In their brief telephone conversations over the years, Stephen had never said so, but Brian now adjusted to the off-chance: "I'm your daddy's brother." Brian knelt. "Care to shake hands?"

The boy snuffled, then wiped his nose on the back of his fist.

"Here—" Brian started to grab his hand, but he rose screaming and ran inside. The screen door slammed behind him.

An instant later Helen appeared behind the rusted mesh, looking as if she expected to find the Manson Family on her stoop. Then a dim smile. "Brian?"

He shrugged. "Just me."

"I'm sorry," she said, coming outside, giving him an airy hug. "Sean's got so timid these past months."

Somehow that pleased Brian: Stephen having a timorous

42

kid. It felt vaguely like revenge. He laughed self-consciously.

Helen had not yet invited him in.

"You look great," he said. But more gray than auburn in her hair.

"You look like . . . Brian."

She had always guarded her opinion of him, yet he had sensed disapproval at the heart of her reserve. What does your brother say about you behind your back? Nothing glowing, for sure.

"Won't you come in?" she suddenly asked as if she'd forgotten her manners. She hadn't. For some reason, she didn't want him to enter her house.

"Sure."

The inside of the house smelled different than what he recalled from having lived here while he slowly flunked out of Northwestern. That smell had stayed with him. He couldn't quite put his finger on this new one. More feminine, maybe.

"Coffee, Brian?"

"Please." He followed her into the kitchen, where Sean was cowering under the table, clinging to a leg as if a hurricane were closing in.

"Come out and say hello to your Uncle Brian," she said with crabby eyes. Bad morning, Brian surmised.

Sean raced past him and up the stairs.

Helen exhaled, but didn't apologize for him. She went on measuring out the coffee. "We'd about written you off. How long have you been back?"

"Four months . . . I guess."

She stopped spooning and just stared at him, waiting for an explanation.

"I know, I know. I've been awful busy . . ." He rapped his knuckles on the tabletop a few times. Break the mood.

"Yes?"

"I should've called." He paused again. "See, I went back to the academy. Finished it this time. I start Monday, supposedly at Engine Seventeen."

"You guys," she said softly, "you really know how to put each other through it, don't you?"

"I guess."

She sat down across from him and smiled in dismay, showing her teeth. An eyetooth had never come in, but the adjoining teeth had almost closed the space. A person of quiet imperfections. Unlike mine, Brian thought. Mine set off trip-flares, beat drums, rent billboards.

"Helen, I need your help with a little something." All at once he felt as if he were asking to borrow money, and she looked for a moment as if that was what she expected. Didn't he still owe them five hundred? He glanced up the stairwell toward the master bedroom door. It was shut. "Stephen's got it in his head I ought to be at Seventeen."

"You don't want your dad's old station?"

He hesitated. She was on to something there, maybe, but he still felt that Stephen was the real issue. "No, the Seventeen's great. Lot of great memories. But I don't know how well Stephen and I can work together. See, I was originally assigned to the One-fifteen. Across town."

"I know where it is," she said distantly.

"That would've been better for all concerned. But Stephen put his two cents worth in with Assignments, and the next thing I know I'm with his outfit."

"You sure you don't want that?"

"Boy, am I. You know Stephen . . ." He avoided her eyes. "And you know me."

"You want me to say something?"

"Would you?" he said hopefully. "That's all I'm asking, Helen. Just a word with him. He listens to you."

She laughed under her breath. Almost a cough.

"Something wrong?"

"I can't do that, Brian."

"Please, just a—"

"Stephen doesn't live here. He moved out last April."

His head filled with an embarrassed buzz. He should have known. The smell. There was no man living in this house. No wonder the kid was peeking around corners at the world. After a while, he just said, "Christ."

Her eyes had moistened. "You two guys should try picking up a phone once in a while."

Brian parked his BMW beside the Calumet River and shut off the engine. It dieseled before gagging to a smoky death. Next paycheck: a complete overhaul. His checking account was still recovering from first and last month's rent on a one-room walk-up with a view of the CTA tracks, a peek of Sears Tower.

He got out of the car and surveyed the small marina. Not exactly yacht club ambience. A slip of dirty green water enclosed by tin warehouses. He followed the boardwalk toward an old trawler in dry dock. It had been his father's obsession to restore it, to cruise the lakes with the family in summer. He had died before the Arab oil embargo, and so had been spared realizing how pathetic that dream had been.

Yet, there on the stern, with the engine covers spread on either side of him like rust-colored wings, was Stephen, bare-chested, bending over the fuel-guzzling inboard motor.

"Permission to come aboard?" Brian asked, drumming up the accommodation ladder.

Stephen looked down at him, wiped his face in the crook of his grease-smudged arm, then went back to work.

Don't let him see you bleed, Brian resolved. He hunkered down at the edge of the open engine compartment, taking in the various petro fumes, his brother's perspiration smell. A fuzzy moment came and went in which he saw his father instead of his brother at work.

Music was drifting up from the galley. "What's that?"

"Buffalo Springfield," Stephen said. But then his own brittleness must have been too much for him. "Want a beer?"

"Always."

Stephen bound out of the compartment and led him into the galley. Unwashed cereal bowls. Crumpled Budweiser empties. Down the passageway Brian could see an unmade bunk. Sheets so dirty a woman could be induced to lie between them only at gunpoint. What had happened? Stephen had always been so annoyingly neat. "I like what you've done with the place."

"It's coming along." Stephen tossed him a beer from the butane refrigerator. It was only cool.

"I thought you sold this tub."

"I did once. Carried the paper myself. Guy defaulted."

They fell silent, exchanged a glance, and then Brian somehow found the will to say, "Helen told me."

A microsecond of unease, pain even, then the smile. It said that nothing was going to knock him off his horse. "When'd you see her?"

"This morning. Roof'll need some work before winter."

"I know."

"You got a nice kid." But Brian saw at once that his white lie hadn't taken.

"He'll snap out of it."

Move it along now. Brian turned toward the stereo mounted in the bulkhead over the table. "*Buffalo Springfield*?"

"They get the job done."

"So did the Lennon Sisters." Brian picked up a tape. "Eight-track?"

Stephen looked down, still smiling.

"An honest-to-God operating eight-track?"

"What?"

"Let's call an armored truck and get it down to the Field Museum before something happens."

Stephen chuckled. It sounded nice.

Brian drifted around the galley. In one corner were city-issue one-gallon cans of solvent, fire extinguisher foam, brass and chrome cleaner. "Been ripping off the stations?"

"It's all old stuff Adcox saves for me. It just goes in the dumpster otherwise."

Brian nodded. "Good. Better than wasting it." Then he could hold it inside no longer. He stopped directly in front of his brother. "I want to go to the One-fifteen, Stephen. It's where I belong."

"Is that why you came?"

"Not the only reason, no."

46

"But the biggest."

"Maybe," Brian admitted. "Something tickle you about that?"

The smile. "Just you—always showing up with your hat in your hand. Always after something."

Brian swallowed. That all too familiar taste of bile. "Okay. Quick solution to that one—get me out of your hair. Go to Captain Belt and square it back the way it was."

"Nope." Stephen finished his beer and went aft again.

Brian was right on his heels. "Did you get your rocks off messing with my station assignment?"

"Hardly."

"They why'd you go to Belt!" Brian cried. Stop shouting. He isn't shouting. Look at his face. Calm. His hand is relaxed on the torque wrench he is holding. "Why!"

"To pull your fat out of the fire."

"Bullshit!"

"It got back to me—as usual, my little brother had pulled a boner. Tried to bribe Assignments. Well, that case of Cutty Sark almost got you dismissed." Stephen showed revulsion for a split second. "Jesus, did you think Belt was some hayseed prospect looking for a log cabin? Now, I'm not saying everything's squeaky clean here, but Belt *is*—and you left a case of contempt on Mr. Clean's doorstep."

Brian wanted to hit him. He formed a fist, but something wouldn't let it fly. The face was his father's.

"Hell yes, I stuck my nose in," Stephen went on in the same effortlessly controlled voice. "Asked the captain as a personal favor not to report you. He promised not to. On one condition." He paused, let it drag out, relished it. "That I take direct responsibility for you. That's why you wound up with my company. That and the fact you've failed or gone bankrupt in everything you've ever tried."

"You don't know me—"

"I got you down cold, little brother. And the scary thing is that you could've faked it for a while at the One-fifteen. But not for long. See, this isn't peddling surfboards . . ."

Stephen suddenly grinned. "Hell, did you ever even try surfing?"

"Of course I did." Once. A miserable chilly afternoon in which he had gotten up only once. And with that inward admission Brian was flooded with that surefire sense of his own absurdity. He wanted to throw one punch into Stephen's smug face and leave forever. But, again, he couldn't do that.

"Well, you screw the pooch here and there's no place to hide. You have an off day here and somebody dies. If you're lucky, it's you." Stephen went back to work.

"So that's it? Big bad brother rides my ass until I cough blood?"

"You'll be treated like any other probie."

"Thanks for the beer," Brian said acidly. He started for the ladder, but then stopped. Why can't I just go? Why do I always have to make myself understood? What am I trying to explain? "You know, I told myself a million times I didn't want to be a fire fighter. I said the devil with tradition and family and all that . . . to hell with proving every minute that you're a tough bastard . . . who . . ." Infuriatingly, he had lost his train of thought. And he was perilously close to tears.

"Good," Stephen said with tenderness. The transition was startling, almost disarming. "You felt all that and still something brought you back. I want you to hang on to that when things get shitty. And they will. Tomorrow. Oh-six-hundred. Don't be late."

Then he ducked back inside the galley before Brian could say anything more.

· 6 ·

Brian dried his face with a towel, turned it from side to side before the mirror, then dabbed a smear of shaving cream off his earlobe. He stepped back, enlarged the inspection to include his uniform shirt. A burst of self-admiration faded in the discovery of a "gross rope," a thread unraveling from a buttonhole. He snipped it off with the same small scissors he used to clip away another unpardonable lineup transgression: visible nose hairs. The obsessive triviality.

He took one more step backward, waited for the admiration to return. It didn't.

Regardless of the angle, he looked nothing like his father. The poster fire fighter. And that was the look he wanted to parade in front of Stephen and Engine Seventeen this morning, wasn't it? Dennis Patrick McCaffrey, that human eruption of self-confidence? If so, there was something juvenile about all this. The ultimate juvenility: I want to be a fireman when I grow up.

He glanced through the open bathroom door at the digital alarm clock on his nightstand: 6:27.

The child voice began groaning through the radiator pipe, whispering through the crack in the toilet tank lid. Get out. Leave while you still can.

He tried to ignore it.

But it went on needling him to end the masquerade here and now. Cut your losses. Nebraska by sundown.

He locked the apartment door behind him, hurried down the staircase out onto the street. An overcast morning, but it was warm and windy. His BMW had survived one more night: all four hubcaps in place, no window glass in pebbles on the asphalt.

He got in and turned the key. A few sharp clicks, then silence.

6:32. Lineup at seven sharp. A clutching sensation in his chest.

He popped the hood and, trying not to panic, looked over the engine. But his eyes saw nothing except a greasy blur, and he kept hearing Stephen's voice break over him in calm, measured waves: I got you down cold, little brother.

He slammed down the hood, scooped up his fire gear from the backseat and bundled it in his turnout coat, then started up the street at a half-trot. The bundle was too awkward to carry. He stopped at the corner and put on his turnout coat and helmet. A block later he leaned against a lamppost and pulled on his boots. Easier than carrying them. Then panic overcame him and he was running, weathered brick and unflappable Midwestern faces blearing past.

Don't go to the station, the child voice started in again, seeping from the hook holes in manhole covers, from storm drain grates. Go downtown and find Captain Belt in Assignments, apologize for the scotch gaffe and convince him that two brothers shouldn't work together on the same shift in the same station.

Weren't there regulations against it?

Probably not, if Stephen had suggested the option to Belt.

He bounded up the worn iron steps to the El station,

pushed his way through the grumpy, Monday-morning throng to the edge of the platform and was the first aboard when the commuter train clacked and squealed to a stop.

He grabbed a strap with his free hand. A lurch, and the train began moving.

An old man was eyeing him. "You guys short on engines?"

"Fell off the back of mine going around a corner," Brian said, deadpan.

Eyes got bigger. "You're kidding."

"It happens. A buddy of mine fell off a ladder into the back of an iron ore car. Couldn't get off the goddamn freight train until it stopped in Gary."

The commuter was slowing in jerks as if fighting the same inertia that was propelling Brian toward Station Seventeen.

Again, he was first through the doors.

The platform was packed, so he kept saying, "Gangway, gangway, folks," as he plowed toward the stairs, leaving the commuters to rubberneck for a glimpse of smoke.

It had been years since he had seen his father's station. He had done his best to avoid it. He rounded the corner. Had it changed? Yes. A five-story training tower had been erected out back, a concrete minaret jutting up against the Chicago skyline. And no. It had not changed. The same sooty brick facade to the firehouse proper, the same sand-colored gargoyles for roof drains, grimacing as if to remind the novices in this proud and ancient order that the wages of failure were paid for in a hell of perpetual banishment. No check. No fringe benefits. No freebies around town. No stool at Willie's.

Total excommunication.

Brian checked his watch and winced: nine after seven. He ran.

The twin red doors of the station began rolling up, and Engine Seventeen and Ladder Truck Forty-six crept out onto the apron, emergency lights flashing. The passenger side of the engine cab halted Brian's progress, and he found himself face-to-face with Stephen. His brother was smiling, but then he tapped the silver trumpet on his shirt collar as if to say that he'd broach no misunderstanding about their on-duty relationship. It would be lieutenant and probationary fire fighter. Brian had expected nothing more or less, and was about to tell him so when Stephen said, "Sorry . . . you're too late to play, probie."

Brian began: "Stephen, I—"

But the trucks wheeled onto the street, and the sirens moaned up to pitch.

Tim floated past on a tailboard, clinging to the back of the ladder truck with studied ease. He gave a contented wave; he was rolling to his first fire, and Brian was not.

Brian gave chase. He overtook the slower ladder rig mid-block and came up on the engine when it slowed for a left turn. A hand reached out from the riding compartment, gripped his forearm and pulled him aboard.

"Why, look at what I reeled in," a familiar voice said. "A baby McCaffrey."

Brian focused on the flinty face. It had aged, but he had no trouble imagining it grieving, sobbing on that distant day.

"Don't you remember me?"

Brian shrugged. "Sorry."

Instant offense. "Jesus, Joseph and Mary, Kathleen and I spent a year fixing all the crap you and Stevie smashed up wrestling on our living room floor!"

Grinning, Brian gave him a quick hug. "Settle down, Axe. I just wanted to see if you still had that rotten temper. How's Kathleen?"

The smile was too nonchalant. "She dumped me."

"I'm sorry."

"Me too . . . sometimes." Adcox was in the jump seat. He shouted past the fireman drowsing in the next seat forward, "Hey, Schmidt!"

The driver glanced over his shoulder. No matter that the morning was gray, he was wearing sunglasses. "What, John?"

"You know this rug rat?"

Schmidt shook his head, incuriously. Another worthless probie.

"I practically raised him," Adcox went on. "And that hard-ass sitting up there with you."

Stephen rolled his eyes.

Brian knelt, his knee touching the boot of the long-faced fireman who was catching a nap. An intolerant eye opened.

He offered his hand. "I'm Brian McCaffrey."

"I'm sorry." The fireman folded his arms across his chest and faded again. His mouth slowly opened, and he began snoring.

"Don't mind Grindle there," Adcox said. But then a moment later he grumbled, "Jesus, these guys today."

"Here Johnny goes," Schmidt said. He laid on the horn at a driver who figured a green light was a green light come hell or high water.

"I'm serious about this," Adcox said. "You should all transfer to something like sewage treatment. You already got your noses up in the air." He gripped Brian's elbow, hard, his eyes shining a little. "Don't mind them."

"I'm not," Brian said, although his eyes had smarted when Grindle had gone to sleep on him. One of his turnout buckles had popped open. He fastened it, then made sure that Stephen hadn't seen. "I'm just along for the ride, Uncle Axe."

Adcox did not react to the old nickname. "It didn't use to be this way. Used to be family. Something's happening. We're hiring nine-to-fivers. Just a job to them." Suddenly, Adcox pressed his glove against the side of Brian's face and laughed happily. "Jesus, it's like Dennis looking at me."

Brian was surprised. Flattered.

"Your smile is Mary's, but Christ—you look at a man just like Dennis did. Your eyes go for the jugular."

Stephen had turned, his hand poised on the microphone. He didn't seem amused. Adcox was saying too much about family, and Stephen looked as if he wanted a word in private with him. But then he sat forward again and radioed in the arrival of the company.

Brian got out and gaped. A factory with the wind shrilling around its edges. Indecisive smoke, alternating brown and gray, was pouring out of windows along the third and fourth stories. Only a trickle from the roof vents so far.

Schmidt thrust a breathing apparatus into his arms. "It's only rock and roll, kid. Don't give yourself a stiff neck."

Brian wrestled it on with the engineer's help. He opened the tank valve, tested the mask.

Reach back for your academy catechism, he told himself. Be more than a spectator. Size the fire up, just as Stephen could be seen doing. Brian started his own mental checklist. Commercial. Turn-of-the-century heavy timber construction, most likely. A mix of combustible and noncombustible elements. Less prone to collapse than other types of construction, but far from the Rock of Gibraltar. Fire appears to have originated on the third floor. The wind will play havoc with the flames when they reach the roof. No doubt people were inside at this hour, so Stephen would go on the offense, attack the fire rather than contain it. Another alarm should be called in. The size-up already warranted it.

Brian then congratulated himself when Stephen radioed another one in.

"Give me a hand," Adcox said, tossing him the big wrench off the front of the engine. "Open that hydrant over there." The affection was gone from his voice.

Brian raced across the street, then frowned at the late model Mercedes blocking the fireplug. Through the corner of his eye he could see Adcox dragging the suction line toward him. He fumbled to close the wrench around the hose nozzle cap, but his hands were shaking.

Adcox stopped on the other side of the Mercedes. "Take the line from me."

Brian thought that he meant over the roof of the car, but then Adcox smashed the brass coupling through the driver's side window. He reached inside, sprang the latch,

54

then opened the door so that he could crawl inside and bash out the window on Brian's side.

Brian just stared.

"Take it, for chrissake," Adcox barked.

Brian pulled the hose the last remaining feet to the hydrant. Then he struggled to thread the coupling onto the male end.

"Come on, come on," Adcox said, standing over him. "Just like the drill. Everything we do you've already done in drill."

At last Brian got a good fit and turned the hydrant's operating nut with the wrench. The line squirmed and swelled into a fifty-foot erection. Schmidt, manning his panel, gave a thumbs-up that he had pressure..

Adcox was grinning at the shattered window. "What d'you think, Baby McCaffrey?"

Brian shrugged.

"I'll tell you what I think," Adcox said, chuckling at his own handiwork. "This rotten prick can afford a Mercedes and God knows what else. Stuff you and I can only dream about. But ask him to vote yes on a bond issue for more fire stations, and he'll tell us to get hosed. Already got enough firemen on the dole. Enough fire engines tying up the intersections. That's how he looks at the world. You and I got more than enough. He'll never have enough." Then Adcox hiked up his long leg and kicked a dent in the door. His contorted face slowly eased into a grin. "You think I'm nuts, kid?"

Brian didn't know what to say. He had a hollow feeling in the pit of his stomach. His father had had his anger, his resentment toward an indifferent public, but nothing like this. Of course, Adcox was twenty years into his career, and his father's had been cut short at ten. But still, did Stephen know about this?

"Well," Adcox said. "I *am* nuts. You're looking at yourself a few miles down the pike. Ain't pretty, is it?" Then he crossed the street to rejoin Stephen.

Brian followed.

His brother and Adcox were gazing at the roof. Smoke

was gushing from the ventilators; it had crept its way to the top and would now start mushrooming down again.

Workers were rushing outside in twos and threes, choking, wiping their eyes on their sleeves. One Latina had a cloth tape measure around her neck. A garment factory, then. A sweatshop filled beyond capacity with illegal immigrant labor. Didn't some fabrics give off toxic smoke? Brian was trying to recall when Stephen gave him a shove toward the engine. "Grab a couple hose rolls. You're going in with me." But before Brian could turn, Stephen stopped him again, gave a sharp tug on one of the chest straps to his air tank. Brian looked down—in that split second Stephen had deftly tightened it.

Brian said, "It was okay the first way."

"My ass." Then Stephen smiled. "Is it my fault you're always doing it wrong?" He let him go.

Brian grabbed two rolls and hurried back to the steps, where his brother, Adcox and Grindle were already in position on the hose line. He took his place, or at least what he felt was his place—behind Grindle at the very rear—and waited.

Smoke gusted out of the crack beneath the door, and following Stephen's lead, they put on their masks. Hissing sighs after each breath as the overpressure was bled off.

"I suppose we can't wait until the ventilation team cuts a hole in the roof?" Grindle asked, his voice muffled.

Stephen shook his head, and Grindle tossed a glance at Adcox as if for support. The veteran fireman's eyes said nothing.

Stephen motioned for Brian to come forward. "Stay beside me," he said. When Brian didn't respond, he asked, "Can you hear me?"

"I hear you."

"Then acknowledge, dammit. Everything I say, I want to hear you repeat it." Then Stephen eased open the door, and a flood of smoke pressed down upon them. He started inside, and Brian followed. A Venusian atmosphere. He felt as if he were suspended in molten lead. He knew that he was putting one boot in front of the other, but he had no sensation of movement until he bumped against Stephen's back, nearly dropping the rolls.

"Slow down, probie," Stephen said. Then he raised his voice to include the others: "Stairs ahead."

They climbed them on their hands and knees, out of the pall into a lighter stuff that sifted around them like fog. An open window somewhere was creating crossdraft. Brian could now make out his brother's silhouette. Stephen was dragging the 150-foot line by the nozzle.

Brian dropped a roll to help, but Adcox scrambled up and told him to do his own job. "You hear?"

"I hear." Brian had fallen behind Stephen. He rushed to catch up, snagged the hose with the top of his boot and fell on his chest. Grindle picked him up by the collar and pushed him onto the second landing. He wanted to tell the man not to touch him, but a swirling downdraft of smoke hid him from view.

Crouching, Brian climbed again. His breath soughed from the mask. Distracting.

Above, the third landing was aglow. An eerie throbbing that suggested nuclear reaction more than fire. A noxious light.

"Keep going!" Grindle hollered from behind.

Brian realized then that he had stopped midway up the flight, an instinctive hesitation. Something ferocious was lurking up there on the landing. Something that knew he was coming, armed only with dry hoses, shielded only by a coat.

But it also drew him upward. He was curious to see the beast now, to discover the mirrors and wires that were giving it the illusion of life.

He found his brother and Adcox crouching at an open door, cast in red as if they'd been dusted with ochre. But in the few seconds it took Brian to duckwalk up to them, their faces and turnouts dimmed to normal color. Beyond their helmets he could see a cavernous room. Everything within it was whitehot: metal tables, sewing machines, piles of chunky embers that had probably been wooden chairs, and the flooring itself. A few weakened joists had tumbled down and were crackling flamelessly. Dark cherry-colored flickers rippled lazily across the ceiling, then vanished.

Brian sank to his knees behind Stephen, who glanced at him and frowned before focusing on the room again.

Brian could recall his father carrying on about fire as if it were a living thing. Stephen did the same, especially when drinking. But Brian had made up his mind not to personify fire, to magnify it into an enemy. Fire was just light, flame and heat. Something as mindless as the water that doused it. Yet, on his knees at the threshold to the glowing, hissing room, he couldn't shake off the feeling that the fire *knew* they had come up the stairwell. It had crept back into the walls, the ceiling, and was lying in wait.

"Wash it to the windows, Stevie?" Adcox asked, slipping the nozzle from Stephen's gloves.

"No. We'll hit the son of a bitch head on."

Adcox obviously didn't like the idea. He too had sensed the treachery waiting in the walls. "It's going to flash. We got to get behind it."

Brian looked at Stephen. He had read about "battle light" that came into the faces of famous generals. He now saw it brightening his brother's eyes, and didn't care for it. In the last few months he had overheard a thing or two suggesting that the lieutenant at Seventeen played the game too close to the edge. He hadn't believed it, not about his tightly wrapped, commonsensical brother—until now. Something about the fire was exhilarating Stephen; not in the obscene way that it excited a pyromaniac, but still it was doing things to his head, throwing his judgment off kilter. Adcox was dishing out the conventional wisdom, the safe way to do this, and Stephen was having none of it. "It's not going to flash," he said, including a skeptical-looking Grindle in his pep talk. "This one's a pussy. It'll just steam on us. Won't flash, I promise."

"I don't know," Adcox said in a low voice. He was grinning, but there was unease in it. It disquieted Brian: to see fear in a veteran, even if it was controlled.

"Go high in the ceiling," Stephen said. That was that. No more discussion.

Adcox and Grindle snugged their helmets tighter around their heads—turtles trying to crawl deeper into their shells. Brian did the same and rechecked the strap with fidgety fingers.

Then Adcox loosed a blast of water against the ceiling.

A cloud of steam howled back at them, enveloped them.

Brian cringed. All at once, his coat seemed to be as thin as cheesecloth, and a scorching sensation bolted down his throat, spread through his lungs and made him feel incandescent. He gasped, wondered if this were dying.

A swipe of his glove cleared enough wet ash off his facemask for him to see Stephen standing with his arms braced on his knees, bellowing at the fire, "I knew you were a pussy! Come on, you son of a bitch—steam us!" He motioned for the hose to go forward, and Adcox staggered through the boiling cloud, dousing the ceiling and walls.

Brian got up and followed, still lugging his hose rolls. He flinched as cinders and pieces of broken timber tapped against his helmet.

Suddenly, Stephen's facemask was pressed up against his. "Where you going, probie?"

"With you. Staying with you."

Stephen grinned. "You love it?"

And for that instant, caught off-guard by the affection blazing like sunlight through the facemasks at him, Brian did love it. "I'm in heaven, L.T."

The affection faded, and Stephen pointed behind Brian. "Hook us up to a standpipe."

Brian, still clutching the hose rolls, ran to the vertical pipe tucked in a corner of the room. He reached under the hem of his coat and took out his folding spanner wrench. His hands had not calmed down. The wrench kept slipping off the coupling. He paused to gather himself, willed his hands to be steady.

But then Stephen was looming over his shoulder. "Jesus, how about it, klutz? We're going to lose this!"

"Got it," Brian said, but Stephen had already turned for the far side of the room.

A crash of glass spun Brian around.

Tim and three fellow truckies had climbed the extended aerial ladder and broken one of three windows in the room with their axes. They were reaming out the last shards lodged in the frame—when Brian thought he heard a sonic boom. But instead of dying away, it amplified into a sharp vibration that made the floor jink beneath his boots. What a time for the New Madrid Fault to finally let go, he thought with a helpless feeling that the building was going to collapse around him. Yet, the vibration took on a pulsing rhythm that was nothing like any of the earthquakes he had experienced in California.

A huge sucking sound, a rush-rush-rush, began to make his ears ache.

Stephen was calmly talking into his radio handset. Brian approached so he could hear.

"Hey, Schmidt," Stephen said, "is it . . . ?" He suddenly let go of the transmit button and shouted for the ladder to retract. Tim, as probie, stayed in the bucket and dropped out of sight, looking as uncertain as Brian felt. The other three laddermen were already inside the room, hacking their way toward Adcox and Grindle.

"L.T.," Schmidt was sqwaking over the radio, "the bitch is coming. I can see her coming."

"Where the hell are our second-in companies?"

"Nobody down here 'cept us chickens."

Stephen slipped the radio back into its holder and shouted, "Dig in!"

Brian had no idea what he meant. "What—?"

"Dig in, goddammit!"

Brian stood by numbly for a moment, watching the crews hurry across the debris-ridden floor and gather in the middle of the room. He joined them, feeling as if he were being forced to do a dance he hadn't learned yet. Grindle and the lieutenant from Tim's company were overturning the red-hot tables, kicking them into place as barricades. Another boom punctuated the rush-rush sound. It rattled the building to its foundation. And then an even more frightening boom. Something fatal had been misjudged. Stephen either didn't realize it or couldn't admit it, for he turned happily to Brian and said, "You're going to love this, probie!" Again, that strange light in his eyes. "Grab your mask and your ass!" But Brian could see the truth in the grim desperation with which Adcox was hosing the shuddering room. Backing him up with the line Brian had connected to the standpipe was a fireman by the name of Santos. Brian could read the name on his neck guard. He had not met the man. And now they might die together. The rush-rush-rush built to a roar. Brian felt Stephen's hand push him down. Custer's brother had gone down with him at the Little Bighorn. Shouldn't have read as much as I did as a kid, Brian thought, a weakness sifting through his body like a paralytic drug. All that reading had put too fine an edge on his imagination.

The windows imploded. A spray of glass sparkled toward him.

And then he was bowled over. His helmet smacked against the floor, and his vision went to white. He couldn't breathe. Even the air from his tank seemed too hot to inhale. When he could see again, he was swimming in fire. He drew in his arms to protect his face—and saw that his sleeves were wreathed in flame. That made him hold up his hands like a surgeon waiting for his gloves, for he was suddenly terrified that the flesh all the way up to his shoulders had melted and would drizzle out the cuffs if he lowered his arms.

Something seethed around him. Steam. He was cooling down. He could fill his lungs again.

A stream of water pressed against his facemask, cleared it. Tim was outside one of the windows on the aerial ladder, washing down the barricaded firemen with a look that said he didn't know if they were still alive.

Brian waved, and Tim's face lit up.

Men began stirring around Brian. He rose to a crouch. For some reason, the floor felt spongy under his knees. The fire had lurked down there before springing on them.

Where was it now? Then, as he watched in disbelief, a heavy commercial sewing machine sank through the surface of the floor as if it were water. It left a hole that slowly widened, sucking down one of the overturned tables before reaching a fireman. Santos. Grindle dived to catch him, but missed the man's groping hands.

"Oh God!" the man cried as his legs slipped over the edge and a boot dropped off.

Below him Brian could see a nest of salmon-colored flames. At least 1600 degrees Fahrenheit.

· 7 ·

Brian started to move toward the dangling fireman. But then he stopped. Santos was losing his grip. He was already falling. Yet, Adcox, who was closer, flopped down beside the hole—sending tremors through the fire-eaten floor—and seized the fireman by an arm and a piece of his coat. He pulled until the cords in his neck stood out, but Brian could see no progress. "Got you, Santos . . . I got you, babe," he said, although the toes of his boots were slowly skidding across the floor.

Adcox was being dragged in.

Brian started to move a second time, but Stephen shoved him aside and fell across Adcox's legs, anchoring them for the moment.

The floor seemed to wobble, but then steadied again.

Brian grabbed his brother's boots.

Santos was squirming, if only from the heat pouring up around him. His face was tremulous behind his facemask. Each instant he expected to plunge into the flames, so he had no chance to fortify himself, to put on a good front.

Brian was glad that Santos couldn't say much.

Then Santos's personal alarm device, a cigarette pack-sized motion and heat sensor clipped to his chest strap, yelped for an instant. A burst of scorching air, at least 230 degrees, had set it off. Grindle leaned over the opposite lip of the hole as far as he dared and tried to flood the hot spot.

Another fireman stood by with the second hose, looking perplexed, frustrated, as if he were trying to figure some way to lasso Santos.

The steam quit billowing up, and Brian could see Adcox staring at Santos, full-on. The strain in his face erupted into a grin. "You go, we go," he told Santos.

The exhausted fireman clearly trusted him, but he also knew that they were losing the struggle. The tangled, clutching mass of men was being drawn slowly into the hole.

Brian decided he would wait for Stephen to give up first. And if his brother wouldn't let go of Adcox?

Grindle started to add his strength to the chain, but Stephen told him to back off, not to come any closer. The floor would buckle under their combined weight. Brian could already hear it groaning.

The flames below had only been stunned, for they now burst up into long orange twists. Brian thought that he could smell Santos's exposed woolen sock being singed.

Santos moaned. No doubt he could feel himself going faster. Brian wriggled around and tried to brace the chain by planting the soles of his boots against the floor, but they wouldn't catch on the heat-glazed surface.

Then Stephen moved in such a way that Brian believed he was letting go of Adcox. He was. All the links but Adcox were parting. The promise was unraveling. Brian released his death grip on Stephen's boots. But instead of backing off, Stephen lunged forward and jammed his hands under Santos's armpits as he rolled to the side. Stephen's momentum raised the fireman several inches, and Adcox, free of his burden for a split second, grabbed the man's legs and swung them up onto the edge of the hole. Grindle and another fireman looped a length of hose around all three of them and dragged them away from the drop-off.

In a blink it was over.

Brian's admiration would have been complete—except that he had taken no part in it. He had given up on Santos. But Stephen seemed not to have noticed. He was laughing and pounding Adcox's brawny shoulder with his fist.

But then he stopped and listened.

Rush-rush-rush.

Brian tested his mask for a snug fit.

Then the fire exploded over them. Brian was not sure if it had surged in through the windows, as it had the first time, or if it had howled up through the hole in the floor. Whatever. He was thrashing in flame once again, fighting for breath. If it had burst through the windows, it might have taken Tim, dropped him out of the bucket like a moth caught by a candle flame.

But then Brian could feel the merciful coolness flowing over him. The stream shifted to cover the other prostrated firemen, and he could see Tim tooling the ladder pipe nozzle back and forth across the room.

Once more, Brian waved from the floor. Tim feigned wiping sweat off his brow.

Then someone stepped on Brian's back. "Watch it."

"Sorry, man," a ladderman fresh from the street said. "I thought you were dead." *Nightengale*, his neck strap read.

"Not quite." Brian sat up. Despite Tim's wash-down, his helmet and coat were still smoking. How close had his body come to combustion? He looked for the answer in the faces around him, but the others were carrying on as if the last few minutes had never happened. Grindle and Nightengale were taking the hose attack down a corridor. The truck company lieutenant—Pengelly—was waving his handset for Stephen to come over to him. "Stevie—BC's on the radio. Says they finally got a Red Cross worker who speaks Spanish to make sense of what the workers were jabbering about."

Brian rose and stood behind the two officers, waiting for his brother to tell him what to do.

He realized that he was trembling, just as he had occasionally while in lineup at the academy. If he had no breakfast and then locked his knees while standing at attention, he began shaking.

"What's the Red Cross doing here already?" Stephen asked Pengelly.

"They were holding a class for the illegals or something. Thing is—one head ain't accounted for. A female."

"Which story?"

Pengelly told him the third floor, the one from which the fire had just sprung.

"Addie!" Stephen shouted. "Got a civilian somewhere below. Start on the third story and work down. Take a probie with you." He glanced at Brian, his eyes narrowing, then said to Adcox, "Krizminski."

Adcox winked at Brian. "Now don't take it personal."

Tim had crawled inside and was probing the ceiling with a pike pole. He jumped at the chance to do something more romantic than grubbing for the dying vestiges of the fire.

Stephen turned back to Brian. "Don't you fold on me now, man."

"I'm fine."

"No, you're not. You're shook."

"I'm *fine*," Brian repeated. "No breakfast. Just a little weak in the knees, that's all." He hated saying the words, hated the aftertaste of bile they left. He wanted to explain that he had never lived a half hour like this and needed a few minutes to put it all into perspective. Standing blindfolded on the track at Indy on Memorial Day—that is what it had all felt like. But instead of saying anything more, he gave his brother a meaningless thumbs-up. "I'm ready to go."

Stephen didn't look convinced.

Nightengale trooped back, dragging his hose, and Stephen ordered Brian to clear it.

"Done," Brian said, but in the steps it took him to

reach the standpipe he got angry. He reached for the gate valve, but then just clenched it. Something deep inside, something that had nearly been extinguished by the morning, welled up and rushed to his defense. The child voice. It reminded him that, except for his inexperience, he had done all right, much the same as everyone else. A less than stellar performance, but one not to be ashamed of either. As far as Santos, he had not honestly seen how the man could be saved. Now he knew.

Then he heard another dim voice.

But this one had drifted up the stairwell. "Help me," he thought it had said. No one else had apparently caught it.

He started toward Stephen, but the anger made him stop.

His brother was supervising the destruction of a wall, a half dozen pike poles clawing at it, trying to get at the fire that was spitting and hissing at this final harassment.

Brian turned back for the stairwell, then slipped down to the third floor.

A smoky twilight hung in the corridor.

He called out for Adcox and Tim. They didn't answer. He took off his helmet and listened.

After a long moment, he thought he heard the voice coming through a closed door. He felt the steel with his palm. Warm but not hot. He put his helmet back on and entered. Hazy light was filtering toward him from a distant window, outlining more tables, gleaming on the chrome parts of the sewing machines.

The door automatically closed behind him with a pneumatic sigh.

He stepped deeper into the room. "Hello? Anybody here?"

He took out his flashlight, but before he thumbed it on something like fox fire, a bluish phosphorescence, writhed along the linoleum behind him. He had glimpsed it from the corner of his eye, and in the instant it took for him to wheel around, the stuff ignited into a tongue of orange flame that nearly brushed him.

He startled, scuttled backward and landed hard on his butt.

"Shit," he said, waiting for his heart to quit racing.

More fire shot up through a strip of charred flooring and formed a sheet of sparks that stood between him and the door.

He got up and began working toward the back of the room, hoping for another way out, sweeping his beam under the tables as he went. "*Buenos días*? It's the Fire Department . . . not Immigration."

Another door. Warmer to the touch.

He cracked it, and smoke gushed over him.

"Christ." He barreled through the doorway and immediately dropped to a crawl, so thick was the stuff. His kneecaps were sore. And a faint squeal told him that his air supply was getting low.

He went to his belly. Only a foot of clear air was pressed between the floor and the smoke. His facemask, still beaded with water from Tim's wash-down, got murky; ashes were clinging wetly to it. He passed a glove over the plate, but it left more runny soot than it took way.

He kept crawling. His beam played faintly over table legs, abandoned handbags and purses, a broken coffee cup. Everything was obscured by the smoke and his ash-bleared mask. Each object he fixed on was a puzzle to be mulled over for a few seconds. Was that an apple or a pincushion?

The smoke was lowering.

And then, just before the suffocating cloud spread all the way to the linoleum, he glimpsed something that made no sense to him: a charcoal-colored blanket spread across the floor. On it lay a human figure.

He froze.

Glossy auburn hair, like Helen's before living with Stephen had streaked it with gray. Bright pink skin—carbon monoxide in the blood could do that. But only to a corpse.

He decided to take no chances. He went forward, blind now, and groped for the face, ran a glove over it. Pliant features, but no movement. He gathered one end of the blanket in his fist and began dragging the woman toward the dim square of light in the outer wall.

She weighed nothing, or maybe his pumped-up adrenaline was making her feel so.

He reached an enclosure of desks. The square of light shone brighter, but slow, thin flames were shirring across the floor.

He flipped the edges of the blanket over the woman to protect her, then dragged her through the wraithlike fire to the window.

It was better than he had hoped: a fire escape. He threw open the lower sash, then scooped her up in his arms and stepped outside. The sky had cleared, but it was still morning. He was surprised; he had thought hours had passed and it was late afternoon.

He held her, wondering what to do next. His mind was blank, weary. Either she was very light or he was very strong. He would bank on the former, as fatigued as he felt. Thirsty. He would kill for a Coke.

Below, more companies had arrived belatedly, and several firemen were milling around. One of them finally glanced up at Brian and shouted, "What you got there?"

"Got one. Too tired to carry her down the ladders."

"I'll get one of the ladder trucks," the fireman said, breaking into a flat-footed jog.

Brian closed his eyes. He thought to part the blanket and take a look at her face, but he didn't want to see death. He couldn't feel her breathing. He realized that he should probably start CPR, but then he heard the whine of hydraulic lifters. A tower ladder was telescoping up to him. In the bucket was a fire paramedic. He held out his arms, and Brian gave him the woman.

"Is it a kid?" the paramedic asked, looking surprised as he hefted her.

"Don't think so," Brian croaked. He sat on his heels. The gloom of the alley below was full of fireflies. Flashbulbs. The media had shown up in force. A brash voice asked him to stand up and look at the ladder being retracted. He ignored it, then got stiffly up and started down the ladder.

A second paramedic helped him off the last rung. The man was grinning.

"Is she going to make it?" Brian asked.

"Never a doubt."

"Great." But then Brian saw that all the firemen arrayed around the blanket were grinning—and it was not in congratulation. He elbowed his way through them and stared down at the victim. For a split second, his eyes were deceived and he imagined that heat had done something strange to her skin, had left it resembling the vinyl flesh of a doll. But then he *saw*. He had rescued Resusci-Annie, the reasonably lifelike dummy used in CPR instruction. Lieutenant Pengelly had said something about a Red Cross class for the illegals. How had he forgotten? Laughter filled his ears.

He tried to smile, but couldn't. His pride scrambled to come up with something, anything, that might explain away this absurdity, and then it came to him that he should laugh more uproariously than anyone else present and pass it off as a practical joke.

But he could not have laughed to save his life. A bleak exhaustion had him by the throat.

He pushed back out of the ring of men, looking for refuge, privacy, and thought he would find both on the far side of Truck Forty-six. Yet, rounding the tailboard, he came upon Grindle and Tim, ministering to a young Filipina, who was shaken but unhurt.

"Adcox and me found this pretty little lady in a closet, McCaff!" Tim said joyously.

"Good." Brian turned, annoyed, for flashbulbs were popping in his face again. Why did the photographers insist on following him around?

"How's yours doing, McCaffrey?" Grindle asked with a smirk.

"Couldn't be better."

"Was she lying facedown?"

"Look," Brian said, "I'm in no mood for comedy."

70

"Answer me, dammit." Grindle was no longer smiling. "This ain't the Improv out here."

Brian sighed. Suddenly, he felt dizzy. "Faceup. She . . . it was on her back."

"Well, that should've told you the whole story right there," Grindle said. "Somebody who succumbs while crawling or staggering through a smoke-filled space usually falls right on the kisser. What the hell they teaching at the academy these days? They teaching anything at all?"

Brian felt the saliva rush toward the front of his mouth.

"You okay, McCaff?" Tim asked.

Brian reeled—a sickening kaleidoscope of engines, hoses, helmets and turnout coats—and bolted for the entrance to the alley, where he could see a patch of sunlight. He believed that he would feel better if only he could reach that sunlight. But he had plodded only a few yards toward it when he had to halt and vomit. Through watery eyes he had a vision of a young woman in a fawn-colored business suit out on the sidewalk. Pert. Self-possessed. He gave her his back as he puked a second time.

Then Stephen was bearing down on him. His face grew less furious the closer he got. He grimaced at the splattered pavement. "What happened to you?"

"Too much smoke, I guess."

"It happens." Stephen's face hardened again. "You know, you got a short memory for direct orders."

Brian stood up, wiped his lips with the back of his hand. "Yeah, fine—I'm a little busy right now. You mind?"

"Hell yes, I mind. I told you to stay beside me."

"Come on, Stephen." Brian started ambling toward the sunlight. It would still feel good. But Stephen's glove clamped onto his shoulder.

"You split the team, man. I turned around and you were gone."

"Get your hand off me," Brian said coldly.

"I told you to stay next to me!"

Finally, Stephen had raised his voice. Brian almost smiled. The shell had cracked a little. "I was doing it,"

71

he said. "I was up there *doing* it. You don't know what. But I do."

Stephen reined in his anger again. "What you did was drop the ball, probie."

Pengelly came halfway down the alley and snapped his fingers. "Hey, Stevie—they're calling for you."

"Okay." Stephen looked at Brian once again, that level, censuring stare that he had grown to detest. "Thirty grand a year and twenty-two days a month off sounded pretty good five months ago, huh?"

"Maybe it still does."

"Maybe it isn't good enough." Stephen walked back up the alley.

Brian turned and started for the sunlight again—but there stood the woman in the fawn suit, pretending that she hadn't overheard, feigning interest in the clipboard she clasped in her red-nailed fingers. Jennifer. In her work personna. The shyness he had liked was now buried in the interests of efficiency and advancement. This new Jennifer so unsettled him he did an about-face before their eyes could meet.

Someone was calling his name.

He looked up: Adcox, leaning out of a window. "Probie—we're still working here, you know."

· 8 ·

Adcox started to duck back inside the blown-out window, but then something below made him stop. His face got still. Twenty paces behind Brian McCaffrey, Martin Swayzak was promenading up the alley. Beside him was the frizzy young thing he was no doubt slapping belly buttons with at present. "Look at the big man," Adcox whispered. Then he pressed his lips together as if to keep himself from spitting. He failed, and the globule fell like a marble. But it landed nowhere near the alderman and his squeeze. "The big man." Hair like sculpted chrome. Nose like a Roman senator. And maggots for brains. "His Bigness."

The newsmen clustered around him. Their words were garbled by distance, but Swayzak's lofted up three stories as clear as a church bell: "Yes, I realize this is one more destructive fire in my district. But please—let's not refer to it as Cinder Alley. Negative phrases like this have serious repercussions beyond the moment. They affect how a community views itself in the long term and . . ."

"Blah, blah, blah." Adcox leaned back inside.

Nightengale was chucking ash clods through the hole in the floor at the men mopping up below. Adcox let the horseplay go on for a few more moments, then told Nightengale to knock it off and get back to ripping open the walls before the battalion chief wandered in.

Grindle sidled up to him, his long face even more woeful than usual. Burr in his fur. Adcox had known him too long. "Yeah," Adcox asked, smiling, "what is it?"

Grindle hesitated. "Stephen, man."

Adcox took a slow breath.

"What's going through that guy's head?" Grindle went on. "Taking the fire on in the first room. This shit's been happening too often. It could've flashed, Axe. It *should've.*"

Adcox clapped him on the upper arm. A friendly gesture of dismissal. "But it didn't flash."

"That's not good enough."

"The guy knows."

"The guy's lucky."

True. And luck went dry. Adcox secretly believed that Stephen would be taken from him one day, just as Dennis had been. Some would survive; some would be sacrificed. Inevitable. He knew that he himself would not be one of the survivors, knew it in the same way that he sensed he was coming down with the flu, or the same way that he had suddenly realized in the station bunk room that his mother was dead two hours before he got the call from his sister in Libertyville.

"You hear me, Axe?"

"Sure, I hear you."

"We need a little agreement on this."

"What's to agree on?"

"Judas Priest." Grindle drifted off, dissatisfied.

But what could Adcox say about Stephen to the crews? Yes, he was going too far—further than any of the men realized. But Adcox would not step in.

Brian dragged in from the stairwell. First fire. Tension had left him a dishrag. It happened to most everyone.

Adcox patted his cheek, embarrassing him a little. "Baby McCaffrey—first one's the clincher. You did fine."

"Our lieutenant might differ with that."

Always so sensitive, Adcox mused. Brian had stopped speaking for a few weeks after his mother went, and Child Welfare had wanted to hospitalize him. But Adcox had taken the two boys in, and one morning Brian popped into the kitchen and asked Kathleen if he might have some toast and honey. Toast and honey were better than a shrink any day of the week. "Ah, everybody screws up some, Brian. You've got to remember—you're working for the toughest L.T. on the job. He's being nice to you."

"*Nice*?"

"Shit yes. I once saw him pick up a probie he thought was moving too slow. Threw him headfirst into a burning building." Adcox touched his cheek again. A good boy, just too sensitive. Like his poor mother had been. "Now grab a pike pole and act like you're doing something."

Don Rimgale stepped out of the back of the building and found Swayzak leaning against the trunk of his red sedan. "Alderman," he said.

"Investigator Rimgale."

He waited a moment longer, then said, "I need to get in the trunk."

Swayzak uncrossed his arms and stood up. "Forgive me," he said with a courtly gesture of invitation.

Rimgale nodded and popped the lid. Now that he had determined that no fatalities were lurking in the rubble, it was time to lug his kits up the scorched stairwells and start deciding if the fire was intentional or accidental. Seven in the morning on a workday was an unlikely hour for a bankruptcy scam, unless a possible device had failed to ignite on schedule last night. And then again, it could have been a revenge set, a disgruntled worker—and God knew these sweatshops created enough of them—or the competitor down the street.

He looked down at a pair of expensive-looking shoes. Not his own. Swayzak was still standing right behind him.

Stink on shit. "Awful nice shoes to be wearing to a fire-ground, Alderman."

"I don't care where these shoes go."

"Or who they walk over?"

Swayzak kept smiling. "Is that what you think of me, Investigator?"

The Achilles' heel in a politician. Deep-down, he wanted to be liked, even if he himself were an insufferable prick. Rimgale had nothing against aldermen in general. A powerful one with white three-piece suits and discreet mob connections had plucked him out of a gang of Taylor Street toughs and booted him into the fire academy. Old school incentive. Finish or get out of town. A favor for Rimgale's ward heeler uncle, he later learned. Yet, an alderman had made it all possible, given him a respectable life in the end. But Martin Swayzak was nothing like those old pols. They had come out of the neighborhoods, and they stayed in them all their lives. Swayzak was a trans-plant from Lake Forest. He kept an apartment in his dis-trict, but it was about as lived in as a diorama at the Field Museum. His home was still upstate with Mother Swayzak, fifteen rooms and ten acres on Lake Michigan. This piddling local office was no more to him than forty days and nights in the wilderness, and even at that he was doing his camping in a suite at the Ritz Carlton. From here it was on to the mayor's mansion, then to Springfield, and then even Washington. God bless America. Sky's the limit when you look the part.

"Let's not get into what we really think of each other, Alderman," Rimgale finally said, keeping his tone chipper.

Swayzak's female aide piped up. "We wanted to talk to you about Alan Seagrave's death." She had been a mouse, shagging coffee and taking notes until recently, when overnight, it seemed, she had put on maroon claws and started using the editorial "we."

Rimgale grinned at Swayzak, but kept his thoughts to himself. Don't kid yourself, buddy-boy. There's always a price for getting laid; mine is a wife seventy pounds overweight and six kids. He was glad to see that the alderman was a bit flustered.

"Jennifer Corcoran, my administrative assistant," Swayzak hurriedly said.

"We've met," Rimgale said.

"Many times," she added. "We still haven't gotten a report, Investigator."

"Didn't get the incident sheet?"

"We're talking about *your* report."

Rimgale opened one of his cases to let them know that the interview had drawn to a close. He didn't want to be shuffling through a blacked-out, fire-weakened building after nightfall.

"Investigator," Swayzak said, "people are asking how a prominent citizen got stuffed through the windshield of his own car. Now, I ask you—does that even remotely sound like an accidental cause?"

"Under the right circumstances, yes."

"Oh, come now."

"Why don't you come up to the academy the next time I put on an arson class?"

Swayzak ignored the invitation. "Whatever the cause may be, people—taxpayers—are asking me about it, and I'm getting tired of having nothing to tell them."

"Tell them the truth."

Swayzak looked hopeful for an instant. "Which is?"

"The case is under investigation." Rimgale slammed the trunk lid and turned to go back inside. But Jennifer Corcoran was standing in his path, glaring up at him. She was rather pretty from this copulative angle.

"The point is, Investigator—we're starting to get the feeling your office is dragging out this case to embarrass the alderman."

"Why would I do that, Ms. Corcoran?"

"Because of Alderman Swayzak's fire department reorganization program."

"You mean his firehouse closing program?" A good reason to embarrass Swayzak, Rimgale decided, but it had not occurred to him.

"We'd just be *very* disappointed if it turned out your office was playing politics," she said.

Rimgale's jaw muscles started rippling under the skin.

"Because I'm not," Swayzak slid in. "I care about this city, and I care about this department—"

Rimgale held up a hand. "Alderman, I've got a remarkably uncomplicated job. To decide if a fire is deliberate or not, and then see if I can catch the creep who set it." A good, although dated word. Said so much about the typical firebug. "But to be perfectly frank, if my methodical investigative methods just happen to run counter to the campaign plans of a certain mayor wanna-be—well, I guess I can't say I sleep any less peacefully."

Rimgale was getting ready to move Jennifer Corcoran aside, bodily, when Stephen McCaffrey dropped down off the fire escape, and the alderman and his assistant backed off. They had recognized the lieutenant.

Rimgale decided to stick around for a minute. McCaffrey, always Mr. Self-Restraint, Mr. Slow to Anger, Mr. Man of Few Words, a veritable Gary Cooper in a Turnout Coat, had turned into a loose cannon over the past year. The gossip blamed it on his recent divorce, but Rimgale wasn't so sure. Every man has a side he hides from his coworkers and friends, but enough pressure and time will draw it to the surface. Whatever the reason for the change, Rimgale was glad to see it. The lieutenant had been so full of moderation he had seemed inhuman at times.

McCaffrey stuck his gloved forefinger right in the middle of Swayzak's gray silk tie. Ms. Corcoran didn't step in the way this time. "Swayzak."

"Lieutenant, good to see you."

"Hello, Stephen," Ms. Corcoran said quietly. A little shared history here?

Probably not, for then Stephen went on without looking at her again: "We almost lost a whole company up there, Swayzak. Wasn't any backup when we needed it."

"Oh?" Rimgale had to tip his hat to Swayzak: he was standing his ground fairly well for a man with soft, white hands and apparently capped teeth. "Why was that, Lieutenant?"

"Because you closed Station Thirty-three. And we really appreciate it, the guys and me—your inspired plan that makes maximum efficient use of the fire resources of this city. We're proud to have somebody in city hall seeing to it that our tax dollars aren't being wasted on redundant services—like second-in companies." Then pure sulfuric acid: "I know you've got my vote."

"Look, Lieutenant," Swayzak said, sounding as smooth and sincere as a bishop, "I'm on your side. If there's a problem, let's pull together on it. I'm asking you to channel all this wonderful anger into our task force."

"Your task force . . ." McCaffrey's face was contorted; he was really losing it. Rimgale smiled. *Wonderful anger.* Such nice horseshit. Adcox came up and stood behind the lieutenant. Reinforcements. Could get interesting. ". . . your fucking task force killed three good firemen with its recommendations this year!"

Swayzak took a step forward; McCaffrey and he were almost bumping chests now. The alderman lowered his voice; his face was now all stare and gritted teeth. "You see that funny glow that's starting to blink in the corner of your eye, Lieutenant?" He paused. "That's your career dissipation light. It just went into red alert."

Adcox barged past McCaffrey. For an instant, Rimgale was sure that the alderman was going to go back to the council chambers this afternoon with a fat lip. But Adcox, his fists on his hips, spittle flying from his mouth, made do with words. "I don't have any lights inside my head, Swayzak," he said. "I'm just a flunky fireman with no ambitions other than keeping my boys alive. In one piece. I don't even give a crap if I retire." He started to grin, but he was too agitated to make it anything more than a scowl. "You're in firemanland now, Alderman. Do yourself a favor and just walk away."

Swayzak glowered at him for a count of three, but then turned and started down the alley, walking just slow enough to maintain his dignity. Ms. Corcoran followed a half-stride behind him, clipboard pressed to her breasts, her buttocks jiggling just enough to compromise her dignity.

"Democracy," Rimgale said to McCaffrey and Adcox, picking up his cases. "No wonder the Eastern Europeans want it so bad."

Engine Seventeen backed up the station driveway. The brakes bit, and Brian climbed out of the riding compartment ahead of Grindle, who had dozed on the trip back in as well. Brian strolled away from the engine to stretch his legs. They had stiffened on the ride in. He wanted to see the building shadows race across the street toward him as in time-lapse photography, for night to come instantly. He could already feel his bare toes splitting the cool sheets of his bunk.

But then Stephen passed by, saying, "Clean the pike poles, wipe down the ladders and hang some hose. Tim," he said as Truck Forty-six backed in parallel to the engine and the tireless probie jumped off the tailboard, "fill out the alarm card."

Tim jogged inside, still on an adrenaline high, delighted to be of service. Damn him.

Brian was taking a sooty pike pole off the engine when he froze. Something pink, the whitish pink of raw pork, had caught his eye in a second-story window across the street. He looked at the apparition straight-on, then whispered, "Jesus Christ."

She was standing on a chair, her face demurely hidden by the valance to the lace curtains, her great pendulant breasts spread before her like a second pair of arms. Her only visible hair had been dyed a bright carnal red. She stood motionless for what seemed an eternity; then, slowly, poetically, she crossed her arms over her enormous nipples like an Egyptian queen preparing herself for death, and stepped off the chair into the shadows of the room.

Someone gripped Brian's shoulder. He jumped.

"Caught you," Adcox said. "Next time you get a spanking."

"What the hell was that?"

"Be kind. The polite question is *who*."

"Who the hell was that?"

"Franny. Used to be an exotic dancer. Lincoln had the hots for her." Then Adcox turned him by the shoulders toward the station. "Get out of your turnouts before you clean up. It's summer, in case you didn't notice."

Brian glanced up at the window one more time. "Perfect ending to the day. Sums it up. Flashed by a fat lady."

"Hey, be thankful. Franny won't do it for civilians."

"I need a locker."

"Stevie already assigned you one."

Brian shuffled inside the station, too far gone to be sensitive to any lingering presences, too spent to evoke any memories, and hunted for his locker. He could feel the gazes of the other men on him, mocking, expectant. Didn't matter. Didn't care. His ears were ringing, and only sleep would turn it off. He drifted among the naked firemen as if in a trance, stumbling over their shucked-off gear, oblivious to the towels that snapped playfully at his crotch.

He found his last name and first initial scribbled on a strip of white medical tape and gave the latch a yank.

He gasped as a woman tumbled out at him. Her rubbery nose hit his forehead, and her slack arms wrapped around him for an instant before she slunk down and folded over the bench at the midriff.

Brian picked up Resusci-Annie and hurled her at Grindle, who was howling with laughter. He caught her, pumped his pelvis against her a few times, then passed her on to Schmidt.

"I don't want no sloppy seconds," he said, scrunching up his face in disgust.

Brian walked out of the locker room.

Jennifer reached into her purse for a cigarette. Martin didn't approve, but she ignored his slight frown as she lit up. She had held off for hours, and now at last the desperation was too sharp. Delicious. She exhaled and smiled across the backseat at him. She could see that he had already forgiven her, but she felt the need to add, "I'm going to quit soon. Honest. After the campaign—when the pressure's off."

He patted her hand. "Okay." He looked at her tenderly. "Did those yahoos upset you?"

"Only that they were attacking you. How can they be so ignorant? And then so proud of it?"

Martin chuckled under his breath. "I face it all the time with emergency personnel. Cops. Firemen. They think they're the last real men in the world. Ask them to be accountable, to be economical with their resources—and you're attacking their manhood." He looked out the window. Tenements; people out on the stoops to escape the heat—his eyes passed over them without seeing. "I've got to win this one, Jenny. I have no choice but to stand up to Steve McCaffrey and his crowd. The decent ones will come around with time. The yahoos never will—but the devil can have them." She could see the thought suddenly occur to him. "We need to cultivate a few allies here and there. I'm talking about the lower echelons of the department. You know, get our message across at ground level." He stole a glance at his watch. "You hungry?"

"Famished."

Martin leaned forward and said to his driver, "The Ciel Bleu, Ismail."

The patient black face dipped once.

• 9 •

Brian held his face up into the cold stream. Water. Restorer. Ally. Natural enemy to fire. It gurgled over his ears, plopped against the tile floor.

Through these comforting sounds Tim was babbling. "Could you believe that fire, man? First day!" He whooped, and it echoed in the shower room like a dozen exulting shouts. "First *frigging* day, McCaff!" Another ringing whoop, but then he dropped his voice to a whisper: "There I was—Adcox and me—pulling that pretty little lady right out of the fire's throat. Where else but the Seventeenth? I love it here, don't you?"

Brian filled his mouth with water and spat.

"No surround and drown for this company," Tim continued. "This here's the *fighting* Seventeenth. Goddamn, but your big brother's awesome. You see how he took that fire by the balls? I'm going to be that good someday, you watch."

Brian asked quietly, "How will you know?"

"Know what?"

"How good you are."

Tim paused in the middle of lathering an armpit. "Damn what if Stephen didn't say something about that to me. Right when all the shit was coming hard. He said, 'You never know till the moment the fire stares you down if you're just gonna do this job or be *great* at it.' "

Brian smiled.

"What's so funny?" Tim asked.

"Nothing." One of his father's favorite sayings. Immortal bullshit now. He had probably coined it while standing on these very tiles. Brian's eyes clouded. He shut off the finger-worn chrome handles and padded out into the drying room. The light was fading behind the pebbled glass of the high window.

The first day was half in the bag.

He only wished that he felt even a glimmer of satisfaction. Midway through one twenty-four shift. Only two thousand more to go. Forty-eight thousand hours more. His spirits sank at the calculation. The hour and twelve minutes they logged inside the garment factory had seemed that long.

He examined his body. Skinned knees. Eggplant-colored swellings he hadn't even felt yet. Tonight he would acutely feel them, and then for days after in dull aches. Twelve hours down. He wrapped his towel around himself.

Stephen's private quarters were just off the bunk room. His door was open, and he was sitting on his unmade bed in his boxer shorts, rubbing Ben-Gay into a knee that looked to have been operated on recently. A knob in his right collar bone revealed where it had been broken. Injuries since Brian had last seen him stripped—he decided not to ask how. Stephen would only turn it all into a sermon.

"Where's my bunk?" Brian asked.

Stephen pointed. Right outside his door, of course.

"Afraid I might mess up in my sleep, L.T.?"

"God knows you'd screw up a wet dream." He tossed Brian the Ben-Gay. "You and Tim get all that hose hung?"

"Nope." Brian began gingerly kneading the cream into

84

his knees. An overpowering mintiness made him turn his face for a second. "We left it in a big pile on the tarmac. A lawyer just tripped over it. Said he specializes in personal injury. Broke his goddamn leg in two places."

Stephen looked at him impassively, then lay down and draped his forearm over his eyes.

His room was untidy. Probably not enough to warrant a note from the battalion chief, but enough so that Brian noticed. A small wood-and-glass case stood in the corner. In it was an old helmet. Brian rose from his bunk, strode into the room and looked it over. Smaller than what he remembered. And compared to today's models it seemed antique. "I thought this was on display downtown."

"Was," Stephen said without lifting his arm off his eyes. "But twenty years is a long time, I guess. Had to make room in the memorial case for new martyrs. More and more of them every year. And it's getting where only the old-timers remember Dad. Axe tried to get the brass to name the new wing at the academy after him. But nothing came of it. Too many righteous names to choose from. So they named it after the fire commissioner."

"Were they actually going to toss his *helmet*?" Brian asked incredulously. He had always believed that his father's relic had a sacrosanct place in the temple downtown; now he was shocked to see that it had been moved to a lesser shrine. "Just throw it out?"

"Same thing. Dump it in a city warehouse."

"I'm glad you saved it."

Stephen grunted.

The alarm Klaxon sounded.

Brian couldn't believe it. There was no way he could coax his leaden body into answering another alarm. But Stephen had sat up, and his eyes were boring into Brian's. "Ain't World War Three, probie—don't just squat and stick your head between your legs."

Tim raced from the shower room still dripping wet. "Isn't this outstandingly great!" he cried, wiping his sodden hair off his brow.

Laughing, Stephen said, "That's my little moron probie." He rose. "Come on, you two—down the pole!"

Brian and Tim balked. "L.T.," Krizminski said slowly, "we'll need our underwear to fight a fire."

"You pussies." Stephen sat up, reached over and apparently tapped the alarm response button that told Central Dispatch the Seventeen was rolling. Fifteen seconds with no answer from a station would result in another company being paged. "I'll bring down your goddamn undies for you. Go! Now!"

Brian slid down first, losing his towel on the descent, his bare thighs chirping over the brass. Tim followed, spinning as he came. He yelped as he hit the apparatus floor, then doubled in pain.

"You all right?" Brian asked.

He was cupping his privates in his hand. "No . . . Think I burned Lucky Pierre."

"Lucky Pierre?"

Tim grinned with clenched teeth. "Sure, he always gets to sleep in the middle."

Brian tossed his eyes heavenward. The only other probie he had for solace and companionship had a pet name for his privates.

They started for their turnouts hung on the wall, but Adcox stepped out of a side door, roughly took hold of their necks and drove them down the corridor. Brought back memories of being collared by the Sacred Heart nuns for fighting.

"Axe," Tim groaned, "that hurts."

"Does it?" Adcox shoved them through an open door into the kitchen, where ten firemen looked up from dinner. A candlelit dinner. They put down their forks and applauded.

"Don't show Franny," somebody said. "She might ask for their union cards."

"Judas Priest," Grindle said morosely, "and we're having bratwurst tonight." It was spaghetti, but everyone bought the joke.

Stephen swept in and tossed them their trousers. He

then took the end chair opposite Pengelly's place of honor as the other lieutenant. Tim and Brian were given footstools that put their noses level with the tabletop. Schmidt flung a dollop of pasta on each of their plates and smothered the steaming piles with tomato sauce. "No meat?" Tim asked a bit weakly.

"No meat for probies."

"At least these two don't have any," Santos said. He was subdued, maybe inwardly still slipping by the centimeter into that flaming hole. The ladderman didn't join the laughter raised by his own one-liner. He just fixed his gaze on a candle flame.

Adcox noticed. He reached over and rubbed Santos's neck. Uncle Axe. His face was tired and sad in the candlelight. In his early forties and already a patriarch, forever shepherding his charges out of harm's way. Brian had a sudden and intense feeling of affection for him, the man who had taken Stephen and him into his home. He had never been sure that Adcox and his father had been best friends; the difference in ages told him otherwise. But he had always wanted to believe so.

The discussion turned to what precise place in the universe probies occupied. Tim listened as if it all had important career implications. Schmidt likened them to maggots. But that was too cliché. Santos said that they were no better than dried dog turds.

Grindle admonished, "We're eating, so shut up, will ya."

"Whale shit," Pengelly said summarily, tomato sauce dribbling down his chin.

"How's that, Walt?" Adcox asked.

"Whale shit sinks to the bottom of the deep blue sea. Nothing's lower than that."

Acclamation was quick. Whale shit it was.

Tim finally worked up the nerve to ask what the candles were for.

"Ambience, sweetheart," Nightengale said with an acetylene lisp. Tim was so taken aback by the possibility that *here* in their very midst—Nightengale switched to his normal baritone: "Easy, boy. I saw you from toenails to dandruff, and it did nothing for me."

Tim nodded, still not sure.

Adcox chimed his water glass with his knife. "The candles are for special occasions," he explained. With the stealth of a magician, he had somehow slipped a tuxedo dickey over the front of his utility shirt. "A tradition of this station not shared by crasser firehouses. As official toastmaster of the feared and fearless Seventeen—"

"A tradition started when Washington blew the fuse box trying to hook up a satellite dish," Schmidt said.

The offending fireman, a black in horn-rims, hung his head. Mock contrition.

"As toastmaster—"

"Axe," Schmidt interrupted, "I just want these two whale turds to know that they got kitchen duty starting next shift." He turned to Tim. "And if the cooking stinks, you two probies are as good as hog-tied and delivered to Franny."

Tim guffawed—he too had apparently glimpsed her in the window. But then his horse laugh was cut short when Stephen said ominously, "You think he's kidding?"

Brian realized that they were all playing to Tim, the better sport. Most of the crew already liked him. First impressions stuck like glue in a station house. He forced himself to come to his feet. "I believe our esteemed toastmaster is trying to say something." He sat again, his face on fire—but he had done it. Done something. Played along.

"Thank you, Whale Turd Brian," Adcox said majestically. "I think it only fitting that we welcome these two probationary firemen, who this morning were baptized into the world of Old Man Fire. Welcome to our society." Bored, rhythmic clapping. Adcox hoisted his water glass. "To Tim, who despite being a sufferer from Zachary's Disease, that debilitating ailment first identified by that famous Chinese physician of this fair city, Dr. Hung Low—"

"What the hell?" Schmidt prompted. He had obviously

borne witness to all this before, but that did nothing to dim his enjoyment. Venerable forms were being followed to the letter. "What's Zachary's Disease, pray-fucking-tell?"

"Why, the poor fellow's face looks *zachary* like his ass." More forced laughter. "To Tim—who not only took on the beast but pulled from its clutches a sweet young thing he would have married on the spot, had I not stepped in and lied to him—for his own good, mind you—that she had a social disease."

"Yeah," said Pengelly, "Zachary's Disease."

Tim turned toward him and said earnestly, "No, sir— she was as pretty as a picture."

Genuine laughter.

Tim would do well here as the slack-jawed foil to their ribbing. Brian could not yet see a place for himself and was afraid to test his own humor, for fear it wouldn't be understood. Bit cerebral, maybe. And he wasn't about to take on the properties of a fool just to please them.

"To Tim, gentlemen."

They rose. A chorus: "Fuck Tim." They sat.

"And now to Brian," Adcox said, winking at him.

Brian's back straightened in anticipation. He mentally rehearsed a smile for the moment when Adcox would talk about his rescue of Resusci-Annie. The slightest hint of resentment would bring only more abuse. Years of abuse.

"You know, when I heard that both McCaffrey brothers were going to be assigned together here, well, my heart was filled with a . . . a sudden desire to transfer." Adcox laughed, but something was wrong. He paused and gazed vacantly in Stephen's direction, blinking as if trying to figure a way to slide gracefully into seriousness. "No man was more dear to me, or to this station and its boys, than Dennis McCaffrey. God rest his brave soul."

Stephen raised his glass, but he was watching Adcox over the lip as he drank.

Somber-faced now, Adcox went on, "The first friend I lost . . . Dennis. I thought at the time it was fate. Lousy luck. But nothing's ever that simple. Not by a long shot.

You see, we're a brotherhood. We stick together. Or at least we should. Your average politician hates anything he can't count on. If you're a pol, you try to break up any block of votes that isn't in your pocket. You pick off the leaders, cow the rest. I was so stupid I didn't see that that's what happened to Dennis. And Ted years later. They were a lot alike, Dennis and Ted. Brass balls. Big-hearted. Gift of gab . . .'' His eyes began glistening.

Brian looked to Stephen. Was he buying this? Yes. Brian could see it in his faint smile.

Adcox was grinning self-consciously. "Hell, listen to me. I must be getting old."

The table was silent.

"So hoist your glasses again, lads. To Dennis McCaffrey's sons, who despite years of getting on each other's nerves have managed with great effort . . . to still be pissed off at each other. Gentlemen!"

They rose. "Fuck 'em!" They sat.

· 10 ·

There were no major fires after that first morning, but Stephen more than filled the hours for his probies. In addition to kitchen duty and equipment maintenance, Tim and Brian had the latrines to look after. The state of the urinals brought out a martial obsessiveness even in Adcox, who would piss in the alley behind the station if he thought no one was looking. Afternoons were spent on the hot tarred roofs of the district, Brian hoping for the thunderheads looming whitely in the west to blow in over the city and drench him, cut short the task of chalking in the locations of the support members so Tim and he would know where to step and where not to step if ordered to ventilate these expansive commerical structures. They practiced ground laddering on abandoned brownstones, got sore backs and arms from lugging chain saws up and down the rungs. They went with Grindle on a fire inspection tour, which happened to focus on the taverns in the neighborhood. They rooted around musty basements and web-laced crawlspaces with flashlights while Grindle bellied up to the bar to "PR the locals."

91

Through it all Tim's spirits never flagged. Each chore was more engrossing to him than the last, and Brian began to dislike him if only for his enthusiasm. He felt none. He counted the hours to his first stretch Kelly Days.

And then, not a minute too soon, it was 0700 hours, Friday morning. The relief crew arrived, and Brian hoofed it for the El station before Stephen might offer him a ride. He had no desire to see his lieutenant for a good long while.

He dozed on his feet during the ride home. Dreamed a piece of the dream. The beautiful flame snaking along the roof toward his father.

His BMW was no longer parked in front of his apartment building.

"Shit."

He pounded up the stairs and phoned the local precinct. His car had been towed Tuesday afternoon, the watch commander explained. The beat cop hadn't realized that Brian worked for the city. No problem—pick it up at the impound yard, gratis. Maybe you can do a favor for me someday? Sure could use a pair of those rubber fireboots. Going to pour a cement patio at home.

"You got 'em, Sarge." Brian hung up. Bless the brotherhood of self-interest. Karl Marx should have lived in Chicago before having a go at *Das Capital*.

Then he drank two beers and went to bed.

The dream awakened him at noon. He was sweating, hyperventilating. He rose and opened the shade on a vacant street shimmering with heat. Anyone who could sneak away was probably down on the shore. He thought of going himself, lying in the shallows like a misguided whale, but then realized that he had owned no swimming trunks since Laguna, when they had been garnished by his landlord along with all his other household possessions of the time.

So, the lake was out.

He watched "Days of Our Lives" with no idea what was distressing all those handsome and glib people, finished the six pack, and finally turned in again at three.

He bolted upright in bed at five-thirty. He had been falling. Falling in his father's arms.

He got up and made his bed.

The day was no less insufferable. He opened the refrigerator and left the door yawning. Only a whisper of coolness, and it reeked of stale food. Air conditioner. He would buy one with October's check. September's check had to be used to get his BMW back in running condition. He laughed helplessly. October. He wouldn't need an air conditioner when he could finally afford one. Already in the hole. Again.

Had to get out of the apartment. Walls were inching inward, cracked plaster ceiling dropping, buckled floor rising. In a couple of hours the room would be no bigger than Rubik's Cube.

He thought about going to the Cubs game. A series against the Padres. But they would be playing under lights, something new since he had left town, and the very idea seemed unnatural, grotesque.

Had to get out. Out of the city. Too hot. Aspen was as cool as a glacier even in August. So was Laguna, perched above the ocean, rinsed clean each morning by fog. Laramie was high and open and breezy. Even Florida had had its cooling trades.

He stopped pacing. A surprising thought. He had always sought escape from *heat*. That meant something. Should he drive north, then? Canada unfolded in his mind like an idyll: lakes, balsam woods, Mounties in red tunics, the chic women of Quebec. Drive north.

No car, he reminded himself.

But then it seized him. The panic. It didn't care if he had a car that ran or not. Leave, the panic commanded him. It spoke to him in the child voice. Bus, train, plane. *Leave.*

And after a long moment, he relented with a bewildered smile. Born to keep moving. Had the McCaffreys stayed in County Wexford, he would have become a tinker, traveling the byroads in a brightly painted wagon, doing nothing more demanding than fixing a tin pot or two. The heady freedom of the road, gobbling down the miles like uppers.

He took his suitcase from the closet and laid it on his bedspread. He was opening it when—

Three raps at the door: two long, one short—an old code.

Brian bit his underlip, then finally crossed the room and sprang the deadbolt.

Stephen stood in the dim hallway, wearing a blue blazer, scarlet tie and gray slacks. He spotted the suitcase at once. "Going someplace?"

Brian ran his hand through his unruly hair. "No. Just reorganizing."

"You can use plenty of that." He strolled past Brian and looked the room over. He had nothing to say about it.

Brian gestured at Stephen's clothes. "Funeral?"

"Close. Retirement party."

"Whose?"

"Come along and you'll find out."

Brian thought to offer him a beer, but realized that all he had to offer were six empties strewn around the Salvation Army–bought furniture. "No thanks. Not tonight. Bushed."

"Well, you're going. Everybody off-duty from the Seventeen's going."

"Is that an order, L.T.?"

Stephen paused. "It's Chief Fitzgerald's shindig. You broke the poor old bastard this time, and he's going out to pasture." His flushed face softened a bit; Brian realized that he had been drinking all afternoon. "He gave you a second chance. It's the least you can do—thank him face-to-face."

Stephen nursed a canned Manhattan cocktail behind the wheel of the same Fiat he had bought new in 1979 for Helen. The yellow paint had oxidized into something like dried egg yolk, and the sun had slowly shredded the black vinyl seats. Memories curled out of the backseat. Memories of Jenny. Rushed passion. Cokes and cheeseburgers afterward. "When'd this start?" Brian asked.

"What start?"

"Drinking and driving."

Stephen just smirked, no doubt recalling the countless times Brian had done the same. "We're fine."

"Are we really?"

Stephen looked askance at him, then back through the windshield. He braked. The unavoidable rush hour traffic.

"Seen your kid today?" Brian pressed.

"Not today."

"When?"

"Soon."

Then Stephen turned the tables. "Did I tell you? Saw Jenny Corcoran the other day."

"Me too."

"Looking good, isn't she?"

"Looking different."

"Anything going there again?"

Brian borrowed the can and took a sip. "Nope."

Stephen turned into a parking lot jammed to capacity with older Detroit sedans, most of them showing salt corrosion around the wheel wells. A handful of foreign luxury models were cowering near the entrance. Fear of dings and scratches from blitzed fire fighters. Stephen double-parked next to a Mercedes and breezed inside without locking up. An American Legion Hall. "Classy," Brian said, trailing him inside.

Yet, on the stage was an Irish folk band, whaling away on fiddles, timpanis, harps and tin whistles, and Brian broke into a spontaneous jig that got Stephen grinning and a few of the drunks clapping. He ended his little spree at the bar, where he ordered a shot of Bushmill's and a Harp chaser for both his brother and himself. But when he turned to offer Stephen his nip and bottle, he caught him staring off at the dancers milling in the center of the hall. Brian tracked his gaze—and felt a queer pull in his guts. Helen McCaffrey with another man. A redheaded dispatcher named Jackson. He had taught the class in radio procedure at the academy.

He wanted to say something to his brother, something to reassure him, but Stephen spoke first. "I got to change the view." And he melted into the crowd.

Brian finished his own round, then started in on Stephen's.

Santos elbowed up. He was blasted. "I know you."

"Brian."

No reaction.

"I work with you at Seventeen. Whale shit?"

It still didn't completely register, but at least Santos made part of the connection. "Stevie must be damn pissed."

"I suppose," Brian said, thinking that Santos was referring to Helen and Jackson.

"Can you believe it? Didn't make the list for captain— *again*."

That was news. "When was it posted?"

"This morning. Wanted to buy him a drink. Went down to the boat. But he wasn't there. Him and Adcox went out."

The musicians broke into a vigorous slide after lulling the dancers half to sleep with the maudlin "Carrickfergus," and Santos spun on them. He seemed to be scanning for one member in particular. Pasty Mick faces. The newest immigrants, illegals from old Erin living and working in Chicago by the grace of the same Fenian-American patriots who pumped thousands of dollars into NORAID, the Provisional IRA's front.

Don't sour your own fun, Brian chided himself. Let go here. Be Paddy for one night. Enjoy.

"There he is," Santos finally said, pointing at the timpani player. Then he announced that he was going to punch the man out and took a step toward the stage.

"Whoa." Brian held him back by the belt. "Why d'you need to hit him?"

"Let me go."

"First tell me why he pissed you off."

"He called me his darling friend," Santos said in solemn Latin outrage. *"Darling!"*

Brian stifled a smile. "Just an expression. Doesn't mean he likes you. He'd say it to the Queen of England if he thought it'd get him a free drink."

"I'm no queen. I'm no—" Then Santos's glazed eyes lit up. "Oh, *Brian*. Whale turd."

"That's me . . . lowest of the low." He escaped while Santos tried to recall to the bartender what he had been drinking. He made up his mind to get his fake show of gratitude out of the way, but the crowd was pocked with dozens of white heads and jowly faces like Chief Fitzgerald's.

Then he saw Jennifer.

She was across the room, schmoozing with a political columnist from the *Tribune*. Her boss was not far away, surrounded by some fellow pols, his head thrown back in laughter he obviously didn't mean.

On an impulse, Brian went back to the bar, avoiding Santos, and ordered her usual. He carefully carried it to her through the crowd. She smiled uncertainly at his approach—until he offered her the glass. Then she frowned. "What's this?" she asked.

"What else? Bicardi cocktail."

Her eyes shifted to the columnist. "I don't think I've had one of these since I was *twenty*," she explained to him, and they chuckled.

Brian felt heat come to his face. She still hadn't accepted the glass. He was slowly sinking into the floor, just as Schmidt had.

"I don't think so," she said, at last, "thank you."

He downed the cocktail and said, "Well, how am I supposed to keep up? First time I got lucky with you, Jennifer Marie, you were still drinking Shirley Temples."

She glared. The columnist begged off, saying that he had to get an interview before Alderman Swayzak was surrounded by his admirers again.

Jennifer clasped both his hands in farewell. "I know he

wanted a word with you, Michael. Your opinion matters *so* much to him.''

Then Brian and she were alone. Her eyes narrowed, and he knew right away that the gloves had come off.

''Look, I'm not the same girl who had nothing better to do than wrap her legs around you on a Saturday night!'' she hissed so only he could hear. ''This isn't about fun—I am working here!''

''You make it sound like you were working back then.''

She started to leave, but he grabbed her by the wrist. Her eyes blazed, and he quickly let go. ''I'm sorry, Jenny. I didn't mean anything. Honest. Tell me something about your work. I want to hear.''

A pause, then a triumphant smile. ''I will tell you something—Martin Swayzak is going to be this town's next mayor.''

''You think so?''

''I *know* so.''

He had loosed her self-righteous streak without even trying. All this just over a drink. Welcome to old times. Then, once again, his pride made him throw in the towel. ''Nice to see the alderman selflessly giving up his Friday evening . . .'' He paused to smile. ''. . . when he could be doing so many more pleasurable things with his free time.''

A flicker of guilt in her eyes? Maybe. ''Why do you think Martin came here tonight?'' she asked.

He shrugged.

''Because he cares about your department. You have no idea how hard he works. You don't know about his programs helping—''

''Helping firemen into early graves. Three of them this year.''

''You got that from Stephen.''

''I'm not capable of independent thinking?''

''No,'' she said triumphantly, ''otherwise you'd never have come back to work under your brother.''

He felt the moisture rise in his eyes. He wanted to walk

away but could think of nothing to say in parting. Something witty and cutting. Trump her.

She must have realized that she had clawed too deeply, for she lightly touched the back of his hand. He had forgotten how delicate a touch she had. "Brian, I have two cousins on the job. Martin's plan is about efficiency, a stronger department. Do you think I could work for him if I didn't believe that?" They were interrupted by a well-heeled couple who just had to say how much they were behind the alderman, and Jennifer switched flawlessly into her schmooze mode. "Tom, Betty—how lovely to see you. I know Martin wants a word with you as soon he can break away. Thank you so much for the donation. Seen the polls?" She crossed fingers on both hands. "This *is* the year." The couple moved on to have a privileged word with Swayzak, and Jennifer picked up where she had left off as precisely as if she had hung a bookmark in the air. "The thing that really makes me mad is the way your union has gone after Martin without—"

He was laughing at her.

"*What?*" she demanded.

"Oh baby, you've added a few moves since shaking the dust of the old neighborhood off your Gucci pumps."

She lifted her chin a bit. "Thank you. I like to think that I have. How about you?"

"Just the same old moves. Here's one you're really familiar with . . ." And he strolled away from her. He ran into Adcox within a few paces.

"Why, baby McCaffrey!" He was in the same condition as Stephen, although he made no attempt to hide it. He introduced Sally, his date, and pinched her bottom. Wide-set eyes. Too much blue shadow.

"Nice to meet you, Brian." She stood on her toes whenever she spoke. Either it was a ploy to draw attention to what she said or a reaction to Adcox continuously pinching her.

Adcox gave him a hug. "Having fun?"

"Not exactly."

A worried look. Uncle Axe. "Why the hell not?"

Brian nodded toward Swayzak and his entourage. "Made the mistake of stumbling in his outer defenses."

"What a scumbag," Sally said in her overly cute voice. "You know him?"

Adcox answered for her. "She got transferred into his office three months ago."

"Out of parking violations," she said. "My supervisor didn't feel I had the moral fiber for such a position of public trust." She giggled.

"Now I gotta pay my own damn tickets and she's stuck with a prick for a boss."

"Oooh," Sally cooed sarcastically, "why there's Miss Corcoran. Used to eat her lunch out of a paper sack with the rest of us, but now that she's the alderman's—"

"I just skated on a parking impound," Brian interrupted.

"First time, Baby McCaffrey?"

Brian nodded.

"They'll pop for a freebie the first go," Adcox said. "But you're on your own after that. Times have changed. A world with no loyalties." He shook his head sadly. "Getting where—"

Brian felt bodies closing around him. Fractured images of a long-ago evening on John Paul II Boulevard, walking away with a bloody mouth—but still standing. He braced, then saw that it was some men from the Seventeen: Grindle, Schmidt, Nightengale and Tim, all grim-faced. He nodded at Tim, who didn't respond.

Grindle thrust a magazine into his hands. "Have a nice read, probie."

Brian turned it into the light slanting down onto the dance floor. The pages were folded open to two pictures. One of Brian on the fire escape Monday morning, offering his blanket-wrapped bundle to the paramedic in the aerial ladder bucket. The second was an inset, hauntingly more familiar: a dazed little boy in his father's helmet.

Brian glanced from face to face. A burial detail. "What's this?" he asked, suspecting a hoax, a practical joke.

No one said anything.

Brian checked the cover: a legitimate-looking copy of the *Tribune* supplement. All too elaborate to be a station house hoax. He flipped back to the photographs and started to read silently, but Adcox asked him to do so out loud. " 'Probationary Fireman Brian McCaffrey, on his first fire, risked life and limb to search a burning floor alone. He emerged with Anna Vasquez, a seamstress for North Shore Garment Company, wrapped in a blanket to protect her from the flames McCaffrey had to brave to extricate her from the building . . .' " Brian chuckled. "Jesus H. Christ."

"Go on," Grindle said.

"Who did this?"

"Read," the fireman said more insistently.

Brian took a breath, then: " 'McCaffrey first gained prominence as the subject of a 1972 Pulitzer Prize winning photograph—see inset—at the scene of his fire lieutenant–father's death.' " He tossed the magazine back to Grindle. "It's bullshit. I had nothing to do with it."

"Me and Adcox brought out the little lady, McCaff," Tim said, aggrieved. "You know that."

"What the hell you want me to do? Write a letter to the editor?"

"Nobody reads the letters," Tim said. "They look at the pictures."

"What're we going to do about it?" Grindle asked, as if only pistols at ten paces would settle the affair. Santos staggered up and Grindle showed him the magazine, but he said reading made him sick.

"Lighten up, you guys," Adcox said. "There's a union bylaw for everything under the sun. If a fire fighter gets his name in print, he buys his officers a drink. If it's bullshit, he buys everybody a drink." He reached over and fished Brian's wallet out of his pocket. Two twenties were extracted and handed to Grindle, who—looking no less disgruntled—led the others back to the bar. "Sorry, baby McCaffrey," Adcox said when the posse was gone, "but it was either that or have one of them bang your lips with a fist."

"My lips I don't need. The money—"

"I think you have nice lips," Sally said, standing on her toes once again. Her legs took on more definition. Maybe that was the reason.

"Back off, honey," Adcox said, good-naturedly. "You got only one name on your dance card tonight. It begins with A and ends with—"

"Cox," she finished for him, giggling, still looking at Brian.

File away for future reference. Brian started toward the bar two paces behind them, but then someone tapped him on the shoulder. He turned and faced a smiling Martin Swayzak. "Brian McCaffrey?" Jennifer was standing on his right, obviously ill at ease.

"Yeah."

She briefly closed her eyes as if he had already muffed something on which the fate of the world hinged.

"I'm Marty Swayzak." He didn't look like a Marty. Nothing blue-collar about him. "Jennifer has been telling me some pretty surprising things about you."

Brian resisted the urge to say that that had been a long time ago, that they had just been horny kids casting off their Catholic inhibitions in the backseat of his brother's Fiat. Instead, he muttered, "How's that?"

"The *Tribune* spread."

So she had been aware of it and said nothing.

"I'm surprised your brother didn't mention your heroism to me at the scene," Swayzak went on. "But then again, your brother and I aren't on the friendliest of terms. I hope that won't color our own relationship."

Then that was the plan: divide and conquer. "What relationship?"

The alderman clearly had something in mind, but he just went on smiling. "Really incredible work you did. You and your brother, fighting that fire together. Helluva image, isn't it? You must feel lucky to be assigned to his command."

Brian glanced at Jennifer. "Every perpetual juvenile's dream." Then he added, "And that's all it was—somebody's dream. I didn't save that woman."

"Brian's too modest," Jennifer quickly said.

"That's me . . . just a modest little man." He ignored her killing glance and went on to Swayzak, "I saved a dummy."

The alderman blinked in confusion, but then said confidentially, "Well, I suppose they're not the *brightest* people . . ." Good old politicos. Confess to them that you're a child molester, and they'll wink and say that they do a little molesting on the side too. "But the point is, Brian, you have some special qualities that can be put to better use than they probably are." A pregnant beat. "I'd like to offer you a job."

"I already have one. Thanks."

"This will still be with the fire department. One of our best investigators, Don Rimgale—know him?"

Brian shook his head.

"Well, Don's working on a very difficult case right now. High visibility. This on top of everything else he has to do. We think he could use another pair of hands. And you're exactly the kind of guy I want representing us in Arson, a—"

"A stupid probie who doesn't know his ass from a hole in the ground."

Swayzak had stopped smiling. "You're too hard on yourself. Maybe what you need is a little sunlight. You know, step outside your brother's shadow?"

So Jennifer had revealed that much when she cooked up this one. Why had she suggested him to Swayzak? Was she honestly looking for a way back to yellow Fiats and twelve dollar dinners for two at Leonardo's Pizzeria? Her eyes told him nothing.

"You'll soon learn that to stay in the sunshine," Swayzak said, "you've got to keep advancing."

"I'm happy where I am," Brian lied. "Fire engines run in my family. Politics don't."

Then some well-wisher glommed onto Swayzak's hand,

and Brian threaded his way toward the front door. Time to leave. Take the El. He was mildly surprised to hear Jennifer's voice behind him: "Not bad—took most of thirty seconds to blow that one."

He stopped and slowly exhaled as she came around and blocked his way. "Come on, girl—he's just another Northside jag-off with French cuffs and a sassy mouth."

"Is he now?"

"Yeah."

"You were the sass-mouth." Then she asked, her voice full of all the weariness of their past, "Why do you always have to be so stupid?"

"Look," he said, "Let's just walk away from this. I'll say lousy things. You'll say lousier things. And everything we say to each other gets chiseled in stone."

"No. I want to talk. I've been waiting six years to talk."

"Okay—you sleeping with him?"

She looked away in disgust. "You're right. We can't talk. I was trying to do something nice for you back there. Give you the one thing you always screw up. Your own future." She hurried back toward Swayzak.

Brian headed directly for the door, but then decided to tell Stephen that he was leaving. If he told his brother he was going home, he knew he wouldn't skip town tonight—like he wanted to.

· 11 ·

Stephen cut across the dance floor, through the light and body heat and reeling couples, and thrust his hand out to Eamon Fitzgerald. The academy chief was with his wife, as always, a small pretty woman with laugh wrinkles around her eyes and a way of looking at each guest as if his congratulations would be the most cherished. "Eamon," Stephen said slowly—he suspected that in the past hour his speech had grown sloppy—"I wish you and Maureen every happiness in the years to come."

"Did you come up with that yourself?" Fitzgerald asked, holding back slightly, as most people do with a drunk.

After a moment, Stephen smiled. It had been a joke. He was at the point of missing them now. "And I want to thank you for my brother."

"Came out at the top of his class."

"I know. He been by to thank you himself yet?"

Fitzgerald shook his head.

He hadn't been much of a fire fighter, but still he deserved every courtesy from the McCaffreys. A favor like Fitzgerald's turned into a promissory note. And if Brian defaulted, Stephen knew he would have to make good on it.

"He'll be by in a couple minutes," Stephen said firmly. "So help me." Throttle the little bastard.

Then he turned and started back across the dance floor feeling as if his right leg were slightly longer than his left. It suddenly hit him that he had not said anything in parting to the Fitzgeralds. Or had he unconsciously mumbled that he was going to throttle his brother?

He faced them again. They were smiling at each other. Indelible affection. He wanted to point this out to Helen, as he had pointed out so many things through the years, but he realized that she was not at his elbow. He had somehow imagined that she was for a moment. The usual presence, taken for granted until now.

He looked for her.

She was no longer dancing. She was at a table crowded with men. A hard, preemptive glance. But before he could respond to it, she turned and laughed at something Jackson had said. It could not have been that funny.

"You look like you've lost your last friend," a voice boomed at him.

Stephen stopped and looked down at a table. Pengelly and the guys from the Seventeen.

The truck lieutenant then realized that he had accidentally said something significant, for he added with a glance in the direction of Jackson's group, "No accounting for taste, Stevie."

Stephen sat and picked up the nearest drink. A buzzer went off deep inside his head: he could no longer tell what he was downing; it could have been anything from straight sour mash to crème de menthe. "Suppose not."

"Help yourself, L.T.," Schmidt said.

"Jackson's an asshole. A lousy dispatcher, too."

"Stop it," Stephen told Nightengale.

"Stop what?"

"Talking about Jackson." They were making him feel like an also-ran. He tried to think of something light and sarcastic to say to them, but nothing sprang to mind. A hateful, sad feeling was beginning to settle in around him. Drinks arrived. He took one for himself without asking.

"Look at that. Will you look at that now?"

Stephen kept his eyes on the table. He knew Grindle was talking about Helen and Jackson.

"Knock it off," Pengelly quietly warned.

"It's okay," Stephen muttered, stealing a look at the dance floor. They were embraced together there, as he had known they would be. An unexpected eruption of phosphorous behind his eyes: he had just seen them together in bed, entwined, the bed he had bought in installments from Halloran's Furniture. Thirty-six months at ten bucks a payment. Chasing checks. Macaroni and cheese and hot dogs three nights a week. Had they actually been that strapped? A dim glow of misplaced pride that they had somehow weathered it all. Only to sink in a safe harbor. "Would you stupid clowns mind your own business?" he heard himself saying. Was he whining?

"That's right," Grindle said with a cautious smile, "give them some privacy."

Stephen glared at him. "What're you saying here?"

"Just that a woman's always a risk."

"What's that supposed to mean?"

"A woman is like everything else," Grindle said. "Push your luck, and you just might lose everything."

"That's enough," Pengelly said.

Stephen bolted up, knocking his chair down behind him.

The sound created an island of silence several tables deep.

Smack Grindle. Stephen had risen with this aim, but now that he was on his feet, right hand fisted, he realized that Grindle wouldn't do.

He started for the dance floor, blood rushing in his ears.

"Stevie . . . ?" Pengelly's voice trailed after him, then died away in the music.

Helen saw him coming. Her hands had been clasped behind Jackson's freckled neck, but now she let go, and Jackson was forewarned.

"Stephen, how are you?" The man took a defensive stance.

Just as well, Stephen thought, I'm no Sunday puncher. Give him his fair chance. "Hello, Jackson." He faced Helen, held her eyes. I want to go home. Want to rise from our bed in the morning, have breakfast with you, then fix the roof, and watch a game in the afternoon with Sean in my lap. I want my normalcy back. Nothing would be sweeter. Nothing else would do. But then he heard himself say, "Where's Sean tonight?"

"Home."

"Who's watching him?"

"I don't like this tone, Stephen."

"I don't like your company." He could feel Jackson glaring at him. "I deserve an answer. And the court would agree." Why bring the court into it? Bed, breakfast, roof, game, Sean—these were the things that he needed to talk about. Persuasion had given way to accusation. When precisely had that happened? How could it be reversed? What had gone wrong so soon?

"Heard about your brother," Jackson said.

"Stephen, I'd appreciate it if you would just go back to your table. You're in no condition to discuss Sean's welfare."

"You saying I'm not much of a father?"

"I'm saying nothing of the sort. You're just spoiling for a—"

"Saved a goddamned dummy," Jackson interrupted. "How moronic can—?"

Then it was done.

Stephen had thrown a roundhouse, and Jackson was standing dazed with his arms spread, gaping back at him with blood trickling from a nostril.

Stephen had expected him to go down, but the man came back down off his heels and shouted, "You out of your mind, McCaffrey?"

"Yes," Stephen said.

And then someone jumped on his back, tried to clamp an arm around his neck and choke him out. "Got him!"

Stephen lost his balance and pitched forward, hurling Jackson's buddy into him. They fell in a heap. Jackson tried to throw a punch from the floor, but missed Stephen's pelvis. His buddy lumbered up, but Brian was there, grabbing him, trying to restrain him.

When that failed, Brian coldcocked him. A job so neat and quick Stephen had to laugh.

An off-duty paramedic leaned over the body, then pronounced that he was just stunned.

Stephen laughed again, then scrambled to his knees so that he could have another go at Jackson. Too late. Several pairs of hands were holding him back. He sank into this many-handed clutch and tried to catch his breath. Fuzzy movement all around. Adcox had him by the lapels of his blazer.

"Hello, Axe."

"Axe my ass!" He was furious, but talking low. "You dumbshit—never know when to quit, do you? We don't need the attention."

"Little attention's good now and then. I could use some lately, you know?"

"Ever wonder why your career's in the toilet? You want to stay the rest of your life an L.T.!"

Stephen cradled his fist in his armpit. It was throbbing. "You're still a Fire Fighter Specialist Two."

"That's different. You got *potential*."

"I got nothing."

"Oh, listen to the poor—"

"I'm out of here." Brian knelt before Stephen, the pocket ripped out of his shirt. "Got to go, big brother. Still on probation. Our battalion chief's trying to squeeze through the crowd. Take names."

"Meet you outside."

"What're you going to do?"

"My keys. Take them out of my pocket." Stephen brushed his knuckles over Brian's flushed cheek. Looked like Mom, especially when he was scared. All eyes. "Now get the hell out to the car." Then he raised his voice so the firemen still holding him could hear: "I'm okay . . . it's over . . . time to apologize.'' They released him, congratulated him on his good sense.

Stephen stood up, brushed himself off, shook his head with self-disgust in Helen's direction—and then lunged at Jackson. A quick jab bloodied the man's lips as well.

A roar went up, and the hands had Stephen again. The band broke into ''The Wearing of the Green.'' ''Mood music,'' Stephen mumbled as they pinned him to the floor. ''It's over. Let me up.''

''Bullshit,'' somebody said, panting.

Brian started the Fiat and pulled it around to the front door. He leaned across the seat and cracked open the passenger side door, then sat up again and waited. Sultry night. The humidity visible as a bug-ridden halo around the globes of the street lamps. He rested his forehead against the steering wheel and groaned: Jennifer had seen him on his dash outside, her face tightened by that familiar revulsion. ''Run and tell sister,'' he had snapped, and it had visibly hurt her.

Adcox and Pengelly came out, dragging Stephen between them. He could no longer walk.

Brian jumped out. ''Is he hurt? Did the bastards hurt him?''

''No,'' Adcox said, opening the back door, protecting Stephen's head with his hand as he and Pengelly eased him inside. ''He just finished the affair by puking.''

''On the BC's shoes,'' Pengelly added.

''Christ. Is he fired then?''

''No, no.'' Adcox chuckled and shut the door after making sure Stephen's feet were clear. He had lost a shoe, just as Santos had lost a boot. ''Sad but true—there's a double standard in this lousy business, Baby McCaffrey. One for probie screw-up and one for veteran screw-up. You did good by hightailing it when you did.''

Pengelly started back inside. ''He sure as hell won't make captain for a long time,'' he said over his shoulder.

Adcox said to Brian, ''I'll follow in my car.''

''No need, Uncle Axe. I can drive okay.''

"I *said* I'll follow."

"What're you afraid of?" Brian asked.

Adcox jogged for his car at a steady gait, his head held high. It was hard to believe that he had started drinking at the same time as Stephen this morning. Iron constitution. A kind of strength more durable than Stephen's, less frenetic.

Brian glanced into the back. They had laid Stephen on his belly with his face cocked over the edge of the seat so he wouldn't aspirate. His eyes opened into slits, but after a moment he gave out with a soft, rumbly snore.

Then headlights flashed over the rearview mirror, and Adcox tapped his horn.

Brian pulled into traffic. The skyscraper lights slid off to the north, and he put his mind to driving without drawing a Traffic cruiser out of hiding. Adcox flashed his high beams.

"What now?" Then he glanced at his speedometer. He was fifteen miles an hour over the limit. He eased off the pedal, sat back and tried to enjoy the breeze gushing in the windows—but it smelled of raw sewage.

"What call he got?" Stephen groused.

"Who?"

"What call he got to say that?"

"Go to sleep, Stephen."

But his brother had sat up, and his booze-swollen face was filling the mirror. "Hit my head."

"You hit your head?"

"No, no, no . . . *he* did it, for chrissake."

"Lie down," Brian said. "I think the McCaffreys did all the hitting tonight."

Stephen flopped down. "Grindle."

"What about him?" Brian's eyes shifted to the mirror; Adcox was still on his bumper. "He was nowhere near you."

"He hit me . . . below the belt. Blindsided me, for chrissake."

Brian made up his mind to ignore him. No use trying to communicate with a chemical. But then he heard a *pfft* and glanced over the seat. Stephen had found one of his canned Manhattans. He slurped with the back of his head propped on the armrest. Sweating heavily.

"Think maybe you've had enough, Brother?" Brian asked.

"Throw out the empties . . . before home . . . she won't know."

Brian smiled sadly. "She already knows."

"Grindle had no call."

Brian rolled his eyes.

Then, surprisingly, the fresh injection of alcohol made Stephen a bit more lucid. "He said some shit. Put me at a disadvantage."

"How could he do that?" Brian couldn't imagine anybody from the Seventeen putting Lieutenant McCaffrey at a disadvantage. Most of them tiptoed around him.

"He just *did*, for chrissake. What do you know?" Stephen sat up again. He rested his forearms atop the front seat. His breath smelled of bitters and stale vomit. "You don't know anything. Don't even know how to couple a goddamn hose to a standpipe."

Brian wanted to snap back, but he resisted the urge. "What does Grindle have against you?"

Silence for a long moment, then morosely, "Doesn't trust me."

"You're kidding. They all adore your egotistical ass."

"Used to. No more. None of them trust me." In the mirror, Stephen's eyes were glazed, disconsolate. "I blew it."

"You sure you're not just upset about the captain's list?"

"Screw the list!" But then, as if out of sheer weariness, he calmed down at once. "List don't matter. It's the trust. Don't you hear what I'm saying?"

"No, Stephen, I'm sorry."

"The *trust*."

"I don't see the problem."

Stephen exhaled and sat back. "Blew it just like Dad did. It's what killed him."

112

And suddenly Brian was angry. He had been there that day, not Stephen. "What're you talking about?"

"Starts easy. Doing something spectacular."

"What're you saying? Spectacular's easy?"

"Shut up! I'm talking about my *life*, for chrissake!"

Brian's ears were ringing from his shout, but he kept quiet. Let him thrash a little.

"They trust you because you can do things they can't. Or won't. But the things got to keep getting bigger, better all the time. Always a rung up. Need a way out. Always—" He stopped and stared out the back window. "We're being followed. Make the next right. Quick."

"It's Adcox."

A pause. "You sure?"

"I'm sure."

"How can you be? Don't even know how to couple a hose to a goddamn standpipe." Stephen chuckled.

"You're home," Brian said. They had come to the slip on the river; beaded reflections were strung across the dark water.

"No, I'm not. Not yet . . . not even close." Stephen sprung the door latch, got out and collapsed onto one knee—all before Brian could help him.

Adcox came trotting up from his car. "Christ, that's his bad knee."

"One of my bad knees," Stephen added with a giggle. "Bad legs. Bad hips. Bad heart—"

"He having heart problems?" Brian asked Adcox, who shook his head, winking. They helped Stephen up, and they started toward the dry dock area, arms hitched around Stephen's back.

"Got to get the sons of bitches, Axe, before everything goes bad."

"We will," Adcox said casually. "First thing in the morning. Sleep."

"I don't dream no more," Stephen said. "Now that *has* to mean something."

"You're tired, Stevie. Your mind's just too tired to fool around at night."

"You dream, Axe?"

"All the time. It's what keeps me going."

"How about you, little brother?"

Brian didn't answer.

They put Stephen to bed, and Adcox offered to sit with him a while before he went back to the party.

"You sure?" Brian asked. "What about Sally?"

"She ain't exactly the love of my life."

Brian had had just enough to drink to ask, "Was Kathleen?"

Adcox shut off the reading lamp mounted in the bulkhead. It was making Stephen scrunch his eyelids. "Yes," he finally said.

"I'm glad. I liked her."

Adcox nodded, but said nothing more.

"Tell Stephen I'll bring the car back tomorrow afternoon." And Brian left.

He then drove to the station, telling the on-duty crew just returned from an alarm that he needed something from his locker. After getting his spanner wrench, he slipped into the storage room and carried a hose roll out through the back door into the alley, where he tossed it into the trash dumpster. Then he said his good nights and drove to a coffee shop around the corner for a late supper of eggs and bacon.

At midnight, he drove halfway up the alley to the station, parked and walked the last hundred yards to the dumpster, where he climbed in and retrieved the roll. From there he went to the academy, clambered over the chain-link fence surrounding the compound and crossed the darkened courtyard to the practice standpipe. He had not wanted to use the one in the training tower behind the Seventeen. Someone might have seen him.

He took a breath, threaded on the hose coupling, tightened it with the wrench. Seven seconds. He did it again. Again. Six seconds. And then again.

From then on, he did it every night of his remaining Kelly Days, always with a silent clock running against him and Stephen's carping eyes trained on him from the darkness.

· 12 ·

Chicks. Thousands of yellow puffs scurrying like leaves before a breeze. Brian's turnout coat, which he had shucked and folded into a makeshift sack, was cheeping from what he supposed to be a hundred of them. Schmidt had given up trying to take them alive. He ran in front of Brian, using his coat to flail them. "Easier to sweep up the little turds later."

"I see!" an old Lithuanian woman shouted from the corner, a babushka knotted tight around her plump face. "I see you there, you murderer! You . . . you *communist*!"

"It's not what you think, ma'am," Schmidt said politely.

But as soon as she had turned, he stomped a stray under his boot, then went after a thick covey of them, thrashing again.

Tim stood in the middle of the street, rubbing his chin, no doubt trying to figure out some way to herd them all back, without casualties, into the jackknifed trailer that had come to rest on its sidewall after the tractor had collided with a garbage truck.

"Come on, probie," Adcox said to Tim, "just go through the motions, okay?"

115

"But I don't see where we're doing much good, Axe."

"Exactly. We're just scaring 'em out into the neighborhood, where the kids will scoop them up for pets—believe me."

"Well, if you say . . ." Tim began tramping around as if he were the Frankenstein monster.

"Would you be less obvious, for crapsake?" Adcox sighed, then approached Brian. "Morning, Baby McCaffrey."

Brian yawned, if only to give his opinion of this "alarm." It had been dispatched as a possible toxic spill. *Toxic?* Did the chicks have Newcastle disease? And why hadn't the Street Department been dispatched? Why did the Fire Department always get the ludicrous ones? He yawned again.

"Maybe you should get more sleep on your days off," Adcox said. A smooth grin that gave Brian pause.

"What makes you think I'm not?"

"Nothing in particular." Adcox shook a chick off the toe of his boot. "It's just that a dedicated probie seldom does." He handed Brian a list.

"What's this?"

"Shopping list. What's it look like?" Adcox took out his wallet, peeled a fifty off a wad and pointed at the mom-and-pop grocery on the corner. "I'll take your gear." He hefted the coat and frowned. "You been messing with the dog on me."

"I'm offended, Uncle Axe."

Brian assumed the list to be for the station kitchen until he got down to a box of tampons. "Look out, Timmy," he muttered to himself, "now they're really going to get rough on us."

"Is there a problem, sir?" the Iranian owner asked, grinning with a desperate will to please. Maybe the Tehran Fire Department had been in charge of water torture.

"Where are your feminine . . . ?" Brian's voice trailed off. He would do his own aisle search. "Avocados?"

116

"Ah, we have both Hass and Fuerte varieties. But I am sorry, sir. I am not familiar with the kind you name."

"No problem."

"No problem, sir . . . very good."

Adcox met him at the door with the utility panel truck he had brought to the scene. Up the street, Schmidt, true to his word, was sweeping dead chicks down a storm drain grate.

"Come on," Stephen said, emerging from the back of the truck and sinking into the passenger-side bucket seat. He had been in a foul mood all morning, but now Adcox was infected by it as well.

"Yeah, let's get a move on, Baby McCaffrey. What took you so long?"

"Couldn't find my favorite brand of vampire tea bags."

Neither of them laughed.

Adcox checked the mirror and pulled away from the curb. Stephen stared vacantly through the windshield, still in his turnout coat despite the September warmth. He looked close to being asleep when he suddenly wetted his lips and shook his head. Spacey today. Distracted.

Brian sat on the engine cowling. "I thought the shift kitty was to take care of our own meals."

"It is," Adcox said.

"We got a female probie coming to the station?"

"God forbid." Adcox turned to Stephen. "Jesus, I've already forgotten the number. Thirty-two . . . thirty-two—"

"Oh-nine."

"How could I forget something like that?"

"Happens."

"I mean, all the *times*. The barbecues. We helped frame and drywall the spare room." Adcox turned a corner, and Brian braced himself with his free arm. A spray of lettuce jutted out of the bag and tickled his face.

Brian asked, "Care to let me in on the purpose of this detail?"

"Nope," Stephen said.

Adcox was craning for the house number. "We call this the *job*, but it's nothing like a job," he said solemnly.

"People who work in the Mercantile Exchange or Sears Tower have *jobs*. They get amnesia at five, and it stays with them until eight the next morning. It's not a person next to them. It's a desk." He set the parking brake; then both Stephen and he bailed out, leaving Brian to tail them up the cement walkway.

On the patch of lawn a boy of five or six years played with a toy fire engine. Adcox knelt to say hello to him, but his eyes stayed fastened on the tiny wheel he was rotating between his fingers. Brian remembered this kind of engrossing solitude, and the fear of having it disturbed by people who threw big shadows and talked too pleasantly.

Stephen made no attempt to chat with the boy. Instead, he hurried up the steps and rang the bell. A minute later, the door glided open a few inches. "Lucy," he said quietly, "it's us."

"Is that my girl?" Adcox rang out, rising stiffly to face her.

"Oh, Axe," she said, "you boys shouldn't have." A weary voice. Tennessee accent. Brian had yet to glimpse her face, as she kept to the shadows of the small entryway. "You just shouldn't."

"Now, we had a deal," Adcox argued, going through the forms, knowing that she could not afford to refuse. "You keep sending us your list for the last week of each month."

"When will it end?" she asked, her voice fading up a flight of stairs. "You fellas can't go on doing this forever." Adcox motioned Brian to follow Stephen up. "I rented out the lower floor," she was explaining above. "It helps."

Brian reached the top and stepped into a small kitchenette. The woman stood at the sink, filling a tea kettle. Early forties. Rawboned. Far from pretty. But she had a sad smile that pierced, that raised an instinct to shelter her. "And who's this now?"

"My brother, Brian," Stephen said. He had sat at the table and folded his hands on the oilcloth. It had been repaired with white vinyl tape. Adcox took the bag from

118

Brian's arms and began putting the perishables in the refrigerator.

"Why, I would've known you're a McCaffrey right off. I knew your daddy. My Teddy just loved him. Two peas in a pod, those guys." She gave Brian a quick hug that was so sincere he felt no self-consciousness. "Welcome to my home, Brian."

"Thank you, Lucy."

"Sit down now, please. Get comfortable like your brother there."

Brian glanced across the table. Stephen looked anything but comfortable. The obligation had been met and he wanted to be off again. Somehow Lucy had the grace to realize this, and what she did next was probably more to ease Stephen's restlessness than benefit herself. "I hate to ask . . ."

Stephen perked up. "Yeah, Luce?"

"But that trap's dripping again under the sink. If it's not too much trouble . . ."

"No trouble at all." Stephen rose but then hesitated. "Ted's tools?"

She went back to filling the kettle. "That's why I have to ask, Stevie." An embarrassed smile. "See, stupid me, I had a yard sale, and somebody offered a hundred dollars cash . . . and all I could *see* was that bill."

"No trouble. We've got everything in the truck." Stephen darted down the stairs.

She had turned off the tap but was staring out the window.

Adcox noticed. He closed the refrigerator, crossed the worn linoleum to the sink and slowly took her in his arms. A father to his child, it seemed—although they could not have been more than two years apart. Nothing happened for a moment. He went on smiling down at her, and she up at him. The sunlight glinting in through the window found the flaws in their aging faces. Then she rested her temple against his shoulder and closed her eyes.

"You need something," he said. "You call. Don't go waiting until we drop by."

For the first time there were tears. Brian realized that he had been expecting them from the moment he had stepped inside the kitchenette. And then a more jarring realization: he had watched Adcox play out this same scene with his own mother. He felt a bit nauseated. Off-balance. The floor had rocked and tilted, and he was sliding back into helplessness—when his mother had slowly begun to die. He had to get out of this cramped kitchen that opened onto an equally cramped living room with cheap furniture and a dime store portrait of the Pope. He needed to go downstairs, outside into the sunlight—and see if it was Brian McCaffrey who was playing on the walkway with a fire engine, refusing to talk to his dead father's friends.

But he waited until Stephen returned with a toolbox before quietly excusing himself.

Brian sat on the warm engine cowling and listened drowsily to Adcox say that they were a family, all the firemen and their dependents, their survivors, and that the bonds were inviolate, eternal. Stephen added that the city council had murdered Ted by closing the station that could have backed his company on a big apartment building fire. From the get-go the chances were stacked against a fire-man, Adcox went on in his suddenly fierce and unforgiving voice, and for every cop who was killed in the line of duty five fire fighters died. Compound that with an antagonistic city council, and the chances for survival dwindled to nothing. A litany of anger. But, at its end, when Brian asked them what could be done, neither of them said anything. Anger without hope. That was dangerous, Brian realized.

They found the station in celebration, the firemen passing around a bottle of champagne. "What's up?" Adcox asked, smiling.

Santos explained that Pengelly had made captain.

Adcox—and everyone else—looked to Stephen. He stood motionless for a split second, then walked over to

120

Pengelly and offered his hand. "You'll make one hell of a captain, Walt."

"I wish it could've been both of us."

"That's the breaks." Then Stephen withdrew into his room.

Pengelly thanked everyone but called an end to the revels. Brian realized that he didn't want to rub it in; Stephen had five more years of service than he. Most of the men returned to the soap opera that had been running in the background, but Tim went down the pole, perhaps in the hope of a late matinee in Franny's window. Brian tried to concentrate on the soap but was quickly bored by the phony dialogue. How could people feel so bad and look so good? He strolled downstairs and outside.

Tim was perched on a pipe railing. "Ain't right, is it?"

"What?"

"I'm taking nothing away from Pengelly, but Stephen's twice the fireman he is."

Brian shrugged.

"Maybe he doesn't want to be captain," Tim said hopefully.

"Oh, he wants it. He just—"

Stephen had swept out the door and was standing in front of them. "You guys look bored."

Brian knew better than to say anything, but Tim fell into the trap. "You know, L.T., I am. Sorta. Except for chasing those chickens, it hasn't been much of a day."

"Let's see if we can do something about that." Stephen motioned for them to follow.

They filed through the station and emerged out back at the foot of the training tower. The concrete shell soared five stories up into the milky sky, just wide enough for a stairway and a small room on each level.

Adcox stood by, his boot planted atop a stack of hose rolls. "Should we test them for steroid use first?" he asked Stephen.

"You kidding?" A humorless grin. Stephen was obviously working off his disappointment, and for the first time Brian actually hoped for an alarm. He found his

121

brother's mood ugly, desperate and juvenile. "Just look at them—they look like marathon runners. *Female* marathon runners."

Tim snorted.

"You think I'm funny?" Stephen asked, fishing a stopwatch out of his pocket.

"Well sure, L.T."

"You ain't seen nothing yet. All right, probies—you should know the drill. If they had enough bananas, the academy could teach a monkey this drill. Ready, Axe?"

"Ready."

"Go!" Stephen clicked on the watch.

Tim picked up a roll, then ran for the base of the five flights. Adcox kept up with him, slapping him on the fanny, telling him how pretty he was with strain in his face. In a flash of brass and deft hands, Adcox had joined the hose to a dummy standpipe, and Tim was dragging the other coupling up the concrete steps, trailing the flat, cotton-jacketed ribbon behind him.

Brian grabbed another roll and held it against his chest, waiting.

"On your shoulder—not your goddamn titties," Stephen growled.

"That's not the way we were taught. Grip a couple folds and carry by hand—"

"Go!"

Brian pounded up two flights to Tim, dropped to his knees and coupled his length onto Tim's. "Nice touch, McCaff," Tim said in admiration of his speed, then started down the stairs for another roll.

Brian continued lugging hose toward the top.

"Having fun, probie?" Stephen's voice wafted up to him.

"Damn you," Brian answered, under his labored breath. He dropped the coupling and hurried down again, passing Tim on the way up. He was scuttling on bent legs and an arm, like Quasimodo tugging a fresh rope up into the belfry. For once he was not grinning.

"You two aren't breaking any records," Stephen said

as Brian reached him, panting, his leg muscles twitching as the burning sensation from the climb wore off.

Brian took the next roll, but Stephen wrenched it out of his grasp. "On your shoulder—like this!"

"I'm off balance that way."

"Fuck your balance." Stephen picked up another roll, his eyes furious. One hundred pounds.

"I'm serious. I can't—"

"Take two and let's go at it!"

Brian shook his head, smiling.

Adcox said from some shade, where he was squatting, "Your knee'll give out, Stevie."

"Like shit. Come on, probie!"

"You know, when I'm real disappointed, I just turn in early and say to hell with the world. Works for me."

"Take two!"

He had to prove something after revealing too much last Friday night. Had to erase that moment of weakness, of self-doubt. Brian finally understood, although he didn't condone. And what if Stephen couldn't have this satisfaction? What if he found out that he couldn't triumph all the time? Might be interesting. Might do some good.

At last, Brian leaned over and picked up two rolls. "I'll spot you three strides."

"My ass." But Stephen took off first.

Brian caught up with him on the second flight. Stephen gained on him with a burst of speed but began losing ground as they charged over the third landing. Brian thought to goad him but didn't have the wind. The rolls dug into his shoulders like manhole covers.

Stephen took the inside of the turn by bashing Brian with his elbow. "Give up?" he grunted, a school-ground taunt that gave Brian a surge of anger just when he had been on the verge of walking the rest of the way up. He gradually left Stephen behind.

"Shit!" Stephen cried.

He had fallen, but before Brian could stop to help, he was on his feet again, giving chase, his face inflamed.

Brian sprinted headlong up the last flight and burst out onto the roof a few inches ahead of Stephen, who dropped against the hot concrete and rolled on his side away from Brian.

He didn't move.

"You . . . you okay?" Brian huffed, lightly touching his brother's forearm.

Stephen shook off his grasp and quickly sat up. That dauntless grin. Is that what Helen had eventually tired of?

Then Brian saw the blood. On Stephen's trouser leg over the shin. "Jesus."

"It's nothing." Stephen pulled up the pant leg and examined the deep, bluish gash in his tibia. He dropped the cuff at once and squinted up into the sky, ground his teeth together. "Can't leave all this hose unrolled."

"What? Just Tim and me? We got supper to cook."

"Tim can get going on supper. You roll the hose."

"Christ, I've learned my lesson."

Stephen glared at him. His shin was obviously beginning to ache in earnest. "What's that?"

"Don't beat big brother up the stairs."

"You got a problem with drilling, probie?" Stephen got up, grabbed the rail that ran around the edge of the roof, and tested his injured leg by putting his weight on it. He winced.

"No problem, L.T."

"Good."

"Except—why one drill for the company and another one for me?"

"Let me get out my violin."

Brian rose, looked out over the southside. It looked hazy, malodorous under the late afternoon light. "You know, you were on to something the other night on the drive home . . ."

Stephen kept silent.

"This is the kind of shit that killed Dad. And it's killing you too, Stephen. Sucking you in by the inch." Brian expected an outburst, but his brother was strangely unfazed. He even chuckled.

"We can talk about this when you learn how much effort it takes just to be mediocre around here. Roll the hose, probie."

· 13 ·

Schmidt braked too sharply as he rounded the corner, and Brian nearly flew off the tailboard. "Hey, I'm riding back here, man!" He jumped down and trotted forward to give the engineer hell, but then he saw the young black woman standing in the middle of the street. She was gazing up at the smoke that was trailing flatly out of the uppermost windows of the tenement. Cataleptic eyes, an ashen cast to her skin. "Miss," he asked, "are you all right?"

Nothing. She was breathing shallowly through her mouth.

"Probie!" Stephen shouted from the engine. "Give a hand here!"

Brian ignored him. He gently turned the young woman toward him. Her eyes were red-rimmed. Somewhere in these last several minutes since the box alarm had been pulled, she had found the time to cry. And with that he understood.

"You were afraid, weren't you?"

The eyes snapped to life, focused on his lips.

"You saw the fire, and you had to run."

"Yes . . . oh yes . . ." Her face crumbled. "I left my baby. I left her up there 'cause I was so scairt."

A chill went up Brian's sweaty back. "Which apartment?"

"Three-fifteen." And then she fainted.

Brian caught her as she folded forward, although her head knocked against his helmet. "Axe!"

Adcox let go of the clamp holder to the length of hard suction hose he was taking down.

"Got one in shock here! Roll paramedics!"

Adcox ran for the radio microphone, and Stephen appeared at Brian's side. "What d'you have?"

"Her baby's still up there. Unit three-fifteen."

"Shit." On the run, Stephen ripped an axe off the engine and started toward the entrance.

A voice squealed over the bullhorn. The battalion chief's. "Hang on a sec, Steve, we got a hoseline coming."

Stephen waved, but went through the door.

Brian hesitated, then put on his mask and followed. A chaos of smoke. He could hear Stephen's boots drumming up the stairs. He caught up with him just as a wave of fire gushed down the well and broke over them. Brian lost his footing, crashed backward and slid down to the landing below.

Stephen had stood through the worst of it, wrapped in tendrils of flame. "Don't take that kind of crap from it!" he shouted through his mask. "Don't let it know you're scared!"

"If it can smell, it knows I'm scared," Brian said, scrambling up to Stephen's side again.

"Come on!"

"I'm coming, for chrissake."

Brian had the impression that the fire was withdrawing just a few feet ahead of them, and that Stephen, by slapping the walls with his axe and hammering at the flaming boards, was keeping it on the run.

Brian watched a wooden door slam shut as if by a spirit hand.

It began creaking. Massive breaths pressing against it.

Stephen knelt on one side and motioned for Brian to wait on the other.

The wood seemed on the verge of splintering. The fire had stopped running. It wanted to roll out at them again, cartwheel them down the stairs, leave them dazed, senseless and drowning in its wash of flames. They would be carried from this building like blackened statues of boxers, arms and legs coiled for an attack that had been cut short because Stephen wouldn't wait for a hoseline.

Stephen suddenly grinned at him. His calm, measured breaths were sighing out the overpressure valve. "You okay?"

Brian nodded. But his own breath discharges sounded like a locomotive at full speed.

"Ready?"

"Stephen, let's wait for the hose team."

"Listen to it, probie . . ." The fire was exhaling against the door, scorching through the wood to get at them. "Jump when I say."

"Stephen—"

"It *won't* get us." Stephen stood and tightened his grip on his axe. "Watch!" He imbedded the blade in the jamb near the upper hinge—and wrenched. Then he ripped free the lower hinge, kicked the door in and dropped to the floor.

Flame whooshed out at his helmet, but curled upward before reaching him. It played itself out in blue streamers along the smoke-darkened ceiling.

Stephen picked up the flattened door and, using it as a shield, charged the fire.

Brian tried to follow, but a huge flame appeared to part around Stephen. These two roaring tongues then clapped together around Brian's chest. He was suspended in pain, paralyzed. And then flat on his back.

When he could move again, he crawled out into the hallway.

Adcox and Grindle stepped over him, a delicious mist leaking from the nozzle of their hose, cooling him. They washed down the room, raising billows of steam that hid Stephen from sight.

Brian rose weakly on his elbows. Dazed, he watched through the foggy doorway.

Nothing stirred inside the room. Gone. Swallowed by the fire.

It finally hit him in a split second that went from icy and shocking to strangely quiet. Loss always presented itself as a sea of dark glass. A modicum of relief. It was over. The worst that could possibly happen had finally happened. He waited for the guilt to sift through the numbness, and it finally came with thoughts of Sean. How could he hope to explain . . . ?

Yet, a figure was barreling through the spray toward him. Long, easy strides. No panic. Less possibility of tripping. Stephen passed between Adcox and Grindle without halting, his outfit smoldering from the heat that had nearly taken him. His coat bulged. He whipped it open to reveal a baby. Pink ribbons in her cornrowed hair.

Stephen dropped her into Brian's arms.

He shook off a glove and tried to feel her breaths on the back of his hand. Nothing. And no brachial pulse, as far as he could tell in his excitement.

He pulled off his mask and immediately covered her mouth and nose with his lips.

"No," Stephen said hoarsely, taking her out of Brian's arms, resting her flat on the floor. He touched two fingers to her sternum and started the compressions before sealing off half her small face with his mouth.

"Probie!" Adcox was waving for Brian to take his place on the hoseline, so he could help Stephen.

Brian stood beside Grindle, who ignored him as he continued to pour water into the room.

Adcox called on Stephen's radio handset for the paramedics to come up. Then he counted out loud for Stephen. Five compression to one breath. Again. And again. Stephen was a machine. Perpetual motion. Blind to disappointment. He could go forever.

Brian stopped watching. He listened to the hiss of the dying fire.

•　　•　　•

Stephen found him sitting on the tailboard, staring down the crowded street at nothing in particular. "Brian?"

His brother's glassy eyes clicked toward him.

"I thought you should know. She's going to make it. Just got the word from the hospital."

"Great." A croak.

"You doing okay?"

Brian started to nod, but then stopped. "I wanted to wait."

"Yeah?"

"I would have waited for the hoseline . . . forever, I guess."

Stephen sat beside him. Brian was finished. He had seen probies in this zombie state before; the signs were unmistakable. Let him down gently. "There was a kid up there. I went in because that's what I do. It's my way. It isn't everybody's. I'm just asking you to pull your weight. Show a little spirit. You don't have to be me."

"This was Dad's way too."

"Maybe, maybe not," Stephen said, although he felt the dodge catch in his throat. "We'll never know. We were too young to really know him."

"I saw him die." Quiet adamancy. Brian was staring down the street again, out into a bank of dirty gray clouds hovering over the lake. "Yours is the same way. I just don't have it. Don't want it, maybe."

"Time to move on?"

Brian gave a noncommittal shrug.

"You know, there's no shame in not being suited—"

"Okay—you win, Stephen." Brian stood. "You're the best man. Cut the soft sell." Then he ducked inside the riding compartment and slid shut the door.

Jennifer's phone rang. The intercom line. She set aside a fire department manpower study that seemed unnecessarily complicated and punched the glowing button. "Yes, Sally?"

"Call for you, Ms. Corcoran." That saccharine voice. Sally had actually put it on her employment application:

her career goal was to become a professional cheerleader for the NFL. But worse than that, Jennifer had the suspicion that she was spying on Martin for the fire fighters union—she was their favorite groupie. "A Brian McCaffrey on line two."

Frowning, Jennifer coiled the telephone cord around her index finger.

"Are you in?" Sally asked. "Do you want me to take a number?"

"No, it's all right. I'll take it." She fortified herself with a quick breath, then depressed line two. "Brian?"

"Hi."

He sounded sober. So far so good. Let him know that it will be all business from now on. Put any dealings on terra firma before he leads you down into another bog of accusation and counter-accusation. "Is there something Martin or I can do for you?"

"Maybe." He sounded exhausted, or depressed. "I've been thinking about what you said the other night. About working with Don Rimgale, I mean."

"Are you saying you want the job?"

"Kinda."

"Yes or no, Brian."

"Well, I was wondering if we might talk about it over dinner. If it's convenient."

She vacillated, but then glanced through the open doorway that connected her office to Martin's—and saw his handsome face inclined over his work. He looked vaguely worried. "Yes or no. Please."

Pause. "Yeah, I guess I'll take it."

"Okay. I'll arrange things with Assignments."

"Just don't try to arrange things with a case of scotch."

"Pardon?" she asked, already making herself a note to phone Captain Belt first thing in the morning.

"Nothing. Private joke. Maybe I'll see you sometime."

"Maybe."

"Yeah?" Surprised hope in his voice.

"Lots of campaign functions coming up in October. May I send you the list?"

Another pause. "Sure." Then, without another word, he hung up.

Stephen drove past the brownstone, its facade smoke-blackened, as dark as the night except for the sheets of plywood nailed over the openings. It would never be refurbished again. Not in this neighborhood. He parked the Fiat along the next side street and walked up the alley by which Don Rimgale had approached the building the night of the fire. Good man, Rimgale. An eye for detail, but none of the pretensions to intellectuality that made most investigators a pain in the ass. He had been a decent engine company man as well. He would find out why an accountant named Alan Seagrave had wound up charred atop the hood of his new Porsche.

One of Stephen's coat pockets was heavy with a crow-bar, the other with a dry-cell flashlight. He stepped quietly up to the back door. There was enough starlight for him to see to pry loose a corner of the plywood sheet.

He slipped inside.

He stood for a moment in the blackness. It smelled sooty, violated. A suggestion of burned flesh came to him, although that was impossible: Seagrave had died outside the stoop, not inside his offices. Yet, a man had perished on the premises, and Stephen had smelled so many burned men, the precise stench could be summoned on command. It clung to nose hairs for days, to the memory forever.

Brutalized. A gutted building always seemed brutalized. Raped. Debris crunched under his shoes.

He switched on his flashlight and ran the beam along the charred beams, across the crazed glass of a mirror and over the ruined baseboards that had so intrigued Rimgale.

Already his hands were dirty. He should not have come. Soon his clothes would be as filthy as if he had slept in the weeds like a bum. He was breathing in the sooty corruption of this place, and nothing about him would be clean from now on. That is what suspicion did.

But he went on searching.

· 14 ·

Brian wiped the rain off the shoulders of his blazer, his clip-on tie, then stepped inside the old Chinatown station. A year before, its ladder apparatus had been demolished in a traffic collision. Instead of replacing it with a new truck, headquarters—in the spirit of tightfistedness sweeping city government—had seen fit to partition off the storage room and convert it into several Arson offices, freeing more space in the fortress downtown for the administrative functions of the department.

This much Brian had already learned about Arson.

He smiled through an arched opening in the glass separator, at the receptionist in her cubby.

"Don Rimgale?"

She waved him toward the back as if anybody who wanted to see Rimgale was a gust of nerve gas.

He strolled past the solitary engine that had survived the cutback. Less than state-of-the-art. No tarp over the hose bed. Tiny riding compartments. Open doors drifted past. Airless pigeonholes with just enough room for a desk, two chairs, file cabinet and wastebasket. Harried-looking investigator on the phone or reading reports. The door with Rimgale's name on it was slightly ajar. Brian started to knock on the jamb but then overheard some conversation inside.

"Stop me if I get this wrong," Rimgale was saying with an utterly insincere tone of reasonableness. "The fire's almost out."

"Yes, sir."

Brian shifted his view to include the young man in the chair set before Rimgale's cluttered desk. An obvious probie. Blond crewcut, florid complexion—unless he was utterly mortified, and his high color would fade as soon as he escaped the Grand Inquisitor.

"You're upstairs on the unburned floor checking for heat."

"That's right, sir."

"Good, so far. Very good. But you've been told by your battalion chief, your captain, and by *me*, Lord of the Flame, Master of All Who Tread in Rubber Boots, not to do anything up there until ordered."

Silence.

"Am I on the right track?" Rimgale asked.

"I believe so, sir."

"But now the itch starts, and all of a sudden comes the Glory Boy Flash—I can be a hero. Heroes just don't stand around. So on your lonesome, you decide to punch out a window for a little ventilation. Is that it, son?"

"Yes, sir—I guess I was thinking along those lines."

"*Thinking?*" Rimgale gave him a merciless chuckle. "Was this before or after you noticed you were standing in a lake of gasoline?" Silence, of course. "You could have crisped half your company with that stunt. But to hell with your company, you wrecked the physical evidence *I* use to prove that a fire's arson. You have made my day longer, probie. You have heaped one more straw on my tired back." A scrape of chair legs as Rimgale rose. "So get out of here, already, before I forget my manners."

The probie shot past Brian, a red-faced blur.

134

"Who's lurking out there?" Rimgale barked.

"Brian McCaffrey." He stepped inside. He had always seen the investigator from a distance. Rimgale was tall, like Adcox, and small-waisted for a man in his fifties. Arms so long he could probably scratch his shins without sitting.

"You selling that crappy disability insurance for the union?"

"No, I'm your new assistant."

Rimgale sank into his hardback chair, his brilliant dark eyes never leaving Brian's face. "You must be Dennis's kid."

"That's right."

"Well, I work alone, Dennis's kid. Shut the door on your way out." He picked up an incident report. His lips moved as he read.

Brian stood his ground.

After a while, Rimgale glanced up. "You still here?"

"Get used to me. I'm not going anywhere."

"Oh . . . a real stalwart." Rimgale abruptly rose and took off his sports shirt. His undershirt whipped up, revealing a patchwork of pink mottles stretching over his belly. Skin grafts. He caught Brian staring. "That's right, they pasted part of my ass onto my stomach."

"Then how d'you know if you're coming or going?"

Rimgale smirked as he put on a fresh white shirt that had been hanging off the handle of the uppermost file drawer. He grabbed a tie out of his pencil drawer and started for the door. "I'm going."

Brian tailed him down the corridor. "I think we should get something straight here." His voice was jiggling from trying to keep up. "I was assigned to this office by the city."

"Look, I knew your dad. Had a helluva reputation on this job. But that don't mean you get any slack. Now, may I correct you on something?"

"Please." They hurried past the receptionist and out into the light rainfall.

"Cities don't assign," Rimgale said. "*Assholes* assign.

Swayzak sent you down here. You go back to the alderman and tell him I got neither room nor a purpose for you. Jesus, I got to step outside my cubicle just to change my mind." His red sedan was parked in a small lot across the street. "You think you're the first Quisling an alderman tried to dump on me, McCaffrey?" He waved to a string of fellow investigators trickling back from coffee at the nearby Chinese coffee shop, then unlocked his door and got inside the sedan, rocking the chasis with his weight.

Brian's door remained locked. He tapped on the glass.

Rimgale gunned the engine and curled his fingers in a little wave of farewell.

Brian began walking away. He flapped his arms. Nothing to be done except call Jennifer and try to put pressure on Rimgale from that end. But then he recalled the effect Nightengale's antics had had on Tim. Worth a shot.

He stood in the middle of the exit. Rimgale braked within inches of taking Brian's legs out from under him with the front bumper. He tapped the horn.

A few of the investigators had stopped on the sidewalk to watch. The continuing saga of the Rimgale and His Probies, no doubt.

"Don, please!" Brian cried, passionately, slapping the wet hood with his palms. "I beg you!"

Rimgale rolled down his side window. "Hey, what's with you?"

"Don, I just don't think a positive HIV test should come between us like this!"

The investigators quickly turned and moved on.

Rimgale's chin sank. He slowly exhaled. Then, without looking, he reached over and flipped up the latch to the front passenger door. Brian got inside, snapped on his seatbelt.

Rimgale was smiling. "Nobody they sent ever tried *that* before. You must be the cream of the crop."

"You mean I get brownie points for resourcefulness?"

"Maybe." Rimgale pulled out onto the slick street. "But first the ground rules."

"I'm all ears."

"You're all balls." Rimgale absentmindedly turned in front of an oncoming bread truck, and its horn brayed at him. "Fuck Swayzak, you work for me. Pipe anything to him without me knowing, I'll cut off those balls and drop them in the pickled eggs jar at Willie's. I don't care who you know, what you think you can do to me, I'll swing the hammer."

"I don't owe Martin Swayzak anything."

Rimgale pinned him with a hard glance. "You just *think* you don't. That's because he hasn't come around to collect yet. If I know that bastard, you can count on it."

Brian looked out the rain-speckled windshield. Rimgale was right. And what would he do if it were Jennifer who called in the debt for the alderman? He shook off the thought and asked, "Where we headed?"

"Joliet."

"Why?"

"Pest control."

A guard brought him into the interview room, a slight man in his early forties with thinning black hair. A bony ledge hooded his eyes. He looked at Brian with suspicion, then turned to Rimgale. A glimmer of a smile. "Shadow."

"How're you doing, Ronald? Staying comfortable?"

"Comfort?" Ronald asked with a weak laugh. He rested his hands on the table. They were fire-withered. "With all the screaming in this place?"

"How's that, buddy?"

"These goddamn crazies scream all night. Scream when they bang each other. Scream when they can't. I'm dying in here, Shadow."

There was something peculiar about his face. After a few moments Brian realized what it was. Ronald didn't blink. As a consequence, maybe, his eyes were watery.

"Who's this person?" he asked, meaning Brian.

Rimgale said, "He works for me."

"Fireman?"

"Yes."

Ronald finally looked away. "I don't think I like him."

"Oh, come on."

"Sorry, I just don't."

"Hell," Rimgale said, "you like me, don't you? And I'm a fireman."

"That's different . . . we got a history." Ronald leaned across the table and read the badge Brian had been given at prison intake. "Brian McCaffrey." Something clicked into gear behind the runny eyes. "Any relation to Dennis McCaffrey?"

Brian sat up. "How'd you know that?"

"Ronald knows all about fires in Chicagoland. Starting with Mrs. O'Leary, right?"

A guarded nod. "There was no cow. The bitch set it."

"He's writing a book about all the big fires, the fatal ones."

"Trying to write it," Ronald corrected. "But this screaming. I'll get some real work done when I'm paroled."

Brian hadn't liked him knowing about his father. He felt as if his past had just been burglarized. He decided to goose him a little. "How come you don't blink?"

"I do. When I'm alone. But one shouldn't blink too much around strangers."

"How's your mother?" Rimgale quickly asked.

A listless shrug. "They won't tell me where she is. They never will, you know." He suddenly shifted in his chair like an antsy child. "Have you told Brian all about me?"

"Do you want me to?"

A roll of his eyes. Complete indifference now. "I don't care."

"Ronald here likes telephones," Rimgale said. "Used to tape wooden matches to the bell striker and wrap it in cotton . . ." Ronald's head bobbed in agreement. "And when he got restless, he'd just started making calls. Retirement homes."

"Not always," Ronald said.

"That's right. We finally met in a factory. What'd they manufacture there, Ronald?"

"Orthopedic shoes."

"Oh, yes," Rimgale said, "same brand your mother wears, isn't it?"

"I forget. How do you expect me to remember *everything*."

"Sorry. But what matters here is that you actually torched it for the owner."

"Exactly," Ronald said. "I heard he was going under, so I suggested it to him over drinks. Mama doesn't like me drinking, but I figured it was for business. A business lunch, you see." He turned to Brian. "I'm not what you think I am. I'm doing a book, you know."

"Back to the fire," Rimgale prompted.

"Just your basic bankruptcy torch," Ronald said, dreamily at first. "In and out in five minutes for five thousands bucks. A grand a minute. Not bad, huh? How much do you make a minute, fireman?" he asked Brian.

"About thirty cents. But there's no screaming at my place."

A coy grin. A sense of humor was buried somewhere in all that psychological offal. But then the eyes clouded, seeing the fire again. "The animal . . . it turned on me. My hair, my hands . . . everything in flame. Shadow was on stakeout in the alley. He barged inside. Tried to help me. But he didn't see the open drum of adhesive next to me . . ." He glanced down at Rimgale's midriff. "Shadow suffered for me. No one ever suffered for me before Shadow. Except Mama."

The intercom speaker on the wall buzzed to life: "Ronald Bartel to the hearing room."

"I want to find my mama," he explained, rising.

Rimgale and Brian took two chairs at the back of the room.

A female psychiatrist was testifying to the members of the parole board. Portly men in their fifties and sixties with earnestly bored expressions. "No, gentlemen," she was saying, "Mr. Bartel is not a pyromaniac. While his profile fits a few of the cluster characteristics—his father abandoned the family, his mother reared him in what can only be described as a pathological environment, he has manifested feelings of inadequacy all of his life—Mr. Bartel lacks the key behavior of this type of pathological arsonist . . ." She paused for effect.

Ronald was listening intently; he looked as if he were in love with her.

"And that, Dr. Norris?" the spokesman asked.

"According to the investigative reports, Mr. Bartel did not impulsively set fires. He didn't use combustibles on hand at the scene. On the contrary, he exercised considerable forethought . . . and this led me to a different appraisal of his profile when he entered this institution."

"And that, madam?" It was going on lunchtime.

"Mr. Bartel exhibited the behaviors of a paranoid schizophrenic."

"Past tense?"

"Yes, in functional terms. As supervising psychiatrist, I would describe his progress as remarkable. Taking into account his cooperative attitude in therapy, his six years already served under the control of my department, and his painful physical disability as the result of his own actions—I recommend parole."

Rimgale chuckled.

She stepped down, and Ronald gave her a long look full of sexual hunger. Vaguely incestuous. It was his turn, next.

"Mr. Bartel," the spokesman said, "do you regret your crimes?"

Ronald looked down at his grotesque hands. "It's been a long road. A difficult road full of bends that brought me face-to-face with myself. My past." A long beat. But not too long. Stomachs were rumbling. "I finally understand the pain I caused."

"If released, will you commit such crimes again?"

"I will not, sir. God is my witness."

"Do you consider yourself ready for society?"

"Yes."

"Very well . . ." The spokesman was ready to dismiss Ronald and huddle up with the other members, but Rimgale had risen and strolled to the middle of the room.

"Yes, sir?" the spokesman asked.

"Don Rimgale, sir. Investigating fire officer in the four cases of arson that led to Mr. Bartel's incarceration here."

"Do you have something to say, Mr. Rimgale?"

"If the board pleases."

A nod for him to proceed.

"I believe you know me, Mr. Bartel."

Ronald smiled at him. Sweetness and light. "I do. You saved my life, sir."

"And that's what I'd like to talk about."

Ronald raised an eyebrow.

"Are there any circumstances under which you might set another fire?"

"Can't think of any," Ronald said. A twitch tugged at the corner of his mouth. "No, absolutely not. No, sir."

"What about saving your own life?"

Ronald thought about that one. "Well, I suppose . . . like most human beings . . . I'd do most anything to save myself. I don't get what—"

"Where's your mother, Mr. Bartel?"

"My mother?" he echoed.

"Yes. Any idea?" Rimgale took a butane lighter from his trouser pocket, spun the striker wheel with his thumb, then adjusted the flame as high as it would go.

Ronald was squinting. He clearly wanted to turn his face, but couldn't. "I . . . I don't know. A retirement home somewhere, I suppose. They won't tell me."

"Have you asked?"

"All the time. I keep asking, but nobody will tell me."

"Let's say that you *are* released—"

"That's my hope, Shadow. My dream." And then staccato with panic. "What's this about? What do you know about Mama?"

"I know where she is."

"Christ, man—tell me." A growl. "You saved me once. Tell me."

"What would you do if I told her where *you* live?"

Ronald's unblinking eyes became enormous, threatened to burst. "You . . . you wouldn't, Shadow. You're my friend."

"I'm afraid you've been a bad boy lately. Making eyes at one of the new punks in your cell block. I'm going to have to tell her."

"Then . . . then it's just as you said. I'd have to defend myself. Hit back." Ronald was close to shouting now. "Find where she lives and burn her out." He shot to his feet. "I'd have to burn the bitch out!" He spun on the board. "So would you, dammit! All of you! Help me burn the fucking bitch!"

Rimgale gently pressed him down into the chair again. Ronald whimpered, bit his knuckles.

"It's okay," Rimgale said. "I'm not going to tell her." Then he approached the board. Stunned faces. He took a folded sheet of paper from his inner coat pocket. "A death certificate, gentlemen, for one Earline Bartel." He dropped it in front of them like a bomb. "She died in a retirement home fire of suspicious origin. Ten years ago." He patted Ronald's shoulder on the way out. "See you next year, buddy."

In the hallway, Rimgale did a little victory dance and said to Brian, "Getting where I look forward to this."

"Jesus, I thought for a minute that he was going to walk."

"No way. Not while I'm still alive."

They were interrupted by the warden's secretary, who gave Rimgale a message to phone his office without delay.

"What's it mean?" Brian asked on their jog to the parking lot.

"What d'you think it means when they say no delay?"

· 15 ·

Three engine companies had already knocked down the fire. Among them Brian saw the Seventeen's rig with Schmidt at his panel. He waved, but the engineer looked right through him.

So much for alumni.

Stephen trotted up to the engine a moment later, grabbed a pike pole and, turning, saw Brian. He paused, a stillness coming into his face. Another snub on the way? No. He touched two fingers to his helmet in salute.

Brian nodded, and Stephen rushed back inside.

Vaguely grateful, Brian wiped the drizzle off his face with his blazer sleeve. An oddly pleasant realization: from now on, Stephen would probably go out of his way to be kind to him.

"Hey, hotshot," Rimgale called from the open trunk of his sedan, "quit rubbernecking and make yourself useful." He tossed Brian one of his heavy black cases, then jerked his head toward the engines. "Wishing you were back riding a tailboard?"

"Not on your life."

"You will before long, believe me. Come on . . ." Rimgale strode under the marquee and into the theater. Brian paused to read the letters UNDER RENOVATION—OPENING CHRISTMAS, then followed, the case bouncing against the side of his leg as he hurried to catch up.

The attack hoses branched off from the Deco lobby, two sloping down into the auditorium, three snaking up the streamlined chrome staircase.

Rimgale barged through the curtains next to the empty refreshment counter. "Where is he?" he asked Washington, who was down in the orchestra pit, hunting for the source of a thin layer of smoke that had crept into the vaulting room.

"You missed it. Take the mezzanine stairs."

"Not much fire then?"

"Nope."

Rimgale tore past Brian on his way back to the lobby. "Come on, come on. About-face, already. The way you move—no wonder your brother dumped you on me."

"Nice theater."

"You should've seen it in the old days. A palace. Maybe that's what they're trying to do here. Make it more than a dark place to jerk off."

"Yes," Brian said, "I'm sure that's how it was put in the prospectus."

At the top of the stairs was a black metal door with gold script: Mr. Donald Cosgrove. A hose kept it from completely closing, and a bittersweet scorched smell wafted out of the crack.

"Who's Cosgrove?" Brian asked.

"Good for you," Rimgale said. "You'll make an investigator yet." He started to reach for the latch, but the door swung open and an engine company lieutenant stood before him. "Hey, Don."

"Doesn't look like much of a fire."

"No, we were lucky with this one. Could've taken the whole structure, but the explosion blew out most of the flame. Good for us . . ." The officer stepped out of

144

the way so Rimgale and Brian could see the smoldering inner door on the far side of the small foyer. Ripped off its hinges, it covered all of the corpse except for a blistered hand jutting out from under an edge.

"Turn it over," Rimgale told Brian.

"What over?"

"The door, whiz kid. What d'you think I meant?"

It resisted movement.

"Harder," Rimgale said, down on one knee, shining his flashlight underneath.

Brian asked, straining. "What's stuck to it?"

"The poor dumb bastard it smacked in the kisser. There. Now it's coming."

The door gave with a sound like Velcro strips being torn apart. Brian gaped at the body, but Rimgale turned his attention to the doorknob. "Look here."

A key was still inserted in the lock.

Then Rimgale asked, "What's with you? I told you to look. Learn something."

"Jesus," Brian said, feeling a little light-headed. He couldn't take his eyes off the corpse. As far as he could tell, the victim had lost most of his face.

Rimgale smiled. "Quit thinking like a medical examiner. Stay on your own turf and you won't get sick. Now, instead of mooning at the gore, start thinking about the story all this fascinating physical evidence is just begging to tell you." Then Rimgale noticed something on the edge of the door, a smear of goo that he tested with a finger. Brian could see that it was still tacky. "Get me a glass vial . . . and don't flash inside any of my cases."

"I'm okay."

"Well, excuse me if I failed to notice before that you're an albino with hepatitis." Rimgale snatched the vial from him, used his penknife to scrape a sample of the goo off the door. He deposited it in the tube. "Tag it."

"How?"

"What d'you mean . . . *how?*"

"This is my goddamn first day, remember?"

Rimgale sighed and did it himself. Then he began strolling around the room in a clockwise fashion, murmuring into a hand-held tape recorder: "Heavy smoke stains observed in the entryroom . . . demarcation line high."

"What's that mean?" Brian asked.

Frowning, Rimgale turned off the recorder. "Fire never got hot enough in here to cook the soot off. It started someplace else."

Brian pointed toward the inner office, then looked to Rimgale.

"Doesn't take a genius," Rimgale said, stepping over the body and into the office. He began talking to his recorder again. "Less soot within the inner office. More heat." He penetrated deeper into the room, swept his flashlight beam along the walls. "And very little soot here. Stand back—you're in my light."

Brian withdrew to the threshold.

"Get that couch out of the way."

"Which is it?" Brian asked. "In or out?"

"That's what my wife said on our wedding night." And suddenly Rimgale laughed. An uproarious laugh that told Brian more about him than anything so far. Rimgale had made peace with his violent and absurd world. He sobered himself. "Come on, move that thing."

The portion of the wall protected by the couch showed no soot.

"So the fire was happy here . . ."

Brian said, "Pardon?"

"Use your head, hotshot. It was warm and cozy and in no hurry." Rimgale flicked on his recorder again. "Soot high, clean and unburned wall low—indicates slow burn in thermal balance . . . Find me some glass."

"Glass?"

"Do we have a language barrier here? *Glass*. A fusion of silica with flux and stabilizer. I'm sure you've seen some before."

Brian went to a blown window high in the outer wall and stood on his toes to retrieve some shards off the sill. The little liquid sounds of the rain and a moist coolness poured in around him. Nice, when compared with the rank stuffiness lingering inside. But he wanted to get the sample back to Rimgale before he snapped at him again.

"Glass found in ignition room is in small, thin pieces, indicating explosion. Lack of discoloration indicates a long, slow burn. Explosion came *after* slow burn . . . after . . ." Rimgale lowered the recorder to his side. "Okay . . . okay . . . started in this room. Took its time. The air eventually ran out. It couldn't breathe. So it snuffed out. Died." In a blink, he shook his head and said, "No, it *hibernated* . . . still all that trapped heat sifting around. Laying low. Waiting for some sucker to open the door and revive it with one gulp of air."

"Backdraft," Brian said.

"And what precisely is that, Mr. Top of the Class?"

Brian was inwardly pleased that Rimgale somehow knew his academy ranking. Another insight into him: he revealed less than he knew. "Backdraft is a static condition in which a fire has consumed all of its oxygen and will not go anywhere until the supply is replenished."

Instead of congratulating him, Rimgale turned to the plaster wall and began probing with his penknife. Then, into his recorder, he said, "Finish coat is burned away. Severe spalling of the rough coat—"

"Spalling," Brian said in an obstinate singsong. "Intense heat makes moisture within masonry elements collect into steam pockets. These burst, leaving the surface pitted or pockmarked."

Rimgale turned an eye on him. "The recital's over, dipshit."

"Sorry, nobody told me to go back to my seat."

Rimgale crouched to inspect a ruined wall socket. "That's our ignition point." He stood up and stepped aside. "Grab that hatchet I got in the big case and dig it out."

Plaster dust flying, Brian chopped the receptacle free.

"I'm getting the idea you do better on the unskilled stuff," Rimgale said, accepting it from him. Brian rose and looked over his shoulder. Rimgale pulled a copper wire out of the congealed mess. Its tip had melted and then hardened into a nuggetlike blob. Rimgale sniffed the receptacle, but then looked disappointed. "Hand me my recorder there." He gathered his thoughts for a moment; when he spoke again he sounded far more tentative than before. "All indications point to temperature in the inner office reaching about two thousand degrees. But the copper wire in the outlet on . . ." He glanced up, oriented himself. ". . . on the south wall melted, which required at least five thousand degrees." And then Brian could see him visibly come to a solution: "An accidental short in the plug could've created a spark of seven thousand degrees. Hot enough to melt the wire and start the fire."

"No, it couldn't," Brian said quietly.

Rimgale shut off the recorder and glared at him. He was speechless. Brian could understand. Years on the job and he was being called by a probie with all of six hours in arson investigation. But he was still wrong.

"I mean, you'd be right," Brian went on, "if we were talking about normal wire. But that's ten-gauge in that plug—industrial stuff. Who knows why the electrician installed it in here. But it won't melt at anything less than twelve thousand degrees. And no natural spark short of lightning gets that hot. Honest."

Rimgale continued to glare, his eyes as hostile and unblinking as Ronald Bartel's had been.

"In another life," Brian added a bit weakly, "I was in high-end electronics."

Rimgale went silently to his cases. He scratched something on the back of the plug with the point of his knife, then dropped the receptacle into a small cardboard box, which he promptly labeled.

Brian could hear him breathing, nasally, angrily, as he wrote. But still he refused to talk. Finally he snapped his fingers for Brian to follow and went down the stairs, through the lobby and into an exit corridor Brian guessed to lie directly beneath Benton's office.

He slowed until he was trailing Rimgale by several yards: his former station mates were mopping up.

"Check for burn patterns," Rimgale said. He tossed

him the flashlight without breaking stride and continued on toward the exit.

Brian advanced along the wall, his left hand in his pants pocket. He came to Tim first, who was probing the ceiling with a pike pole.

"Well," Brian said, "you surviving without me?"

Tim didn't stop to look at him. He kept lancing the wet plaster overhead. "There's been no replacement."

"They'll send out some fresh meat."

"No, they won't. Thanks to all the cuts your boss is making."

"Swayzak's not my boss." Brian said, his voice flat. He moved on. A depression in the floor had filled with dirty water that had percolated from the office above. He balked at wading through it in his Oxfords, but then realized that Nightengale was waiting for him to come to this decision.

He sloshed forward.

"Nice tie," Nightengale said, going back to work.

"Mind scraping down that wall for me?" Brian asked. "I would myself, but the tie, you know."

Nightengale hooked into and pulled down a section of wall, dropping it into the puddle and splashing Brian's slacks. "That do, McCaffrey?"

"Perfect." Then Brian could no longer put a good face on it. Tight-lipped, he continued his inspection, making no effort to speak to the others. But it was Grindle, sour-faced Grindle, who disarmed him.

"How's it going, Brian?" A sincere tone if only because it was halfhearted.

"Okay."

"Rimgale got you looking for patterns?"

"Yeah."

"It's his favorite make-work to give to a probie while he ducks out for a cup of java. But for once, there are some down here. Textbook funnels."

Brian hid his excitement. A vee, or funnel, indicated a point of ignition at the apex, with the flame and heat spreading laterally as they rose. Finding these patterns

down here meant that the arsonist had not trusted his handiwork up in Benton's office to conceal his homicide, but
had set backup fires below as well. Or the original fire
itself. A whole new equation could emerge out of this.
One that might dovetail with his observation to a skeptical
Rimgale about the ten-gauge wire. "Where are they?" he
asked Grindle.

"That way . . . yeah, in there someplace . . . to the
right . . . further . . . further."

Brian backstepped, finding nothing. A pike pole was
leaning against the bulging wall. "In here?"

"Yeah, right there somewhere. Don't you see?" Grindle asked. "Maybe that pole's in the way. Toss it here."

Brian knew as soon as he grasped the haft that the pole
was propped against the distended wall, not leaning
against it.

But it was too late.

The plaster collapsed, and a freshet of sooty water
poured over him, knocking him flat and holding him
against the floor until it had slopped away into the
depression.

"Sorry," Grindle said, "maybe there weren't any funnels after all."

It would have been better if the men had laughed, Brian
decided, but they looked at him with a quiet satisfaction
that retribution had been served. He stood up, resisted the
urge to wipe his face.

"That's enough, guys," Stephen said, coming down the
corridor with Adcox. "Wrap it up. Let's go."

The men began trooping past. Brian tried to stare each
of them squarely in the eye, but most looked at the floor.

Adcox offered his handkerchief. Brian shoved it aside.

"Hey, knock it off," Adcox said. "What the hell's the
matter with you? Stepping in the shit again. You could've
made it with us. Made it just fine." He glanced at Stephen, meaningfully. They had obviously disagreed on this
point. "Fine and dandy." He gestured at Brian's sopping
civvies, his clip-on tie that had come loose and folded
over the tack. "You don't want this, Baby McCaffrey.

What you got now is a job. Just a nine-to-five excuse for a life. Wake up. Come home, okay?'' Then he ambled after the others.

Stephen took a towel from his turnout coat pocket.

Brian grabbed it, dried his face and his hair. Then he held up the dirty towel as evidence. "So you knew."

"I knew."

"And didn't try to stop it?"

"Wasn't my place to."

"You're my brother, for chrissake!" Brian's voice came back at him in echoes.

"Keep it down." Stephen checked the corridor. Empty but for the two of them. "You made yourself fair game for this."

"How?"

"Cleaning out your locker at the station like you were getting out of prison. Whistling. Rubbing it in about upward mobility. The fast track."

Brian wanted to explain that the bluster during his departure from the Seventeen had been purely defensive, that when failure started squeezing him, he invariably showed little grace. It was him. His baggage. But he didn't know how to begin to talk about this.

Stephen's face softened. "How's it working out with Rimgale?"

"Okay, I guess."

"Is he square with you?"

"He's getting there." At least he had been until a few minutes before.

"Just don't let him get carried away."

Brian paused. A funny thing to say. "What d'you mean?"

"I don't know." Stephen had been caught off-guard, for he suddenly smiled. "He's a typical investigator, that's all. They get so wrapped up in their theories, they go out on a limb over nothing sometimes. See you on days off?"

"I doubt it. Rimgale's working straight through until he gets a handle on this."

"Good," Stephen said distantly, "I'm sure you can use the overtime."

Helen no longer relished her time alone. Her loneliness wasn't acute enough to make her want to change anything, but the delicious sense of privacy she had once taken from such moments was gone. It was simply an autumn Saturday morning with a certain emptiness to the warmth. A fading without vivid colors and scents. Burning leaves. She had lived all of her life in the yardless city, yet she dreamed of retiring in a tranquil place where the chill-crisped leaves were burned in heaps in backyards as big as parks. She had smelled this once, on a fall trip with her mother to visit an aunt in Wisconsin. She could still smell it . . . if she closed her eyes.

Hammering from above made her start.

She glanced at the kitchen phone, thought 911, but then found her courage and rushed up the steps, into her bedroom, and opened the dormer window.

Stephen was out on the gentle slope of the roof, replacing the ice-frayed shingles. "What're you doing?" She knew at once that she sounded angry, but it was more from being startled than finding him there.

"Fixing my roof."

"It's not your roof anymore. You got the Fiat. I got the roof."

He nodded, thoughtfully. Acceptance at long last? "Where's Sean?"

"Piano lessons."

"When'd this start?"

"When you caught up with the child support." She realized that she had found him in a strange mood. He had no anger left, and she wasn't entirely sure that this was good.

"My dad could bang the keys like a demon. Maybe it's inherited." He gazed down across the neighborhood. Fondly, she realized.

Pull back from doing this. Don't goad him when he's so low. But the past wouldn't let her. Memory, salted away in hurt and betrayal, wanted to exact something for the things that had happened. "I doubt it's inherited, Stephen. He doesn't bang. He's got a nice touch."

"So he wants to be a musician?"

"No, he wants to be a fire fighter."

A look of triumph. Damn him.

"Stephen, I don't like you just climbing up on my roof like this. Did you think to ring the bell?"

"Yes, I did. Started to twice. But I knew it'd feel so damn odd, I couldn't do it." Stephen idly tapped the hammer against the heel of his boot. He was wearing a black T-shirt. Showed off his powerful shoulders and chest. Jackson was a soft, pale man with no definition to his body. But he was kind, she reminded herself, guiltily.

"I won't do it again," Stephen said at last. "Sneak like a thief."

"I didn't mean that."

"It's just . . ." He looked at her, fully, with all his attention—something she could not remember. "I wanted to find some way to apologize for the other night at Fitzgerald's party. Even if I don't remember much of it."

"You remember."

"Yeah . . . you're right." He suddenly drove in a nail. Pounded hard three times. "Sorry I lit after Jackson like I did."

"You both were in the wrong. He shouldn't have made fun of Brian. I've tried to explain about the problems—"

"He treats you okay?" Stephen interrupted.

"Okay."

"As nice as I did?"

"You treated me like shit." But then she felt herself smile: the surprised look in his face had done it. "You want some coffee?"

"Nah, I've got to go."

"No, you don't." She held his eyes until he lifted out the screen and climbed into the bedroom. Her bedroom exclusively now, yet his mere presence, the commanding smell of him, took possession of it once again. He stole a glance at the double bed. Was that sad look regret or envy? Or just lust?

"Why do you always do that?" she asked, starting down the stairs first.

"Do what?"

"Change the subject whenever we get on Brian."

"Didn't realize."

"Remember me? Helen?" She poured him a cup at the stove, topped off her own. "I helped raise him in this house for two years—tried to put him through college."

"And he bombed at that too. How can somebody so smart fail at *everything*?"

She didn't have an answer. At least not a safe one.

"You were just a kid yourself, Helen. But you were good to him. Patient. I won't forget how good you were to my brother." He took a sip. "He's out."

"I heard. With Arson now. But how's he doing?"

"I don't know." That inappropriate smile she had once despised. Maybe it was no more than a facial tic. Someday a big medical school would come up with a name for it, and she would feel awful. "He hates my guts," Stephen went on. "I treated him better than any probie I've ever had, but he hates me. Bad. Still, I did the best thing for him—made him finally look at himself in the mirror."

"Didn't happen to get a glimpse of yourself while you were holding it up to him, did you?"

Still no anger. "What's that mean?"

"Remember the time he really got spacey?"

A cautious nod.

"And how he kept calling you *Dad* without realizing he was doing it?"

A little coffee had slopped over the lip of his cup into the saucer. Stephen reached for a napkin. "Not really. If you say. Does all this lead to—?"

"He doesn't need your approval, Stephen. That's what he wants from your father, but that can never come now."

A pause. She didn't know which way he would spring from it.

"Okay," he finally said, agreeably enough, "I can buy

154

that. But what're you trying to say about me here? It's me we're talking about, isn't it?"

"Brian needs your friendship. He wants a brother. But you keeping pushing him away."

Stephen shook his head. "He irritates me. I can't help it, he just does."

"It's more than that. I wish you'd talk about it someday, Stephen."

They sat together for a while longer, but in heavy silence now. He abruptly said something about coming back tomorrow to see Sean, if it was all right, then went out to the Fiat without another word. From the screen door, she watched him drive away.

He had left his tools on the roof. She would have to ask Jackson to take them down. Or they would rust.

· 16 ·

Brian had never stepped inside an autopsy room, but it was everything he had expected. Anemic neon fixtures plus powerful operating lights. Lots of porcelain and white tile. Stainless steel scales, like those in the produce section of a supermarket, dangling on chains from the high ceiling. And a corpse on each of two trayed tables, covered with gray plastic sheets. Everything was in place except the ghoul in a blood-splattered smock to conduct Rimgale and him through the horrors of the municipal charnel house. Ricco, the pathologist's chief technician, was a slender Hispanic with gold-rimmed glasses and a blank stare. He had dispensed with the bloody smock in favor of a polo shirt and a pair of stone-washed Levi's. "Okay," he said, pulling off the first sheet and exposing the shrunken, blackened remains of "Alan Seagrave." He turned to the other table and whisked off that sheet. "And Donald Cosgrove . . . until recently, certified public accountants of this city."

Cosgrove's corpse was in better shape than Seagrave's, although the outer layer of all visible skin had been sloughed off the underlying tissue by the searing heat of the explosion.

Brian felt less anxious than when he had first stepped inside the morgue. He had seen the elephant and was still in possession of his breakfast.

"Both deaths due to close encounters with stationary objects," Ricco went on. He seemed less blasé than intent upon conveying a great deal of intricate information as clearly as possible. "A Porsche windshield for Seagrave. An oak door for Cosgrove—"

"It had his name on it," Brian quipped, although with a subdued voice.

Ricco either had not heard or knew every morgue joke in existence. "The attitude of both trajectories is consistent with explosions. No non-relevant traumas. No significant blood toxicology."

Brian found himself staring at Seagrave. Is that what his father had looked like? They had brought him down to the street in a zipped-up body bag.

"Do you have today's return from the crime lab on that residue you scraped off the two doors?" Ricco asked Rimgale.

"No, not yet."

"Then it's waiting for you in your in basket, Don, because I just got my copy ten minutes ago by courier." Ricco apparently didn't want to ruffle any feathers. "The stuff is a combination of plumber's putty and rayophene gum."

Rimgale asked, "Does rayophene burn as hot as I think it does?"

"Right. Burns almost completely away when you light it. But we're straying outside my arena. You can ask the lab guys if you have any more questions about it." Ricco pivoted and leaned over Cosgrove. 'Here's something kind of interesting . . ." He began to lift the head and shoulders, but then he realized that he couldn't elevate them and point at the same time. He looked to Brian. "Mind giving me a hand, guy?"

"Have some spare gloves?"

"Jesus Christ," Rimgale said, "Cosgrove isn't going to try to sell you life insurance. Lift him."

Brian took a breath, then hefted the upper torso. The flesh he was forced to touch felt sticky, like barbecued chicken. Make a stab at nonchalance. Say anything. "How come he isn't stiff?"

"Rigor mortis is usually completely gone within forty-eight hours of death," Ricco said, not pleased at being sidetracked over the obvious. "See that patch of shirt there, Don?"

Brian stared off across the room, pretended he was holding a hundred-pound sack of dog food.

Rimgale said, "What's commingled with the flesh?"

"Yeah, right around there. We wondered about the slight discoloration, so we ran a spectro. Got lucky. We picked up some traces of trychticholorate."

"Trycht-o-what?"

"Nobody around here had ever heard of it either."

Brian fought a rising panic that his hands were clotting to the corpse.

"Trychticholorate," Ricco said, trippingly on the tongue, "is an absorption catalyst used for cleanup in toxic waste accidents. It's pretty rare, and on evidence that it's carcinogenic, they stopped making it a couple of years ago."

"You getting sick?" Rimgale suddenly asked.

Brian shook his head, although he had started trying to breathe through a stuffy nose. Autumn hay fever. Bring on the snow. Clean, white, odorless snow. He fixed on the image of an unbroken field of snow. But Rimgale's voice brought him back to the echoing room and the unstirring thing in his arms.

"So this stuff probably got in Cosgrove's clothes in a gas state from the fire?"

Ricco shrugged.

"What the hell was a rare toxic cleanup substance doing in two fires a mile apart?"

"That's your job, Don."

Suddenly, Brian felt movement in his grasp. He was sure of it, but he was afraid to tell Rimgale. The story would live longer than his rescue of Resusci-Annie. Maybe it was his own arms shaking. But then he had no further doubt—a low, gassy moan broke from the gaping mouth and bounced eerily off the tile walls.

"Jesus!" Brian cried, letting the slack head and shoulders fall against the table.

Ricco and Rimgale were laughing.

"Putrefaction gasses," the technician finally explained. "Gets everybody the first time."

"I told you to hold him," Rimgale said, wiping his eyes with a handkerchief, "not feel him up."

As Brian drove away from the morgue, Rimgale tossed an open fire chemical book in his lap. "Read."

"I'm behind the wheel, for chrissake."

"So what. Easy to drive, isn't it?"

Brian admitted as much with a hike of his shoulder.

"And it's easy to read—especially for a big valedictorian type like you. Right?"

"Sure."

"You go to college?"

"Two years," Brian said, taking a glance down at the pages.

"What in?"

"Philosophy major, English minor."

"Sounds like you were jerking off."

"With honors."

"Read."

"And what're you going to do?"

"Meditate." Rimgale began to stretch out, but then recoiled and reached down to the floor mat for something. An uneaten McDonald's cheeseburger he had mashed under his shoe. He unwrapped it, contemplated the possibility, but then tossed it out the window.

Brian checked the rearview mirror, then. "Trychticholorate is a binary structured—"

"Go the bottom. Under heat properties."

Brian jumped at the sound of a car horn but then was surprised to see that it had been meant for a bullying bus driver and not him. "During heat episodes of two thousand Kelvin or higher, trych breaks down and dissipates—" He caught a winking of brake lamps in his peripheral vision and slowed down just in time. "Also says it will consume magnesium."

Rimgale whistled. "Ever burn magnesium? It's so hot it takes water molecules and—" He clapped his hands together next to Brian's right ear.

"Why don't I just slam into something, Rimgale, so we can get it over with? The suspense is killing me. What d'you say?"

"Tears them molecules apart just to eat the oxygen. Wouldn't take much at all to melt ten-gauge wire. Problem is—burnt magnesium leaves a powder trace . . . unless . . . unless you could find something that would eat its own residue."

And then it fell into place for Brian. Despite his anger. "Trychticholorate," he said. "Put that in your opinions and conclusions, and Swayzak can announce to the world that Seagrave and Cosgrove were murdered. The public's off his back, and he's off yours."

Rimgale was staring at him.

"What's wrong?"

"I was starting to have hopes for you."

"What?"

"The difference between finding it as a vapor in Cosgrove's clothes and in the outlet is proof. With our luck, some shyster lawyer will be able to prove that Cosgrove moonlighted cleaning up toxic waste. Poof goes our arson case."

"Then why was the putty worked in all around the doors?"

"Even if it was used to seal the air off, that doesn't tell us why somebody would go to all the trouble of using a backdraft. A gun's a helluva lot easier."

"But the right guess is—it's arson."

"I don't guess."

"Then what do we say when Swayzak rings up again?"

"Nothing. We say nothing. Dead men tell no tales."

Brian pulled into a gas station. "I got to wash my hands."

"Again?"

Jennifer picked up the receiver, dialed six digits with the cap of her ballpoint pen, but then hung up. She took a gulp of cold coffee, went back to work. Eight-by-ten glossies of Martin were spread over her desk blotter, each shot from a different angle—as she had instructed the portrait photographer to do for the second go-around at something suitable for the new campaign poster. Full front from straight on. From above. From slightly below—no, no, that only magnified the quality she was trying to avoid. A quarter left. A quarter right. Even with modestly downcast eyes. Yet, Martin's portraits invariably projected something she sensed would not play well in the city with the brawny shoulders: a patrician aloofness. Unapproachability.

She glanced through the open door into his office. He was courting members of the Urban League, smiling at them from the Louis Quatorze chair that dominated the sitting arrangement in the sunniest corner of his office.

My God, she thought, it's not just in his portrait!

And now something morbid was compounding that arrogant look. In the past week dark circles had sprouted under his eyes, and against her advice he had insisted on hiding them with makeup. The pasty result made him appear as if a mortician had worked on him.

Go ahead—phone.

She picked up the handset again, but put it back in the cradle right away.

She was being too sensitive.

Martin had been distant toward her these past days, and she was taking it personally. The effects of a long and bitter campaign were finally taking their toll on him. He was snapping at everybody on his staff.

He suddenly realized that she was staring at him. He looked away without sharing even a flicker of warmth, then smiled insincerely at his guests.

161

She finally dialed all seven digits.

"Arson," his quiet voice said, "Don Rimgale's office."
Refreshing to hear someone who was not trying to project
something.

"Brian?"

"Yeah." A pause. *"Jenny?"*

The sudden brightening of his voice encouraged her,
but then she heard Don Rimgale in the background,
demanding to know who it was. A rustling sound followed
as Brian palmed his receiver.

"Brian?" she asked after a moment.

"Yeah . . . I'm here."

"How're you doing in your new job?"

"Not bad." He sounded as if he meant it.

"I'm glad." She hesitated, wondering how to frame
this. Then, suddenly, she lost her nerve. "There's a fund-
raising party tonight. Martin would really like you to
come."

"I don't know . . ." He was begging off, she just knew
it; mention of Martin had done it. "I'm working a lot of
overtime right now—"

"I'm lying," she quickly said.

"Pardon?"

"Martin knows nothing about this. *I* want you to come,
Brian. And I don't care if you give ten cents to the
campaign."

Nothing but static over the line. She was pressing her
fingertips against her forehead when he finally spoke.

"Where and when?"

Her hand fell away and she smiled. "Dock off the
Michigan Avenue Bridge. Seven-forty-five. Sharp."

"The party in some Marina City restaurant—or am I
expected to walk on water?"

"You'll see. But no walking on water. And we have
enough wine and fish for everybody." She looked again
at Martin and felt a twinge of guilt. Was she only using
Brian to force some unspoken issue with Martin? The pleasure she felt said otherwise. Then she realized that he

162

might have taken the El to work this morning. Did he even have a car? "Do you want me to pick you up?"

"That's okay. Don can drop me off."

"My ass," Rimgale said in the background. But did she detect a budding camaraderie in his grizzly tone? She hoped.

"Thank you, Brian. Looking forward to seeing you."

"Me too."

The Urban League had left. She quickly rose, trying to catch Martin up on a few matters before tonight. But she was too late. A party ward boss had arrived, and the inner door swung shut against her.

"So you and Jennifer Corcoran," Rimgale said with a droll smile. The refuse from his metal trash can was strewn around his shoes.

"Something wrong with that?" Brian asked.

A tiny shrug. "No. Sounds healthier to me than what I had figured."

"And what was that?"

"I thought maybe it was Swayzak who was sweet on you. This puts a whole new spin on it." He had placed a circle of sheet metal atop the can's lip and was tamping plumber's putty around the gap. "So how well do you really know the alderman?"

"Met him all of once. At Fitzgerald's party."

"Was this before or after you and your brother tried to clean out the place?"

Brian smiled. "Before."

"And how long have you and Jennifer been getting it on?"

"We're not."

"Shame."

"We went with each other from the seventh grade until six years ago."

"What happened?"

"I split."

"Good thinking. I tried that. But her brothers came down to St. Louis and brought me back. At gunpoint."

The alarm Klaxon vibrated through the walls. Brian could hear the crew of the engine company overhead, running across their bunk room toward the pole.

"Still don't miss it?" Rimgale asked.

"Nope."

Rimgale scooted the can across the floor to him. "Peel the top off."

Brian examined it with suspicion.

"Go ahead," Rimgale said, "take it off already. You think I'd hurt you or something?"

Brian finally ripped off the lid.

A billow of flame whooshed past his face, but blew itself out before reaching the ceiling. Brian touched his hair. He had heard it sizzle. "Christ!" Then he turned on Rimgale, who was clapping his hands together. "You are off your nut!"

"That's it!" Rimgale cried. "Oh, this son of a bitch is different. Can't you see?"

"I see that you need a stress disability!"

"Clam down. The point is—our torch doesn't love fire."

Brian couldn't see what relevance this had, but he sat again. The engine siren was wailing away into the distance. "So what?"

"Look at your different setters. The pyro wants creamy shorts from watching it roar. Your schizo, like Ronald, wants to watch the whole world burn for what it did to him when he was a kid. Your arson-for-hire gumba wants to light up the entire block. Give his client his money's worth. Don't you get it? They all want to make as much fire as possible."

"And this guy doesn't."

"Bingo. The fires that took out Seagrave and Cosgrove never really got going."

"Because the burns were all lit in outlets surrounded by double firebreaks in the walls."

"And because he made his burns backdraft," Rimgale said, still excited.

"But he killed these accountants. He dropped the hammer on two human beings."

"But he could've tried to kill everybody *there*. Firebreaks kept down the spread, backdrafts blew out the flames. That's it." Another sharp clap. "That's the reason."

"What reason?"

"Why backdrafts instead of a more straightforward ignition method. Whoever fried these two guys went to a lot of trouble to make sure they died by fire. But he also made sure the fire blew itself out."

"Then we've got a torch with a conscience?" Brian asked.

"A what? No such animal." Rimgale scowled. "Who saw to your moral upbringing?"

"The nuns at Sacred Heart."

"You're kidding?" Rimgale looked taken aback. "Same here."

"Are you going public with this?"

"No way."

"Why not?"

"Do that and I guarantee he'll dig himself a nice warm hole and crawl in. I don't want him hiding. I want his butt *now*—not when he surfaces again three years from now and I got to start from scratch." Rimgale suddenly reached out and poked Brian in the chest with a finger. "I am hereby ordering you to tell the Honorable Martin Swayzak nothing. Jack shit. Do you read me, probie?"

Brian let out a breath, then nodded.

"Now get me out the Seagrave file."

Brian squeezed behind Rimgale to get to the cabinet. He saw that the lock was depressed. "I need the key."

"No you don't," Rimgale said. "I drilled out the pins. Lost the key years ago."

Rimgale let him off on Wacker Drive, grumbling about being late to dinner, and Brian walked down to the dock through the gathering nightfall. The Chicago River reflected the lights of a dinner cruise boat, but the water still smelled like tomato juice that had turned sour. As he strolled across the parking lot, a Ford Taurus darted into an empty space in front of him. Jennifer stepped out of it, dressed to the nines. Somehow he had expected her to own a fancier car, and he was reassured by the domestic compact.

Do more than think it, he reminded himself—*say* it. "You look great, Jenny."

"Thank you." She clipped on an earring that had probably fallen off during the drive. "Don't get seasick, do you?"

"Always a first time."

"Don't think negatively."

"Sorry . . . old habit." He smiled as she stepped close. "You also smell great."

She took his arm. "You too. What is it—Old Spice?"

"No. Rayophene gum."

"Sorry?"

"Later . . . long story."

They rushed up the accommodation ladder, for the boat's air horn was echoing off the front of the Wrigley Building. He immediately lost her on the quarterdeck to a flawlessly handsome young man in a ski sweater.

"Be gracious," he said, wrinkling his nose at Brian, "and let me borrow her for a few minutes, will you?"

"Sure, how about six years?"

She gave him that fighting-again-on-the-school-ground look and went to the railing with Mr. Aprés-Ski. An animated conversation ensued, although she seemed in complete control. She, who had lost sleep before having to do a book report, who hadn't eaten anything on their first date because she was so ill at ease. It seemed a little as if that person had died. But no use mourning her.

He eventually drifted over to the hors d'oeuvres table, humming to himself to show that he did not consider himself jilted. He avoided anything with caviar on it. A cocktail waiter swept by, and Brian snatched two white wines off his tray. The boat was moving.

Jennifer found him again.

"Sorry about the six years crack," he said right away.

She smiled. "You can't help it, can you?"

"No, I guess not. Must be how I work off stress." He inclined his head toward Mr. Après-Ski, who was picking through the hors d'oeuvres as if his monogram might be on one of them. "Did he promise you breakfast in Paris?"

"Only if I gave him the city contract for toilet paper. Or microchips. I forget which."

"It's just one big food chain with these folks, isn't it?"

"Some of them are nice."

"I suppose. Is this the last of these shindigs?"

"Meaning?" she asked. Her defenses were going up. A harmless question had done it. Chitchat.

"I was just saying—this must be one of the last cruises of the season."

"Yes." She relaxed a little. "And we were sweating tonight's weather. After all the rain recently. Thank God for Indian summer."

"Yeah, Indian summer." An inane echo. His stomach tightened. He said nothing for a while, trying to predict what was safe to say. What wasn't. There were things to be said well. This was an audition. A trial balloon. "I wasn't so sure . . ." He paused, looking ahead. The boat was entering the locks.

"Sure about what, Brian?"

"That I'd like the new Jenny."

"Do you?" A sip to hide her anticipation.

"Yes. I'm not quite comfortable around her yet. But she sure knows herself—and her way around these people."

"I got the impression you don't think much of them."

He shook the last drops out of his glass into the lake, then smiled. "If they like you, they can't be all bad."

She bowed a little. Pleased. "Thank you."

They fell silent again. The boat began to swing ponderously around to the north. "We're going to pick up some more people off the Navy Pier," she said. "There wasn't enough parking at the dock."

"The alderman's doing pretty well, then?"

"Couldn't be better, young man."

Martin Swayzak was standing behind them. He looked

167

exhausted, even his voice was beginning to go, but he managed a smile for Brian. "How's the new posting?"

"All right."

"Any progress to report regarding Seagrave and now—who's the new one?"

"Donald Cosgrove."

"Yes, Cosgrove."

"I'm afraid I'm not the man to ask. Busy enough just trying to learn the ropes."

"You should go into politics, McCaffrey," Swayzak said with an irony that didn't suit his smile. He turned to Jennifer. "I just talked to a couple called Green. Roger and Sandra. He's a vice president for Allstate up in Northbrook, but lives in town. She's an attorney. I think they're good for a pledge tonight if you press them—"

"Sorry, Martin," she hurriedly said, "I didn't get a chance to tell you. The Greens came through with a check this afternoon."

"How much?"

"Ten thousand."

Swayzak's hand flew to his forehead. "Christ."

"I tried to tell you. But the Urban League and then—"

"Do you realize," he started slowly, under his breath, "I brushed them off after thirty seconds when I should've invited them to sit next to me at dinner! No wonder they looked miffed!"

She looked stricken, but gave Brian's hand a sharp squeeze when he started to say something to Swayzak.

The alderman glowered at her a moment longer, then threw up his hands melodramatically and walked aft.

Don't add to it, Brian told himself. "Ready for another glass of wine?"

"We're all so tired," she said. "It's turned into such a grind."

"I understand, Jennifer Marie. You okay?"

"Fine." But she was chalk white, and he was afraid she was going to get sick.

Yet, when the boat docked at the Navy Pier, she seized his hand and led him at a fast clip down the accommoda-

168

tion ladder and then along the pier toward Lake Shore Drive. "Let me buy us some dinner," she said, her voice faltering. "And some drinks. Lots of drinks."

Over their second bottle of wine, she asked him about all the things he had done in the last six years. He started out breezily, lots of one-liners, anecdotes about California surfers and Wyoming ranchers, but eventually it felt like testifying against himself. Guilty of gross failure on all counts. He grew glum, so deeply so he didn't want to hear what her life had been like without him.

She covered his hand with hers.

"Things will be different from now on," she said. "You'll climb fast. Trust me. The sky's the limit for someone as sharp as you." Then she caught the look in his eye. "If that's what you want."

He leaned back. The room had grown small and stuffy over the last few minutes. Swayzak had the power to make her unhappy now. He himself didn't, and he wanted to get even with the man. But he didn't know how.

"Brian?"

"Yes?"

"Tell me what you're thinking. Please."

"Remember Sister Beatrice?" he blurted.

"Who could forget? I slept with my hands outside the covers until I was fifteen—because of her."

Brian laughed, but it quickly faded. "One of the times she caught me slugging it out on the playground, she said something. It stuck, somehow. God knows why; the rest went in one ear and out the other." He looked away, slightly embarrassed. It was corn. Yet it had indeed stuck: maybe because it was the perfect credo for a failure. " 'He who conquers his own soul is greater than he who takes a city.' "

She was moved. He could see it. "Is that why you came back?"

"I don't know . . . maybe. I don't even know why I just said that."

"Yes, you do." She signaled for the check. "Show me

169

where you work, Brian McCaffrey.'' Then tenderly: ''I want to see where this battle for your soul is being fought.'' She closed her eyes. ''But first, do you have any idea where I left my car?''

· 17 ·

"Where's everybody?" Jennifer asked in a voice bright from all the wine. Two bottles between them over dinner, plus the two rounds in the lounge while waiting for their table. She had made a point of ordering Bicardi cocktails.

Brian shushed her by pressing his fingers against her lips, then pointed overhead. "Bunk room," he whispered.

"Asleep?"

"Let's hope."

He led her past the engine, across the apparatus floor toward the Arson wing. Her heels tapped over the concrete to his back. Then silence told him that she was no longer following. "Jenny?"

She was staring up at the ornate ceiling. Nineteenth-century pressed tin. And a trapdoor. "Where's the pole?" she asked, catching herself after a slight lurch, from tilting her head back too far.

"Behind you—and careful."

She glanced over her shoulder, her eyes shining in the dim light. "Can they hear us up there?"

"Probably."

She craned her neck for another puzzled look at the trapdoor. Finally, she started whispering. "What's that for?"

"It used to lead to the hayloft."

"Really?"

"Yeah, when they had horse-drawn engines." He smiled at her slack-mouthed expression. A little girl looking for ponies. "It gives me a funny feeling sometimes," he said. "These old stations. Manned for over a hundred years. Night and day ever since they were opened after the Great Fire. Know what I mean? All the lives that've passed through?" She smiled too. "And the guys then, given some time to adjust to the new equipment, would probably fit in fine today. Same macho attitude. Take Old Man Fire by the balls. Same bad jokes about the food. Same contempt for probies."

"Do you miss it?"

The words shut down in his mind for a few seconds. He didn't feel like explaining. Success was a joy to explain, but failure a chore.

"Seems like you do, Brian."

"When I came back, maybe I did. But things got confused."

"Stephen?"

"Oh, more than him. I can't blame Stephen, although he's been no prince."

She turned his face toward hers, rocked it gently between her hands. Her touch. Lovely. "Why do you always wind up blaming yourself?"

Good question. He had no answer.

"You know," she went on, "when you left . . . I didn't feel like I'd failed. Call it pigheaded, but I didn't. Maybe I knew that you'd taken all the blame with you. I was just hurt that you wouldn't talk it over with me."

"I talked about it with you, Jen. A thousand times. I just didn't have the guts to do it face-to-face." And then he was on the verge of telling her what would have been unthinkable only a few hours before when—

Footfalls above, the quiet slapping of bare feet around the pole opening.

He grabbed her hand, led her back into Rimgale's office and locked the door behind them. A hum from the ceiling fixture, then a wash of face-blanching neon. She blinked.

"Not much in the way of romantic atmosphere," he said.

"Anything in here to drink?"

Booze had always made her amorous. An expedient years ago. A vague disappointment now. But maybe he was asking for too much too soon. "Sure." He took a squat fire extinguisher off the bookshelf and set it on the desk. A twist of the valve freed the base, revealing a quart of Jim Beam.

"Does Rimgale hit it pretty hard?"

He stared at her a moment, then took two tumblers from a file cabinet drawer. "No. I've never seen him touch a drop."

"Then why the—?"

"Business entertainment. And debriefing for weak-kneed probies."

"Debriefing?"

"Like after our field trip to the morgue."

She made a face, hid it behind her glass. A gulp, then a dribble down her chin. She was drinking for a reason. None of this would be happening if Martin Swayzak hadn't dumped on her. "Was it pretty horrible?"

"I suppose. But it helps to concentrate on the evidentiary aspects." He felt like a phony, sounding so worldly-wise. It had been ghastly.

"Seagrave and Cosgrove?" she asked, lighting a cigarette.

It was her careful unconcern that put him off. He slid the quart back into the dummy extinguisher, replaced it on the shelf.

"What's wrong?" she asked, exhaling smoke.

"Let's go."

"We just got here."

"Yeah. And we've already worn out our welcome."

"How—?"

"This is Don Rimgale's office. He's not as gracious as the people on that boat tonight, but he plays it fairly straight with me. He deserves the same."

"Brian—"

"Lock the door behind you."

She caught up with him beside the engine, stopped him by grabbing his arm. "I wasn't asking about your cases." She dropped her cigarette and crushed it underfoot. "Screw your cases. They don't mean a thing."

"I wish I believed you."

Her eyes moistened. A direct hit, then. "Why won't you?"

"Martin Swayzak, that's why. You'd do anything for him."

"Maybe." She stepped back. "You still don't get the picture, do you?"

"Probably not."

"I admire Martin. He's one of the finest men in this city. The only politician who really intends to do some good for it—and not just line his own pockets." She crossed her arms and looked away, tears welling in her eyes. "But I love you. Dammit. Been in love with you since I was twelve years old. It's a crummy life sentence, Brian McCaffrey, and I keep looking to get myself paroled. But it just never seems to happen. And I always wind up back inside."

He stood looking at her a moment, a little stunned, then lifted her face and kissed her. He realized that his mouth was dry, but hers was moist. He broke away for a breath. "Why do I wind up crapping out on everybody I love?"

"Shut up." Her shaded lids slid down over her eyes. But then they snapped open, and she nipped his underlip with her teeth.

"Ouch."

"Were there lots of others?"

He hesitated, and that was enough for her to step away from him again.

"Christ, Jennifer." He could see it happening once

174

again: the possiblity slipping away. Evaporating the split second it seemed in his grasp.

"Don't answer that," she said. "I've got no right." And then another lightning shift: "I meant somebody serious."

He watched her, helplessly. "No."

"Why not?"

Jennifer Marie's roller coaster. Yet, riding it had always made him feel alive, important. "I don't know." Glinting chrome caught his eye. "Never had a fire engine before."

A confused smile. "Fire engine?"

"Yeah." He reached up and patted the company logo. "Like our specimen here. Your basic standard issue piece of primary suppression equipment. This area is the pumping panel, which controls the rate of liquid insertion into the hose."

She clasped her hands behind her. An attitude of long ago. On the playground. "Is this your best shot?"

"No, I'll get to deluge gun in a minute. This is a six-inch playpipe, cast bronze to keep it firm during hard flows."

"No wonder you got nothing going all those years."

"I didn't say that. I said nothing *serious*."

Her eyes pinched, and he quickly went on. "That up there, as promised, is our straight bore stang, for bigger jobs."

"And what qualifies as big?"

"A lesser concern, I've been told," he said.

A snigger. "I'm sure you have."

"Easy, lady. This is our hard suction line . . . and this our adjustable insertion nozzle . . . and this . . ." He jerked his head toward the soft folds of hose above them. Then his face grew quiet. ". . . the hose bed."

"I can't see from here."

"Are you sure, Jennifer?"

"Yes. Show me."

"And if I don't?" he asked a bit sadly.

"I'll tell Sister Beatrice you were fighting again."

•　　•　　•

Engine Seventeen stopped before the high rise. Stephen stepped down from the cab and gazed aloft. No visible smoke. Fifty stories of third-generation high rise. Built after 1960. Curtain, or exterior walls, made from glass and lightweight metal panels. Too many synthetic materials and vinyl furnishings to be considered fire-resistant. A potential bitch. But these days he needed an occasional bitch to ream the sludge out of his arteries, to get the warm honey of excitement flowing. That balm of adrenaline that made him forget Helen and Sean and Brian and everything he could not hope to control.

"I've been waiting for this one to go," Adcox said. A flat voice, but worried.

"Then there is a God, Uncle Axe. And He wants to give us this one on a silver platter." Stephen turned in time to see the ladder truck pull up and Tim leap off the tailboard—he stumbled, nearly falling on his face. "Concentrate, goddammit!" he shouted at the probie. And he had thought that Brian was clumsy.

"Sorry, L.T."

"Don't apologize—just use your head!" Stephen grabbed an axe and started for the entrance.

He could hear Grindle behind him, ragging on Tim. "If you're going to get hurt, dickhead, wait till the fire. We need casualty stats for the next manpower report."

Grindle's high tone irked Stephen, but he kept quiet about it. Probies needed peer pressure as well as tons of abuse from above. Abuse was the chisel that sculpted them into fire fighters. Early on, he had tried patience and kindness. It hadn't worked.

The security guard was pacing back and forth behind his console. "Finally."

"Where is it?" Stephen asked, taking the elevator command key from him.

"Don't know. There's alarms going off on three different floors." The guard glanced at his board. "Make that five."

"Starting where?"

"The twelfth."

"Wonderful," Adcox said. Beyond the reach of the eighty-five-foot aerial ladder. And stiff winds aloft often precluded landing a chopper on the roof.

Stephen strode to the lock-out switch set in the lobby wall near the elevator doors and inserted the key. All the cars had been deactivated by the first alarm. Turning the switch put one of them under his direct control.

A pair of doors rumbled open.

"Let's do it," he said, taking the key with him. The four firemen stepped inside. A clank as Tim brushed Adcox's air tank with his own. They all put on their masks. Hisses from exhalations. Stephen went to the control panel, jammed the key into the slot labeled FD Command, then punched the twelfth-floor button.

The car rose, built speed.

Muzak was burbling from the overhead speaker. "With a Little Help from My Friends." Tim was humming along.

"Knock it off," Stephen snapped.

"Sorry." Like Brian. Big doe eyes. Always sorry.

"Mind on the fire. It wants a sacrifice, probie, and you might be what's on the menu tonight."

Adcox said, "Kid wasn't doing anything, Stevie."

Stephen glared at him.

Tim stepped into the middle of tension. Natural peacemaker. Like Brian. Hated discord. "How do we know if the floor's on fire, L.T.?"

"If the doors open and it's hot, don't get out."

"On second thought," Grindle said drolly. "Go ahead and step out, probie. Just don't try to come back in."

Brian looked down at her. Beautiful below him. Smiling with pleasure. "All that sneaking off into dark places," he whispered between long kisses, "when we were young . . . ?"

"Yes?" she asked breathlessly.

"Messed me up in the head."

"How?" She was rubbing the heels of her hands up and down his back. "How, baby?"

"I'm obsessed with unlikely places. Living rooms with

177

relatives griping in the kitchen about life. Backseats of yellow Fiats. Garages with piles of newspaper on the floor.''

That one sparked a laugh. "God, how did we do *that*?"

"I don't know. I'd still take those newspapers over the best room at the Ritz Carlton."

Her arms suddenly tightened around him. Had he said something wrong?

The elevator doors opened on air like steel wool. Stephen had to keep depressing the "open" button to prevent them from automatically shutting against the smoke.

"Shit," Grindle said, "I hate high rises."

Stephen stood a moment in the middle of the corridor, seeking the fire with all his senses, then turned right. It was lurking in that direction. He just knew it. He motioned for Adcox and Grindle to peel off to the left, and they quickly vanished into the pall.

"Stay with me, Brian," Stephen said to the crouched figure behind him.

A moment later, a muffled voice interrupted, "It's Tim, L.T. Not your brother."

"Quiet." Something passed behind the thin steel wall facing Stephen. A sound like BBs rattling on a sheet of aluminum foil. It faded to a whisper and then was gone. A moment later he heard either Grindle or Adcox attaching a hoseline to a standpipe. Adcox, he decided. Grindle was not quite that deft.

"Just wanted you to know it's me," Tim went on, fear making his voice thin. What had gotten into him? Before tonight, he had gone into fires like a wildcat.

Adcox and Grindle dragged the charged hoseline up behind Stephen, then crouched.

"Let's wait for some more help, Stevie," Adcox said. "We're early on this one. It hasn't even broken out yet. And we're one short with Brian gone."

"These high-rise gigs give me the creeps," Grindle said.

Stephen turned to Tim. "Ready to learn something?"

A moment of visible self-doubt. Then the probie gripped his axe like a shotgun. "Sure, L.T."

"Let's go."

Tim and he moved along the corridor. Adcox backed them up with the nozzle ready, and Grindle lugged the line. All at once, Stephen stopped and faced Adcox. "You and Grindle," he said, tossing him his radio handset, "get Pengelly up here and check the other side."

"*What?*"

"You heard me."

"It isn't safe, Stevie," Adcox said. "Don't go splitting us up. Not this one."

"Do you think you can say anything you want!"

Stephen was as surprised as Adcox that he had shouted. But he was tired of the chronic manipulation. Adcox thought he was some kind of informal captain, the way he sorted out commands and did what he damned well pleased.

"I just do what I have to, Stevie. How about you and me leading the way? Put Tim on the hose."

"Goddamn it, John! Just do your fucking job!"

Adcox backed off. Grindle followed him into the smoke.

Never called him John before. That got him. Been slack too long. Now they think my prerogatives are unreasonable. Start fresh with the new generation. He brought his facemask close to Tim's. "You do what I say—or go down to the street. Understand?"

The helmet bobbed.

"Come on." Stephen touched his glove to the wall, felt his way along it. A rattle whispered past. Then a crack sounded down the length of the ceiling. Like plastic being rent by an angry child. "Listen to it," he told Tim, "you can tell when a surface cracks which way the fire's going to jump. You can hear the doors breathe if they're cooking. Fire's like a rattlesnake. It'll tell you before it strikes. But not always. So you've got to develop a sense. An intuition about it. Do you understand?"

Once more the helmet moved, but Stephen wasn't convinced. "Work at this, Brian." He paused, searching the eyes. "You going to fold on me again?"

"Don't think so, L.T." A hurt, muted voice.

"Then show me something!" Stephen crawled on.

He came to a door. He shed his glove and felt the jamb. Heat. But it was distant. Lurking elsewhere.

The door was locked. He wasn't going to fool with a hundred different master keys.

Slipping his glove on again, he reared back his axe— Tim braced against the wall—and dug the blade into the wood near the latch. He wrenched, and the door gave with a shudder.

Nothing, as expected.

The fire rattled and hummed overhead. "Q" deck flooring. Three inches of slab concrete floating on corrugated steel sheets. A construction technique to keep down the total dead weight of the high rise. The fire was using it as a tunnel, moving at will without hazarding the hose Adcox had already charged in the corridor.

Stephen spun around and slammed his axe into a door, trying to ambush the fire as it slunk from room to room.

But it had already passed through.

He paused, thinking. Chess against a mindless grand master. Who could reach across the board and kill you.

The alarm Klaxon made her eyes pop open. Her look of soft pain vanished in a flood of overhead lighting. "Don't tell me," she moaned.

The men of the engine company were already sliding down the pole, climbing sleepily into their coats and gear.

"My underwear, Brian," she hissed, grubbing around in the folds of hose.

"Just put on your dress," he said, kicking up his legs and fumbling into his slacks.

"No, I'm not leaving my panties and bra."

The diesel engine coughed to life. The outer door was rolling open. "Jennifer—let's cut our losses and get down *now*."

"Not without my panties." She had found her bra.

"Don't you see? There could be political ramifications."
She clasped the ends of the bra together between her small
breasts, shifted it around, and looped her arms through the
straps.

Brian waited for a face to leer over the foot of the hose
bed.

The company was shorthanded; otherwise someone
would have jumped on the tailboard—and seen them
straight off. But as it was, the entire crew piled into the
cab and riding compartments. Brian scooted toward the
back on his buttocks, getting ready to help her down.

But she was still hunting for her panties. She seized her
slip and held it up in grim-faced triumph, but the engineer
was already tooling the truck out of the station.

The motion finally convinced her to think about making
do with her dress.

"Too late!" Brian shouted over the siren. Chinatown
was blearing past. Neon tube dragons. The stir-fried smells
of the restaurants.

He climbed back up to her. "What'd you mean by
political ramifications?"

"I don't know." Her skirt was fluttering around her
bare legs, and the emergency lights were flashing against
her face, blue and red. "Something bigger than us."

"There's nothing bigger than us."

She held her hair fast to the sides of her head so she
could look at him without it whipping in her eyes. "Do
you honestly believe that?"

"Yeah," he admitted, then shrugged. "No wonder I
always mess up. Priorities all out of kilter."

But she pulled him down onto her. "Shut up."

· 18 ·

Stephen stopped crawling. He turned on his elbows and squinted down the corridor for a glimpse of Tim. The probie kept lagging behind. Stress had robbed him of his energy. He had shot it all in the first few minutes. Squandered it.

Stephen lifted his mask off his mouth for an instant. "Krizminski!"

At last, Tim emerged through the smoke. He drew up next to Stephen, then let his head droop between his shoulders.

"Lots of smoke—but it's not rolling," Stephen said. "What's that mean?"

Tim glanced up. A thousand-yard stare behind the facemask.

"Come on—it means the fire's hiding."

"Where, L.T.?"

"Behind one of these doors. Either cowering or ready to sink its teeth into our throats." Opportunity or death. The lady or the tiger. How could he make it any clearer? Any less painless?

Stephen brushed his hand over the next door. He paused, frowning, then took off a glove and felt the surface with the back of his hand. More sensitive to heat. Then he sprang up, sank the axe blade between the jamb and the door a few inches above the latch, and twisted the handle. The lock cleared the keeper, and the hinges creaked as they spread open.

A bank of thin smoke hovered beyond the threshold.

The beast had been here only seconds before. He listened. Nothing. Gone again. Then he took his glove from his armpit, where he had clamped it, and put it back on. "You can't hide forever."

He backstepped into the corridor, knelt into the clearer atmosphere near the floor—and saw that Tim had moved ahead of him. Good, was his first thought. The probie was going after the fire. Showing some spunk. But then, through the shifting smoke, he saw that Tim was getting ready to use his axe.

"You check the door for heat?"

Tim started to wind up for a blow.

"Krizminski?"

Stephen scuttled forward. A lazy tendril of smoke had sifted out from under Tim's door; it suddenly sucked back inside the room. "Don't!"

But Tim's axe was already falling.

Stephen lunged, trying to catch the haft in mid-flight. But he missed and fell across Tim's heels just as the blade crunched into wood. A lance of white flame shot out of the gash in the door. Stephen felt an invisible force expand toward him, and then he was skidding clockwise away from the smoke explosion, spinning on his shoulder, caught up in a hailstorm of flaming bits of door. Before his vision went to pixels and the roar deafened him, he saw Tim slam against the wall, clawing at the dazzling air like a wounded bear.

"Oh, God!" Adcox was crying somewhere in the choking fog. "Oh, Jesus God!"

Stephen rolled onto his back, made sure his mask hadn't been blown off.

The fire had taken on human form. Screaming as it reeled and staggered in a circle. Then Stephen realized that it was Tim. The flames were still clinging to him.

Stephen tackled him just as Adcox hit them both with the hose stream. Blinding steam. But he kept rubbing his gloves and sleeves over Tim's head, for Adcox had quickly shifted the nozzle to beat the fire back into its lair—before it incinerated them all.

Tim's helmet was warped. The faceshield was gone.

Stephen ripped off his own helmet to have a look. The steam seared his nostrils, and he gagged from the smoke. But despite burning eyes, he could finally make out Tim's face.

"Shit!" he hollered, wanting to hit something. But his gloves were full of Tim's lolling head. Eyes, cheekbones and nose were encased in melted plastic. His skin, otherwise, was already sloughing off, so deeply that muscle tissue in his neck was exposed in two places. "Shit . . . shit!"

Then Adcox shoved him back and took hold of Tim's body, laid him across the puddled floor. But when he started to try to take off Tim's helmet, Stephen grabbed his arms and held them. "Stop—you'll peel off everything with it!"

"I've got to help him!" Adcox cried.

"Not like that!"

Tim's respiration was coming in uneven bursts. Grimacing, Stephen guessed where the mouth lay and, with a probing finger, cleared the airway.

Tim began breathing easier.

"What happened!" Adcox demanded, his eyes wild behind his facepiece.

"He got froggy on me."

"I counted on you!" Adcox shook his arms free. "To watch after him . . . He's just a damn baby, for chrissake! I trusted you! Otherwise, I'd never have gone the other way!"

Grindle backed out of the door, still pouring water inside. "Hey, there's a fatal in here!"

184

• • •

The fireman was dragging hose out of the bed when a pair of lavender panties fell onto one of his boots. He picked them up in wonderment.

"Oh no," Jennifer whispered.

"I think the jig's up, Jennifer Marie." Brian showed his face and waved. The fireman startled.

"What the hell you doing up there, man?"

Brian lowered Jennifer down to him. She snatched her panties out of his gloves and retired behind the engine to put them on.

"What is this?" the fireman asked.

Brian refused the offer of his helping hand. "I thought I told you just once around the park."

"What park, man? Hey—I know you, don't I?"

Then Brian saw Rimgale, staring at him from across the street. The investigator slowly shook his head, then went back to taking his cases out of the trunk of his sedan.

Brian looked up at the high rise. Steam and smoke were trickling from a row of blown-out windows a third of the way up the glass-and-steel face. He was counting the floors when Rimgale said behind him, "I was going to congratulate you on beating me to the call, but then I saw the dolly get herself right behind the engine." A pause. No smile. "You and Miss Corcoran doing a manpower study?"

Brian ignored the question. "What happened here?"

"Started in an accountant's office. Need I say more?"

Two paramedics, assisted by Grindle and Washington, rushed a stretcher toward a waiting ambulance. The flashing lights of the engines reflected off the safety stripes on the victim's turnout coat.

"That's a fireman," Brian said weakly, then chased after them.

The paramedics slid the stretcher into the bed of the ambulance. The fire fighter's face was hidden by a thick dressing and an oxygen mask. Brian asked, "Who—?"

"You wouldn't know him," Grindle said, then walked away.

Washington said, "It's Tim."

A dizzy, falling sensation. "Is he dead?"

"Not yet."

Brian climbed up into the ambulance. He wanted to hear Tim breathe. He needed to take a carotid pulse, feel the soft thump of coursing blood under his fingertips.

But one of the paramedics stiff-armed him. "Get your ass down so we can get on the road!"

The man was right. Brian backed off.

As he stood watching the doors swing shut, Jennifer came to his side. She took his hand. "Do you know him?"

First day at the academy. Okay if I call you McCaff? This is great. Wanted to be as good at it as Stephen. "Yeah."

The ambulance made a U-turn, then sped off, siren yelping.

"I'll have Dispatch get you a taxi," Brian said. "Rimgale's waiting for me upstairs."

"Brian?" She was shivering.

"Yes."

"Okay if I stay until you're finished? I don't want to leave you. Not just yet."

He nodded, then got her a spare turnout coat from Engine Seventeen.

Stephen was sitting in the corridor of the twelfth floor, his back against the scorched wall and his knees drawn up under his chin. Brian started to greet him, but then saw the look in his haggard eyes and went by him without a word.

A moment later, he looked out into the corridor, and Stephen was gone.

"Same tune, same instrument," Rimgale said, shining his flashlight over the corpse. Like Seagrave, the latest victim had shriveled into the pugilistic attitude. Charring. Split and ripped skin. Yet, these visible ravages of the fire were less horrible to Brian than the sterile white bandages that had hidden most of Tim's face.

He turned away from the body, began prowling around

the crime scene. Try to get your mind on this. Again, an anteroom had been rigged to trigger the backdraft, a small coffee kitchen that gave access to a larger office.

"Apparent white residue on the edges of the surviving door," Rimgale was intoning into his recorder, "to be collected and analyzed for chemical traces, especially for trychticholorate . . . one more preliminary indication of a perpetrator behavioral link with—" Rimgale suddenly clicked off the recorder and turned to Brian. "What's with the paws in the pockets? You know the rigmarole. We got enough sifting and tagging and bagging to keep us here until dawn."

"He was a friend of mine," Brian said.

Rimgale's expression softened. "The probie they wheeled out of here?"

Brian nodded. "I'm not sure he's going to last long. And I'd like to be there if . . ." He didn't finish.

Rimgale looked around the wreck of a room, exhaled loudly, then dug into a pocket for his keys and tossed them to Brian. "One hour. Then back here with your head screwed on straight. The best thing you can do for your friend is to catch the prick who did this to him. You understand?"

Jennifer sat close to Brian, her hands twined around his arm. He drove as in a trance, speeding. After a few minutes, he began to talk. A low, raspy voice. Without being asked, he told her what he had just seen inside the high rise with Rimgale. He talked out of anger. A slow-burning rage that the torch, whatever his purposes, whatever his sickness, had hurt Tim, stolen his face. Perhaps his life. Jennifer gripped his arm more tightly. She quietly asked a few questions, which he answered halfheartedly, seeing no purpose to them. His mind was on Tim, the bandages. "He can't die," Brian said as he turned into the emergency entrance parking lot. "He's too goddamn happy right now to die. Happy to wear a Nomex uniform. Roll to fires."

Adcox was standing outside the sliding doors, smoking

187

a cigarette, filthy from the fire. He watched the couple approach with sunken eyes. Then he flicked his smoke away and embraced Brian, held him fiercely as he said with a strange, haunted expression, "You got to go easy on them at first."

"What's that, Axe?"

"Not too easy. You're looking for a balance. A certain touch with them."

Brian stiffened. "What're you trying to tell me?"

"They can shake apart, you know."

Brian bolted for the doors. The electronic eye was too slow, and he jerked the two glass panels apart on his rush to the emergency room. Dirty swabs and dressings littered the floor. But the examination tables were empty.

"ICU," he demanded at the floor nurse's station.

"You can't go in there."

Then he saw Santos at a distant turning in the corridor. He broke into a run.

"Come back here!" The nurse shouted after him.

And then Adcox farther back. "Brian!"

They were all there, the crew from the Seventeen, filling the corridor with a pungency of smoke and sweat.

Stephen was staring through a door window. Brian pushed him aside. Inside, surrounded by doctors and technicians, was Tim. He had been cut out of his uniform; it lay in shreds on the floor. A surgeon was taking forceps to his face, peeling away plastic and layers of ruined skin, dabbing the raw lesions with antiseptic. Leaky reds and browns and whites. Nothing familiar remained.

Brian turned, looked at his brother. Then he threw a punch with everything he had.

Stephen waited for the blow without reacting—as if he wanted it.

But someone deflected Brian's fist. Nightengale. "Easy," he said as Schmidt and then Adcox helped him restrain Brian.

Stephen drifted across the corridor and leaned against the wall, his eyes turned inward.

Everyone but Adcox let go of Brian. "We shouldn't talk about this tonight. None of us. Okay?"

Brian stopped resisting Adcox's vise of a hug. "Do they think he'll pull through?"

"They're not saying," Grindle murmured. And then he glowered at Stephen. "I don't know, Axe."

"What don't you know?" Adcox asked.

"About tonight's gig."

Stephen met Grindle's accusing stare. "Say it."

"Why'd you split us up?" the long-faced fireman continued. "Why'd you go right in that hallway like you knew exactly where that fire was? Why—?"

Stephen had crossed the floor and was standing inches from him. "Because those are the shots I called. That's my job. I call the shots." He looked from face to face. "I had that fire. The probie didn't listen to me."

Jennifer had approached the cluster of firemen but then stopped short, listening.

"You hear that!" Brian, still in Adcox's grasp, appealed to her with a bitter smile. "Stephen had to take on another fire bare-handed! Had to be the Myth Man instead of looking out for his probie!" She started to cry, but Brian looked away from her and back to his brother. "Is that what happened! Is it, L.T.!"

"Hey, hey . . . Baby McCaffrey," Adcox cooed, wiping the sweaty hair off Brian's forehead. "Not tonight . . . Tomorrow we can sort it all out."

"I'm done," Brian said, forcing his tense muscles to relax. "But the truth's still the truth," he said calmly. "Tim was the candidate. Stephen's responsibility. He burned him."

"Tomorrow."

"Yeah, Axe . . . tomorrow."

Then Adcox released him, and Brian flew at Stephen, catching him alongside the head with a roundhouse. "You no-good fuck!" he cried.

Stephen came back at him with arms spread wide, smiling that arrogant, unassailable smile, and tackled him.

They rolled over the floor and against the wall, locked in each other's grip.

But then it was over.

A half dozen pairs of hands pinioned their arms and legs, and Adcox was hollering for them to knock it off.

"I don't pack guilt just to get some sympathy," Stephen said into Brian's face, breathing hard, still smiling.

· 19 ·

Brian arrived first at the office. He hung his dripping raincoat on the hook behind the door, but then realized that Rimgale would frown on this. Usurpation. He draped the coat over the back of the spare chair, the only property in the room he had a vague right to think of as his own, then went through the incident reports that had been routed to Arson during the night.

Rimgale showed up a half hour later and said, "Get out of here."

Brian looked blandly up from the reports. He thought Rimgale was joking. "I finally got my goddamn car out of the shop yesterday afternoon. Twelve hundred bucks. You can spring for lunch."

"You hear me?" Rimgale was deadpan.

Brian sobered. It occurred to him that Rimgale had found out about Jennifer being in his office the night Tim had been burned. Given his suspicious nature, he had probably dusted his dummy fire extinguisher for latent fingerprints. "What gives here?" Brian finally asked, for Rimgale was still on his feet, staring at him.

A rain-speckled *Tribune* fell from the investigator's big hands onto the desktop. "Take it with you. Read it at your leisure. I don't want you stinking up my office any more than you already have, so I'll summarize . . . " And as Brian scanned the headline—FIRE DEATHS RULED ARSON MURDERS—Rimgale told him how the break had been made through the discovery of "chemical traces" at all three scenes, and that Martin Swayzak congratulated the investigative team on its "imaginative work" in making a "behavioral link" between the homicides. "An arrest is imminent," Rimgale concluded. "Now get your stuff and get out."

Brian was waiting for Jennifer when she came back from lunch at one-thirty. She gave him a peck on the cheek, then—no doubt disturbed by his cold silence—invited him into her office and shut the door. Her eyes darted to make sure an inner door was closed. It was.

Swayzak's inner sanctum, he supposed.

"How's Tim?" she asked, standing her umbrella in the corner.

"He'll live. Not much else."

"How bad are his injuries, then?"

"Permanently blind. Years of reconstruction on his face."

She winced, then sat behind her desk, primly, coolly. She knew. "Forgive me, Brian—but I get the idea something's wrong here."

He flung the newspaper at her. The pages spread apart in the air, then floated down around her. "Yeah, I'd say something's wrong."

She swiped them off her desktop, but then composed herself. Massive effort. "What was that supposed to prove?"

"You told Swayzak."

She took an errant paper clip off her blotter and put it away. "Of course I did."

"That was a confidential lead!"

"Lower your voice, please." Her eyes shifted to the

inner door, then back to Brian. "And sit down so we can discuss this like civilized human beings."

He glared for a moment longer, then flopped into her small leather sofa. "Jesus . . . Jesus . . ." He covered his eyes with a hand, laughed under his breath. "It's my own fault. I should never've trusted you."

"Will you please tell me what trust has been violated?"

"Lady—you took what I shared with you, just you, and put it on the front page of the *Tribune*!"

"Oh Brian . . ." She delicately touched her fingers to her temples as if he had given her a headache. ". . . you're right. I messed up. I misjudged you."

"Me?"

"I thought that night you were finally showing some maturity, some savvy."

"And how was I doing that?"

"By channeling some long-overdue intelligence to the highest levels of city government, of course."

"Jennifer," he said, trying to calm himself, trying not to lose her over this, "you scared the son of a bitch off. We may never bust him now. All for a couple of political points."

She mulled this over. Regret seemed to hover just behind her eyes, but then she said, "I was doing my job."

"Above and beyond the call, if I remember everything that happened that night." There. Done. Blown. He saw the anger spill into her face, tighten it.

But her voice stayed crisp. "Let me ask you something—why do you think Martin had you assigned to Arson?"

He just looked back at her.

"Because of your professional knowledge and years of experience, Brian? Or maybe because he was sick and tired of Rimgale stonewalling and wanted somebody he could communicate with!"

"You're raising your voice."

"Hell yes, I'm raising my voice!" She had stood as well. "You knew what we were asking you to do! So don't suddenly pull out a conscience now!"

The door opened, and Martin Swayzak stepped inside the room. He looked worn, remote, old. Even Jennifer seemed struck by his appearance. "A problem here?" he asked with a disingenuous smile.

"No, Martin . . ." She visibly struggled for the right words. ". . . a difference of opinion, yes."

"Nothing serious, I hope," he said, his smile faltering. "I have high hopes for you, Brian. You've served the city well so far. If it weren't for fellows like you, nothing constructive would get done. All the special interests would see to that." He paused. For so long Brian began to suspect that he had lost his train of thought. "Tradition," Swayzak then said as if it were another name for Beelzebub. "It's killing us all. And for what? Just so we can squat in the same old rut?" And then, as if afraid of the somber mood he had just created, he smiled again and clapped his hands together. "Keeping busy?"

"Yeah," Brian said. "Been running my ass off this morning."

"Good, I'm sure Don Rimgale appreciates having an extra pair of legs."

"I just dropped off a letter at the *Trib*, explaining how yesterday's arson announcement was a fabrication by your office to boost your recent dip in the polls. They loved it. The reporters, I mean. The management and a few of the columnists are still solidly behind you. But the reporters think you're a Lake Forest carpetbagger with noticeable face-lift lines."

Jennifer sank into her chair. "Brian . . . oh, Brian." And then she gave him an unhappy smile. He knew at once that it was in farewell.

The rain had stopped, leaving a deep blue twilight. Rimgale was crossing the street in front of the station, ambling wearily toward his sedan, when headlights sped around the corner. The limousine stopped in the middle of the street fifty feet from him, and Martin Swayzak stepped out, his breath running away from his mouth in the chill air. "Don?"

Rimgale approached him. "*Don* now?"

An insipid grin. "If you don't mind, Investigator."

Rimgale gave a shrug. Swayzak had been drinking. Scotch or Irish whiskey, by the smell of him.

"You know, Don, there's been a terrible mix-up, and I want to be the first to apologize for any unwitting part I may've had in it."

Rimgale laughed.

"Something funny?" Swayzak asked.

"Forget the damage control, Alderman. The ship is already sunk. Now, if you don't mind, I'm late for dinner the fourth time this week. And I got to work tonight."

"I do mind." Swayzak had taken hold of his upper arm. A brittle grasp.

Rimgale glared until he let go. "You want to talk, you tell me straight out. You latch onto me, you better hope I let *you* go."

A high, tinny laugh. "Don . . . Don, what are we doing here? We're snapping at each other like dogs."

"Instead of what?"

"Communicating like associates. Fellow public servants."

Rimgale eyed the alderman's silk suit. "So talk."

"Do you mind if we take a short drive while we chat? I hate standing still. Even for a few minutes."

"There goes dinner," Rimgale said, getting inside the back of the limousine.

"Permit me to take you to dinner, Don."

"Sure. I know just the spot."

"Tell my chauffeur," Swayzak said, lowering the window that partitioned them off from the driver. "Ismail . . . the restaurant at . . ."

Rimgale rattled off the intersection, and the window whined back up.

Swayzak took a flask from his inner coat pocket. "Do you think I'm so stupid as to believe that you've come up with no credible leads?" He offered him a nip. "Some Chivas?"

"No, thanks. And after the stunt your kid pulled, I've got no clear idea how stupid you are, Alderman."

"He's not a bad boy."

"No," Rimgale said, "and that's what really pisses me off about this. Your cute little squeeze wiggled her fanny at him, and he wound up blowing his last chance. God knows his brother's finished with him."

"Ms. Corcoran's not—"

The window glided down. "I don't understand, sir," the driver said. "There's nothing but three service stations and a McDonald's here."

"That's it," Rimgale said, "the golden arches. Use the drive-through so I can get back to work."

Swayzak laughed as Ismail ordered Big Macs and Cokes for the three of them. "I should've brought a photographer, Don. The very picture of the frugal modern politician."

"Yeah," Rimgale said bitterly, "frugality's your strong suit, Marty."

As they pulled back into traffic, Swayzak said with sudden sharpness, "How can you tell me that there's no link between the victims? You must be aware of *something*."

"Other than the fact that they were all bean counters—no, I can't find a thing."

"You're joking."

"No. I'm not."

"Well," Swayzak said, opening his Styrofoam box and quickly closing it again in disgust, "maybe you've got something there, Don. Maybe Seagrave, Cosgrove and Holcomb have nothing more in common than a profession."

Rimgale stopped chewing for a moment. "Oh, this is minor league as far as coincidences go. I once had three female arson victims who, as it developed, were banging the same guy without knowing about the other two. Know what? He turned out not to be the torch. The real fire setter was a drifter who picked these gals to roast because they had strawberry-blond hair. He didn't like strawberry blonds."

"Really?"

Brian heard the key turn in the door lock. He sat straighter.

Rimgale stepped inside, looked blankly at him, fished the last french fry out of a McDonald's bag, then sat, munching as he said, "Tell me every last thing you told Jennifer Corcoran."

"Aren't you going to ask what I'm doing here?"

Rimgale wadded up the bag and tossed it at his scorched waste can. He missed. "You're here because you're an obsessive-compulsive neurotic whose sorry ass is in a sling because he fucked me over. Now you want me, the only person in the world who has ever taken you on your own miserable terms, to forgive you for your sins."

Brian picked up the bag, finished the delivery. "That's about it. Except I want to catch the bastard who burned Tim. That's the only reason I'm asking for another shot. Tim."

"Again, what exactly did you tell Miss Corcoran while you were thinking with the wrong head?"

Brian told him.

"Did you tell her Holcomb's name?"

Brian was confused. "No. That was confidential."

"Yeah, well . . ." Rimgale rolled his eyes. "You remember if Holcomb's name was on the building directory?"

"No, I looked for you. Some corporate name for that suite. I forget what—"

"Hot damn." Rimgale formed a fist and shook it. "Come on . . ."

Rimgale tapped away with a chisel and hammer, gently prying the stop strip off the door jamb to Jeffrey Holcomb's office. He exposed more white residue. "Good. The more of this we identify the better. I want to walk into court and be able testify that we found enough trychtichlolorate to give cancer to China . . ." He suddenly tossed the tools to Brian, who juggled and dropped them. "You can finish later. First things first. Bring the hammer and a punch."

Rimgale picked his way through the debris to the file cabinets, while Brian clattered through the tool case.

"You know," Rimgale said from across the room, "this prick *knows*."

"Knows what?"

"Fire." Rimgale made a sour face. "What else? Listen, will you? He knows how to think like fire. Knows that flame will spread this way and not another across the floor. Not because of the physics of flammable liquids or heat convection, but because it *wants* to. You know?"

Brian realized that he might have argued differently in August. But not now. He had felt Fire breathing in his face, groping for the seams and openings in his turnouts. "I know," he said, tossing Rimgale the tools from a few feet away.

He caught them both and went on, "I got to admire the son of a bitch. He knows fire fighters. In fact, he counts on our engine companies to behave in certain ways."

"Such as?"

Rimgale centered the punch over the lock to the first cabinet. "To be leery of backdrafts. Except . . ." With a quick, square blow he drove the lock back into the cabinet. ". . . something didn't go according to plan this time."

"You mean Tim?"

"Yeah, probie fucked it up." Rimgale glanced at Brian. "But that's not a given yet. We got to ask your brother some questions about what happened." He yanked open a drawer and began riffling through the bloated and charred papers. They fell apart in his hands. "Shit."

Brian thought he was referring to the condition of the files, but then he tracked Rimgale's gaze to the doorway. A thin young woman in an overcoat stood there. "Oops," she said, then turned to go.

"Miss?" Rimgale called after her. "Can we help you?"

She stepped back inside. Sheepishly. "Are you guys cops?"

"*Please*. We're human beings. Firemen."

That made a favorable impression. "Joey let me come up."

"Joey?" Rimgale asked.

"The security guard. We dated for a while. I used to work here."

"In this office?"

"Yeah."

Rimgale looked to Brian with a smile in his eyes. "Awful about Mr. Holcomb, isn't it . . . Miss . . . ?"

"Pastorino. Edith." She stepped deeper into the office. "I don't know," she said about Holcomb, trying to hold a frown in check. "I walked out last week."

"Just like that?" Rimgale said.

"Just like that."

"Mind if I ask why?"

"Long story."

"Two sets of books? Something like that?"

"Long story," she said more adamantly. "You didn't find any checks laying around, did you? That's what I'm looking for. My severance pay."

Brian asked, "Whereabouts?"

"Probably on that desk." Her face dismal, she pointed at a gutted hulk. It was topped with melted plastic and a conglomerate of fused electronics components. "Along with my cassette player, my digital clock radio and my calculator. All personal property. I hope the sleezeball carried some insurance."

"You might talk to the building owner," Rimgale said.

"Jeff Holcomb *was* the owner."

Brian said, "Our book lists the owner as Dekom Trust."

"Yeah, that's right. And this office is—"

"D and T Enterprises," Brian interrupted, recalling what had been on the building directory.

"Who handled disbursements?" Rimgale asked.

She looked at him with large, vacant eyes. "Me."

"You ever write any checks to an Alan Seagrave or a Donald Cosgrove?"

"You *are* cops," she said, then hurried out. The clip of her high heels faded down the corridor.

Brian started to go after her, but Rimgale whistled him

back. "Let the little lady go. She's scared. And there's another way. Nicer than leaning on the hired help."

Brian nodded, and Rimgale turned back to his chore of punching in the file cabinet locks. "Where'd I leave off?" he asked himself, looking slightly bemused.

Brian noticed that the lock to the first cabinet and then those to the last two in line had already been driven.

Rimgale asked, "How many did I do before we were interrupted?"

"Just the first one, Don."

"No shit?" he asked, wide-eyed.

Stephen took to his bunk rather than risk another squabble with his crew. He set his bottle on the floor in the patch of light that spilled in from the dorm room, as if to dare anyone to do something about it. A half hour into his isolation, Grindle appeared at the doorway, noticed the bottle, and quickly went out again. A minute later the fireman's voice drifted up through the pole opening: "The L.T.'s busy. Can I help you with something?"

Stephen couldn't make out the reply. Didn't sound like the battalion chief.

A faint whisper passed through the wall behind him. He startled, then relaxed again, telling himself that it was the old building contracting in the cool air of the autumn night.

Then the room lights blazed on.

Stephen bolted upright, blinked at Rimgale. "Don't they knock on your planet?"

"We don't even care for our young. That's how tough things are." Rimgale scooped up the bottle of Popov and uncapped it. "But we do look out after our friends. Even if they get mad, and we got to knock them on their asses." He opened the window and poured out the vodka. It sounded like a cloudburst on the pavement thirty feet below.

Stephen lay back down and closed his eyes. Nothing left. Not even enough to get up out of bed and take a few jabs at Rimgale. Because Don was right.

Rimgale sat on the foot of the bunk, his weight tilting Stephen's face toward him. "I still haven't gotten your fire report, Stevie." He paused. "On Krizminski."

Just this mention of the name was enough to sober him. Half a quart wasted. "I'm working on it."

"It ain't *War and Peace* I'm asking for. What's the problem?"

Stephen slid his forearm over his eyes. "Go away."

"What happened up there? It's important. He was a probie. Let's begin there. Was he paying attention? Was he listening?"

"He wasn't listening to the right thing."

"And what's that, Stevie?"

"I don't know anymore." Stephen felt that he had been abandoned by the thing, the presence that had always told him before. Now he couldn't tell the difference between the furtive movement of fire and the creaking of an old building. "But it knows us. This one knows us."

Tapping. Stephen opened his eyes. Rimgale was tapping his notebook against his knee, visibly thinking.

"I got your brother with me, Stevie. He's downstairs right now, looking over your engine like a kid on Christmas eve. Why don't I send him up to talk to you."

"No," Stephen said sharply. Then more conversationally: "Not tonight, Don, I'm bushed."

"Let's not quibble—you're blitzed. There's a helluva difference, especially if that Klaxon goes off any minute."

"I'll do okay."

"A string of Kelly Days coming up, Stevie?"

"Five, starting tomorrow."

Rimgale sighed. "I'll need that report before you go on them."

Before he fully realized what he was doing, Stephen had sat up and grabbed Rimgale's pad and ballpoint from him. He scribbled in block letters: KRIZMINSKI WENT TO THE FIRE AND NOW HE DOESN'T HAVE A FACE. Then he flung the pad back at Rimgale. "Turn off the lights on your way out."

· 20 ·

Brian was getting drowsy. The Hall of Records was too much like a college library. Something plopped on the table in front of him. Today's *Tribune*.

Rimgale was standing over him.

Brian unfolded the paper, almost afraid to read.

His letter to the editor, as half-expected, had escalated into a full-blown news story. And, as expected, Martin Swayzak had tried to turn the entire affair to his advantage: he regretted the misunderstanding between his office and the Arson Bureau, blamed no one for it, particularly the investigator, although this was precisely the kind of mis-fired communication between elements of city government he would bring to an end as mayor. A Communicator for the Windy City. A new campaign slogan.

"So far so good," Brian said. "But I'm sure we'll be hearing from our own brass."

"*We* already have. That's where I've been for the last two hours, there and the PD."

"And?"

"I saved your ass," Rimgale said. "For the time being.

But if it's an incentive to work any harder—you better hope to heaven Swayzak doesn't win next week." He sat. "Now, what've you been doing other than snoozing at seventeen bucks an hour?"

Brian closed the record book. "As you know, Jeffrey Holcomb's D and T Enterprises is a division of Dekom Trust. Which is owned by Pan Illinois. Which is majority controlled by Lakeside Dynamics. Which is a division of Calumet Ventures, whose partners are . . ." He couldn't help but to pause. ". . . Alan Seagrave, Donald Cosgrove and Holcomb."

Brian could tell that Rimgale was pleased, even though he simply said, "Cops figured Cosgrove laundered money for the mob before he went into redevelopment. They weren't very high on Seagrave, either."

"So we've got the three of them tied together," Brian said happily. "Wrapped up."

"Not quite. It's a quartet."

"Who else?"

"A certain alderman who was scared shitless last night that we would find out what you just did. Now we've got to link him. And that's going to be the bitch."

"I phoned you at the office," Brian said. "But they said you'd already gone for the day."

Jennifer spun around in the middle of the parking lot, and her hand flew to her breast. That she recognized him at once did nothing to relax her. Her hand crept up to her coat collar, which she slowly closed around her throat. "What do you want?"

"Square things with you."

"I think you've done all the squaring you can possibly do. It'll be some long time before Martin completely trusts me again."

"Consider yourself lucky." He shook his head, exasperated with himself already. "I didn't mean that. Let me walk you up to your apartment."

"No, thank you."

"Then can we just walk for a few minutes?" It was a

203

cold evening, but the chill was helping him to keep a clear head.

Some quick vacillation, then, "A few minutes."

"Thanks, Jen."

They passed through a breezeway and out into Lincoln Park. The moon was rising through some overcast, its dispersed light making the surface of the lake look frozen, even though it wasn't yet. "There's been a legitimate break in the case."

"I don't want to hear," she said.

"I know. And I don't blame you. But it involves Swayzak."

"What d'you mean?"

"We believe he had some connection to the three accountants who were murdered."

She began walking faster. "I doubt it."

"We don't."

"Good for you. I don't know anything about it."

"But you could check his files."

She laughed rancorously. "I don't believe this. So what if Martin knew them? He knows half of Chicago by first name."

"He's hiding his association with them. That's what tipped us off."

She stopped, faced him. "Do you realize what you're asking? How *much* you're asking?"

Let her have her say. Be attentive.

"You know," she went on, "I was set up by a mousy mother and a boozy father to think that housewife and mother was the best I could ever do. Baking cupcakes for the PTA, muffins for the Holy Name Society. Two weeks a year for myself when the kids went off to CYO camp. And the astonishing thing is—I looked forward to all that. Until my dreamboat skipped town."

"Jennifer—"

"I'm not finished. Four years ago I was working nights in a bakery so I could go to school days. Still a little starry-eyed, because I didn't realize that all a degree from a business college gets you is a clerical job in City

204

Finance. Two years ago I was shagging the computer spreadsheets up to Martin's office, and he didn't even know my name. I run that office now. Martin respects me, and I respect him. Believe in him. Now you want me to throw that away because you suspect him of something you can't even prove without my help?"

"Swayzak's falling apart. It can't be just the election. He's too much of a politician for that." Brian guessed that her eyes had turned pensive, troubled, but it was too dark to know for sure. "Something's scaring the hell out of him. Maybe he fears for his life. We don't know. But how can we help him if we don't?"

Helen McCaffrey heard the neighborhood dogs bark twice within ten minutes. She put away the last dish and flipped off the kitchen light. She glanced up the stairs, thinking of Sean asleep in his room, then went to the bay window in the living room, parted the curtains an inch and gazed out. A masculine silhouette on the sidewalk.

She pressed her lips together, then opened the front door. "Stephen?" she called out quietly.

He came up the walkway without answering, and she turned on the porch light. His face gave her a jolt. A disfigurement of booze and pain. "Hi, babe."

Babe. Pushing a quart, then.

"Listen," she whispered, "I'd invite you in, but then Sean would hear your voice—and he'd never go to sleep."

"School tomorrow?" Thanks to his schedule, he never knew what day of the week it was.

"Yeah . . . school."

"Okay, see you."

Yet his disappointment was so profound, so unlike him in that he failed to smile, she said, "I'll get my coat. We can sit on the stoop."

"Okay."

When she came out, her head kerchiefed against the cold, he was already sitting, staring off at the risen moon. A pale blur behind some wintry clouds.

"Hey, lady . . . good to see you." A croak.

She sat, keeping a foot of chilled air between them. Lay down the rules first. His loneliness had come close to suffocating her before. "Stephen, there's no going back. I don't say this angry. If I was still angry, that'd be a bridge for you and me. But all our bridges are gone. We burnt them, and hurt Sean doing it."

"I know." He stirred a little, but didn't look at her. "When we were splitting," he said haltingly, "the job was a refuge for me. A place to forget. But it's not that way anymore."

"What happened?"

"Wish I knew. Then I could do *something*."

She started to reach for his arm, but then checked the impulse. Stupid. Think of Sean: he's just beginning to settle down. "That's the job, then. Jobs can go sour. Even fire fighting. What're you going to do about Brian?"

"I don't know." Desolate.

"Can you talk to Brian?"

Silence for a long moment, then, "I envy him."

She couldn't believe her ears. "What? You're the guy other men look up to. Idolize. He's a boy. And he'll always be one."

Stephen crossed his arms over his knees, then rested his forehead on them. "He rolled with Dad that last day. He was with him at the end."

"I know. And it messed him up in the head. I think of Sean seeing what Brian saw . . . the same age within a year . . ." She took a cold breath, then slowly let it out. The vapor wafted away. And the terrible image went with it; a little boy in a yellow helmet faded into the night sky.

But Stephen was still visibly harboring it. "I should've been there."

"There was nothing you could've done. You were a child yourself."

He looked up, his face puffy, contorted in the porch light. "I'm not talking about that. Just seeing him one last time. It would've made me stronger. Helped me through times like these. Stronger."

"How—?"

"Not weaker like Brian. I would've taken something from Dad before he went away."

She felt her eyes burn. It was like a stranger talking, or a fissure opening in a crust of eons. "What, baby? What would you have taken?"

"His love." Stephen McCaffrey was not smiling. He was crying, pressing the webbing between his thumb and forefinger against his wet eyes, and tears were twining down his wrist. "You know, he always just expected that I'd do okay. But with Brian, it was in doubt. I could see that even way back then. And it made him love Brian all the more. God, his face did shine when he looked at the goofy little kid." Stephen dried his face on his windbreaker sleeve. It was all he had against the chill, a fire department windbreaker. "Pathetic, isn't it? Jealous of a dead man's love after all these years?"

She took him in her arms. He made no possessive move of his own but simply relented to her grasp. Like a child. "I wish you'd told me a long time ago."

"Would it've mattered?"

"I don't know." She kissed the crown of his head. "Maybe. One thing might've led to another." And then it sprang from her lips. "Come in . . . You're freezing."

His coming into the house had always made it seem smaller. But now the walls were swelling away from them, everything becoming spacious and airy and slightly dizzying as they went up the stairs without the long, careful pause she had intended for the kitchen. And then the bedroom door was shut behind them, the lessons of the past already violated—even though he was just looking at her with stark, damp eyes. He cupped her face in his hands and kissed her. She had believed that there was no more secret thrills locked away inside her, but then she shuddered.

"Oh God, Stephen," she heard herself say, as they became one expectancy, one breath, and fell to a clack of bedsprings.

Yet, in the early morning darkness, with the percolator thumping out the rhythm of the once familiar, the irretrievable familiar, she girded her terry cloth robe and said to him, "I don't want to confuse Sean."

He looked up at her from the table, blinked twice, and then the night's tenderness vanished from his face.

She went on, heart pounding, "I think you'd better go before he gets up."

"You're probably right." And Stephen smiled. It scalded. On the way out he batted the front door against the inner wall, leaving it open to the chill.

Martin had turned his chair in to the window. Jennifer hesitated in the doorway. His head remained perfectly still. He hadn't heard her, and she couldn't make up her mind whether to step farther toward him or back out of his office and ease shut the door. Beyond him street lamps threaded into the distance. A slate sky offering no promise for either rain or clearing before the imminent nightfall.

His profile suddenly snapped into view. "Who's there?" he asked as if afraid to swivel around, to open himself.

"Jennifer."

He gazed out the window again.

"I have the latest poll, Martin."

Silence.

"Did you hear me?"

"Just leave it . . . please."

She stepped around his desk, sat on the corner. "What's going on, Martin?"

A flutter of his head, then the same remote stare.

"Something's terribly wrong, isn't it?"

"You tell me. What's the poll say?"

She frowned. "A one-point improvement."

"Hmm."

She glanced down and saw in his lap the packet a captain had delivered from Fire Department headquarters at eight this morning. Everything Rimgale had compiled so far, the officer had assured Martin during the shouting match that boomed through her door. Now, the reports and crime scene photographs were scattered over the desktop, on the floor around his shoes.

"We've come a long way together, Martin. I know what pressure over a police or fire incident can be like. But this is different. This is personal, isn't it?"

He finally looked at her full-on. "No."

"You know nothing more about these deaths than Rimgale does?"

"Nothing."

She smiled briefly. "All right, that's all I need to know. In the morning, then."

"Good night, dear."

On her way out, she scooped up the manila envelope she had just set beside the document shredder. She tucked it inside her purse.

Brian pulled up in front of his apartment at ten, killed the engine and just sat for a while, almost too weary to finish out the long day. He had had no dinner, thanks to Rimgale's insistence that they have a look at the file cabinets in Seagrave's boarded-up brownstone. They hit pay dirt: the lock to one had been drilled, something Rimgale had missed during the initial investigation. This discovery gave rise to a new question: Why had the torch cracked only two of Holcomb's cabinets—and used a noisier, cruder method than drilling? Had he been in a rush? Rimgale could provide no answer, but then had sped off to Cosgrove's theater to check the cabinets there. Alone. Brian had had enough, his body sounding a curfew.

Still, it bothered him. That Rimgale's own file cabinet lock had been drilled.

At last, he sprung the door latch and lumbered out of his BMW. Down and across the street a Taurus was parked.

He walked over, filled with a sudden need to look casual. She had come to his turf. The dirty old neighborhood she had forsaken forever. She had waited for him to come home.

Jennifer cranked down her side window.

He spread his arms and leaned on them against the Ford. "Interest you in a beer, lady?"

"No," she said, thrusting an envelope against his gut.

"What's this?"

"Just take it." She started the engine, gunned it.

"Jenny, I'm sorry."

"That's a stupid thing to say."

"You're right . . . I just—"

"Good-bye, Brian." And she sped off.

· 21 ·

Brian sat alone in his apartment, an empty metal waste can wedged between his knees. He held a book of matches in one hand and a four-inch thick sheaf of papers in the other. He knew what giving it to Rimgale would do. Jennifer herself had suggested the outcome as she had driven away: it would take her out of his reach forever. Never one to let things slide, Jennifer Marie. When in doubt, put things to a vote.

This was a test, then.

And he failed it. He jerked up out of his Salvation Army easy chair, rushed out the door and down the unlit stairs to his BMW—with the Fire Resources Allocation Manpower Efficiency Report undamaged, under his arm.

Rimgale was kneeling in the charred darkness of Donald Cosgrove's office, rummaging through a file folder he had spread open on the floor. His flashlight beam continued to flit over the seared pages as he said, "I'm giving you no more overtime pay tonight. My budget's shot."

"Forget the overtime."

"That's the spirit." Rimgale gingerly closed the file

and came to his feet. "What I got here is a copy of the FRAMER bullshit that shut down a fifth of the stations in this city. Interesting that a tax accountant would have a copy. Must've been civic-minded."

"Which copy?" Brian asked.

Rimgale looked at him for the first time. "What d'you mean?"

"I'm holding three different drafts of the same report. Each with different numbers. I flunked statistics, twice, but it looks to me like they were making it up as they went along. Juggling figures like mad. Each stab at credibility closer to being airtight than the one before."

"You're kidding."

Brian handed him the big manila envelope.

Rimgale perused for a few minutes, his breath whistling softly through his nose, then said, "Everybody on the job knew it was crap, but we could never argue with the numbers. I did a little check on the consulting firm that wrote it. They did exactly one job—FRAMER. For Swayzak. It's not even really a company. No employees, no directors. Just a post office box in Evanston." He suddenly shook his head in frustration. "But *who* put together this garbage for Swayzak? I got some ideas, and so do you. But we need a tie-in. A link—" He paused. Brian had handed him a snapshot.

"Holy shit," Rimgale said at last.

Seagrave, Cosgrove, Holcomb and Martin Swayzak—together on a fishing dock, grouped around a sturgeon as big as a torpedo.

Rimgale said, "It's time the alderman and we had a little heart-to-heart." And, scooping up his tool kit, he started down the mezzanine stairs.

Brian caught up with him on the street. He was about to tell him that no, they couldn't do this without jeopardizing Jennifer, when Rimgale said, "We'll take my car." He jerked his thumb at the BMW. "Who in his right mind would steal that?"

"Don . . . ?"

"Come on. Shake a leg. It's already going on midnight."

Brian got in the sedan and had no sooner shut the passenger door than Rimgale accelerated away from the curb.

"Where's Swayzak live?" Brian asked.

"Good question . . ." Rimgale checked for cross traffic, then blew a red. "He's got an apartment down in this neck of the woods. A model of blue-collar simplicity. But I don't think he's even crawled into the sheets there, unless it was to bang some dolly on his lunch break." He turned up Michigan Avenue. "No, he's got a suite at the Ritz Carlton, when he's not up at Lake Forest."

Brian closed his eyes. A wash of jealousy so intense it left him with a knotted stomach. Light-headed. That look that had come over her face when he idly mentioned the Ritz in the back of the fire truck—no wonder. But he still said, "We can't handle it this way, Don."

"What way?"

"Confronting Swayzak . . . directly."

"Why not?"

"He'll know right off how I got the copies."

Rimgale clapped him on the neck, squeezed hard. "So what? You got 'em like a true gigolo. Just like she got our lead on chemical traces. Fight fire with fire."

Brian brushed away Rimgale's hand. "It wan't like that. She went into Swayzak's files because she thought it was right."

The investigator nodded after a moment. "Okay, I can respect that. But she *did* it, for chrissake—so we've got to assume she knew the chances she was taking." He double-parked in front of the Ritz Carlton and got out. He waited only a second for Brian, then went in alone.

A taxi honked from behind, and Brian slid over behind the wheel. He restarted the engine and parked down the street in front of a hydrant. The Ritz. Ugly mental pictures. He wanted to hate her for it. But couldn't. She had tried to curry favor with her boss by getting him confidential information.

"Make that two of us now, babe," he said quietly.

A sudden panicky thought. Had she trapped him into doing precisely this? *You're no better than I, Brian McCaffrey.* Was she that devious?

Rimgale got back inside, slamming his door. He had only been gone a few minutes. "The son of a bitch went up to Lake Forest. To rest before the final election push."

Brian was relieved—until Rimgale got on the Kennedy Expressway and started north.

"What's with you?" Rimgale asked after a silence that lasted until they reached Skokie. "Does she mean that much?"

"I think so," Brian said.

"What's to think? Either you know or you don't." Rimgale braked and stopped in the emergency parking zone next to the center divider.

"What're you doing?"

"You worry too much." Rimgale reached across him, took a butane lighter from the glove compartment. "You think everything's got to wind up a disaster, so you go around blind to your options."

"What options?" Brian honestly saw none at the moment.

"Always options. If you learn one thing before I kick you back downstairs to an engine company, let it be this—there's always options." Rimgale cracked his door, then held the first few pages of the FRAMER sheaf outside. He lit the upper right-hand corner, let the flame crinkle and blacken the edges, then shook it out. "There. Now Swayzak'll think we got this from one of the torched offices, right?"

Brian gave a tiny smile.

"I just bought your Miss Corcoran some breathing space," Rimgale went on. "The alderman won't search his own files until it's too late—and by then we'll have him by the nuts." Rimgale barged back into the left lane; horns wailed. "What's so goddamn great about Wisconsin!" He hollered, waving his middle finger in the rearview mirror. Then he lowered his voice again. "As for you, McCaffrey—you got to quit half-wanting and half-not-wanting. Either you want to be a fire fighter and get the girl, or you don't. Don't complicate the obvious. Christ, you remind me of the Cubs." Rimgale lifted his eyebrows. "Happy now?"

"Not quite."

"Yeah?"

"The file cabinet in Seagrave's office."

"What about it?"

"The lock was drilled," Brian said evenly. "Just like the one in your office."

Rimgale snorted, sobered for an instant, then laughed uproariously. "You got spunk. Got to admire it." But he fell silent.

"And then you punched the locks in Holcomb's office— just like two of them had already been."

"You want to advise me of my rights now? Or can we see Swayzak first?"

"I want an answer, Don."

"Well, clown, you're not going to get one," Rimgale said. "I took your sorry ass back on trust. Nothing more than your lousy word and your dull-looking face. Now, you're going to have to trust me." He laughed. "Talk about balls. When in doubt, blame your teammates. You *are* the Cubs."

The street lamps hollowed out grottoes of color in the oaks and elms. Leaf litter had drifted a foot deep in the gutters. Mansions floated past, all of them lit to the hilt against burglary. Except one. It was completely darkened. Rimgale started to park out front, but he suddenly stomped the pedal to the floor, rammed through the wrought iron gates and sped up the long driveway with his headlights off.

"What the—!" Brian cried.

"You cover the front door. Stay outside," Rimgale said with an enforced calm. "I'll go through the back."

"What're you talking about?"

"I think our torch is here."

Brian braced himself against the dash as Rimgale hit

the brakes. A strange cobalt-blue light was flashing strobo-scopically through some thin curtains on the ground floor. "You got a gun?" he asked.

"Somewhere back at the office," Rimgale said.

"Want me to use the radio?"

"Don't you dare. Lake Forest PD would wind up shooting one of us." Rimgale got out and raced around the back.

After a moment, Brian stepped out of the sedan.

It was colder than he recalled. Dead leaves crunched under his shoes. The front door was ajar. He wanted to close it, not really knowing why, but then resisted the urge. He held his breath to listen. Breaking glass from behind the house—that would be Rimgale forcing his entry.

Brian widened his stance, expecting someone at any instant to come barreling out the door.

Should he hit him in the face? Try to trip him? Nothing struck him as being particularly effective.

It seemed like ten minutes since Rimgale had gone around the back. Something was wrong. Something had happened inside.

Brian hesitated, then nudged the door all the way open. A dim corridor awaited him. Should he go back to the car for a flashlight? No. A hiss, an electrical snap, drew him on. He thought it was coming from the room in which Rimgale and he had seen the flickerings.

Yet, the door he expected to open on noise and frenzied blue light gave access to a small anteroom. Semidark. He groped for the latch to a second door, under which the scintillas were still pulsing.

Best to sweep it open at once; he made up his mind.

Light smoke gusted in his face. The flashes were coming from an electrical socket in the far wall. A study or library. Sliced images. Books. A desk. A couch.

The burning receptacle had a magnesium intensity.

Movement brushed the edge of Brian's vision. He thought for a split second that the tall silhouette was Rimgale, but then the man hurtled into him, drove him against the couch, overturning it. Hands closed around Brian's throat. He tried to pry the fingers loose, but the man's grip was too strong. He could smell gas. He craned for a look: the couch had crashed into an unlit space heater, ripping it free from the line.

Grayness began to fill his head. Do something. He clasped the man's chest and rolled with him across the carpet and toward the socket. A scream. And then the smell of burnt flesh.

Brian thought that the man was finished. But then he sprang up, lifting a pry bar. The blow was coming fast. Brian twisted his face to the side, and the crook of iron smashed against his neck. He tried to raise his arm to fend off the second blow, but he was paralyzed, floating, watching his father fly between the balconies.

A locked French door stood between Rimgale and the kitchen. Where were the servants? Swayzak had probably taken them with him to his bivouac at the Ritz Carlton.

Rimgale slipped off his shoe and used the heel to smash out a pane. He reached inside and opened the latch. He rushed toward the point of ignition, the ground-floor room. The first door he came to was to a bedroom. He fished in his coat pocket for his flashlight, swept the beam over the unmade bed.

The first thing he saw was a leg in pajamas sprawled over the bloody bottom sheet. Then on the far side of the bed he saw the rest of Martin Swayzak lying crumpled.

Rimgale knelt.

Swayzak had been struck alongside the head, but he was still breathing. What was he doing in this modest bedroom? Rimgale asked him. Then he smirked. Mother Swayzak, the matriarch of the timber and iron ore empire, who would vote by absentee ballot from Monaco according to the papers, probably had dibs on the master suite. Till death us do part, Mama.

Something had fouled up the torch's plan: cracking skulls wasn't his style. Maybe a red sedan smashing through the front gate had interrupted his fire-setting.

A crash from the adjoining room spun Rimgale around. He pulled on the door, but it resisted slightly. Putty, then, had been pressed into the cracks. He instinctively froze. He didn't want to wind up on the wrong end of a backdraft. This is exactly what the three bean-counters had done. Opened a sticky door.

Yet, the continuing racket on the other side told him that the room had already been ventilated. There had been no blast.

He yanked the door and slipped inside. Natural gas as thick as fog. And a figure crouched over Brian, getting ready to bash his head with a pry bar. Rimgale dived. But he was too late: the bar thudded against Brian's neck.

"You prick!" Rimgale roared, catching the man along the jaw with a glancing blow. He had missed the chance to coldcock him, because of the light. It was coming from the socket in disorienting bursts.

A small flame wormed out of the receptacle, tempted the gas with a slow lick up the wall. Rimgale wrestled out of his coat and beat it out, but the socket went on sparking, hissing. He wheeled to meet the man's next attack, but he was gone, his footfalls pounding down the corridor.

"Run, you son of a bitch! You're not home free yet!" Then Rimgale hefted Brian onto his back and staggered out carrying him. As he ran toward the sweet coolness flowing in through the front door, he saw it: the plan Brian and he had interrupted. The telephone in the study. After the torch had silently finished his set, he would have gone to the nearest pay phone and dialed the number in the study. Groggy, exhausted, Swayzak would have stumbled into the bomb of a room. As insurance, the torch would have rigged the anteroom doors as well, so either way he came into the study the alderman was going to die.

Rimgale eased Brian down onto the leaf-strewn grass.

"Stephen?" he murmured.

"Stay put this time," Rimgale said, then jogged back inside the house.

Gas had drifted most of the way down the corridor.

"This ain't for you, dickhead," he grunted to the yet unconscious Swayzak as he picked him up, balanced him on his back. "This is so I can still get into heaven. After the way I treated my old lady when we were first married."

He dumped Swayzak beside Brian and had taken three strides toward the house again when the door and window openings flashed orange. The brightened sky was filled with broken glass and splinters. Something forceful and hot shoved him backward, knocked him on his buttocks.

He slowly looked down at himself.

A long, jagged splinter was lodged in his shoulder. It had penetrated from front to back.

"You're shitting me," he said.

Carla Rimgale, an overweight but pretty woman in her late forties, insisted on holding the ice pack to Brian's bruised neck. Rimgale's five dark-haired sons kept vigil in silence, with the same distrustful look Don wore most of the time. His daughter, Rosalie, wept now and again, but her mother finally made her stop. And she did. At four, the surgeon talked to Carla in a corner, then took her into Don's room. She came back out a few minutes later, eyes wet, explaining only that he was "doped up and talking about Mike Ditka."

First light finally showed through the waiting room windows, and Brian tossed his half-melted ice pack into the waste can. "I'll be back later this morning."

Carla kissed his cheek. "That's it—get some sleep."

But he didn't return to his apartment. He dropped by the office, collected into a cardboard box all the reports on the backdraft cases, then drove out of the city, southwest along U.S. 55. A stream of commuter headlights glimmered against him. Points of illumination. One no different from the next.

At Joliet, he had to wait until breakfast was finished. Then Ronald Bartel was ushered into the interview room, looking as haunted as ever. "What's this about, McCaffrey?"

"Don Rimgale was hurt last night."

A wince of concern. It seemed genuine. Ronald floated down into his chair. "How bad?"

"Pretty bad. Lost a lot of blood before I came around enough to help him."

Ronald ran his scarred hand through his hair, then suddenly smiled. "He's real now, isn't he?"

"Who?"

"You know—your spark."

"Yes," Brian said somberly. "He's real." He had grappled with him. Smelled his sweat.

"What happened that Shadow got hurt?"

Brian picked the cardboard box up off the floor and slid it across the table to Ronald. "This is everything. Even the stuff that's being withheld from the media."

That unblinking stare. "This isn't a new situation for me," he said nonchalantly. "You all know I've got eyes for the animal. I am the animal . . . sometimes."

"Sure."

Wounded pride. "You don't believe me?"

"Look, I don't know what I believe." Brian glanced away from the stark, hooded eyes. "All I know—he's somewhere in this pile of paper. The bastard who hurt Shadow." And Tim.

"Maybe. Now let me read in peace."

Ronald turned over the last page at 11:06. Then, for the first time, he lit a cigarette.

"Well?" Brian asked.

"Well," Ronald echoed.

"What's the story here? Do you have one for me?"

Ronald leaned back in his chair, hands behind his neck. "Only if you have one for me."

"Don't jerk me around."

"I'm not. Fair's fair. I want something from you."

"What? A kind word at your next probation hearing?"

The eyes turned wistful. "You won't do that. I don't even know if I want you to." Ronald stubbed out his smoke. "I need something for my book."

Oh yes, his great tome about fatal Chicago fires. Not

even close to being finished. Unbegun. But anything to get him to explain that twisted darkness he dwelt in.

Brian put up a screen of calm. "What do you want?"

"To show to the world that nobody's immune to the animal. It gets to everybody. And it's my duty to make this clear. As a writer. Everything's got to be clear." Ronald paused expectantly.

Brian motioned for him to go on.

"Twenty years ago. A straight burn. Just an engine and a truck on the scene. What'd you feel when you first got there?"

Brian shifted his weight in the chair. "I don't know. I was just a kid. I loved it. But it was nothing to those guys. Medium deal."

"What guys?" Ronald asked quietly.

"Adcox, my father." Brian shook his head. "I've forgotten the others in the years since. They retired. Died." He tried not to sound accusatory, then. "What's the fascination here?"

"My father vanished too," Ronald said, dolefully. "Okay," he then broke his own spell, "so Adcox and McCaffrey head up the stairs, get out on the fire escape. Your father jumps across . . ."

Brian saw it with blinding vividness. His coat like a cape. "That's about it." His own voice sounded faraway to him.

"No, it isn't You saw him die."

"Yes, I suppose." Brian realized that he had lost control of the interview. "Let's get back to—"

"Awesome beauty."

Brian felt a chill. "What'd you say?"

"I want to know if there was an awesome beauty to it all."

Brian fell silent.

Ronald grinned. "I thought so. There was something to your father's death that still has you by the throat. You want to make it terrible and ugly inside your head, but that won't stick. It was too thrilling. Too perfect. My guess is that you saw the fire coming, sneaking up on him—and found it too lovely to betray.''

Brian felt as if his chair were hovering a few inches above the floor. ''I loved him. At that moment I loved him more than anything. I wanted to be him. That's what I really remember.'' He scooted the ashtray to the far edge of the table. It stank. ''There. That's my end of the bargain.''

Ronald clucked his tongue. ''Close . . . so very close.'' Then he sat forward again, all business, the perverse dreaminess gone from his face. ''About your torch. Your first question should be—who isn't doing this? Not a pyro. Wrong taste to the whole thing for a spark. And no insurance pro. Where's the profit? Passion or profit. Eliminate them, and you got something to work with.''

''All right. How do I get inside this guy's head?''

''Through his tools. It's the way he talks to the fire. The way he summons it.''

''The plugs?''

Ronald frowned. ''That's a probie answer. You're smarter than that.''

Brian smothered his irritation. ''Trychticholorate.''

Ronald held up a jutting forefinger. Shriveled like a cinnamon stick. ''There you go.''

''There what?''

Ronald looked disappointed. ''I can see why Shadow's blind to this. It leaps off every page, but he refuses to see it. He loves firemen more than his life. But you—I can tell you got a little distance on the subject. Love-hate, you know?'' He began piling the reports back into the box.

Brian wanted to grab him by the collar. ''Goddammit, quit the riddles!''

''Riddles? I don't see how I can be plainer. Who has ready access to trychticholorate?''

''Toxic waste cleanup firms. Rimgale canvassed them all from Springfield to the Wisconsin border. Nothing.''

''He should've started closer. Always start close and work outward. Shadow knows that, but his love blinded him." Ronald paused, smiling. "Now who responds to toxic spills? Who answers that first alarm?"

Brian pulled off the expressway and slept for an hour. He awoke cold and stiff. Snowing lightly. The season of snow again and nothing was better. Worse. The long morning at Joliet came back in flashes, like jabs, punches; he kept seeing Ronald's grisly hands poised around the pages. Brian started the engine and drove the rest of the distance to the slip on the Calumet River. A white dusting lay on the tin roofs, the docks, the rust-streaked boats.

Stephen's trawler looked lifeless, and no footprints broke the snow on the decks or the steps of the ladder.

Leave. The voice urged Brian as he walked toward the dry dock. Florida. Now was the time to leave for Florida.

"Stephen?" He called out at the top of the ladder, although he knew that the cabin was empty. His brother was on duty.

He was prepared to force the latch, but it was unlocked.

The interior was heavy with the smell of stale food and mold. Straightaway he went to the surplus chemicals stacked in the corner. He took a moment to steady his hands, his nerves, before trying to read the labels. Still, the first was a blur of fine print. He rose and tossed back a curtain on the gray afternoon. A lagoon of iron-colored water. A gull was hunched on the top of a piling, its head tucked under its wing. Brian knelt again. Armor All. Brasso. Tox-Away. He held the quart can up into the light. The word sprang out like his own name. Trychticho-lorate. The metal crunched inward under the pressure of his grip.

Then the aft hatch flew open, and Stephen stepped inside, snowflakes dissolving on his station house blues. His eyebrows were raised in mild surprise. "What's the occasion?"

"Veterans Day . . . isn't it?" Brian eased the can to the floor behind him.

"You're no veteran. You didn't even make it beyond

probie." Stephen brushed the melted snow off his shoulders. "Actually, I'm kind of glad you showed up."

"Yeah?" Brian hid a surge of wild joy. Stephen was going to talk finally. Say that he was sorry for Tim. Admit everything else. Brian felt strangely honored.

"You can help me clean up a little," Stephen said. "A guy's coming to look her over in a few minutes, and then I've got to get right back to the station."

Brian looked off through the porthole.

"You mind?" Stephen asked when he said nothing.

"You're selling Dad's boat?"

"Yeah." Stephen tossed a tea towel over the dirty dishes in the sink.

"Lots of memories in this hull."

"Too many memories everywhere. I'm drowning in fucking memories." Then Stephen seized an empty Bud can and hurled it against the bulkhead. He laughed bitterly. "Look at your face."

"What about it?"

"It's going to break, you hate me so bad."

"I don't hate you."

Stephen thought about this a moment, then said, "Whatever I did . . . it was in spite of my feelings. You don't want to know those feelings, but—"

"Maybe I do."

Stephen shook his head adamantly. "People say that. Then you tell them and it doesn't change a thing. Their minds are made up from the beginning. That's what makes it all so . . . useless." He started to run a dry mop over the floor, but then flung it in the corner again. "You didn't like me when you were seven years old. And then me trying to raise you put the icing on the cake. Jesus, you ever think what it was like trying to raise you? Me with a teenage wife and bills up to here?" He touched the flat of his hand to his forehead.

"All the time, Stephen. I don't know how you did it."

Stephen hadn't heard. "Dad and Mom were *gone*. What was I supposed to do? What the hell was I supposed to do!"

"Me too," Brian said. "What was *I* supposed to do? I crept around your house like I was trying to make myself invisible." He tried to smile, but failed. "Maybe I'm still creeping around like that."

"Shit." Stephen had heard. A look of raw guilt. "Is that how you felt?"

"Yes."

"I didn't know. That would've made me feel lousy . . . had I known. I feel lousy right now." Stephen visibly tried to decide what to do with his hands, started to raise one toward Brian, but then tucked them both under his arms. "I . . ." He didn't know how to finish, or to make a new beginning either. His eyes were now glistening.

And this discomfited Brian. Seeing his brother so strangely off-balance, so helpless. "You want to grab something to eat?"

"Like what?"

"I don't know. Pizza?"

"Naw, I don't feel like pizza."

"Something else, then?"

"I'm not hungry," Stephen said. "Besides I got to clean up this dump. Get back to the Seventeen." He thrust his hands into his trouser pockets and began wandering around the galley as if he didn't know where to start tidying up. But Brian knew it was more than that. Speaking would be like tearing a bandage off a fresh wound. Yet, Stephen then blurted, "I was wrong, Brian."

Hope again. Confession. "About what?"

"About you. About stepping in and bringing you to the Seventeen. Wrong from the start."

"Then why'd you do it?"

"I can't say."

"You don't know?"

Stephen's eyes turned guarded. "Can't say."

And then a voice from outside said, "Hello the boat!"

225

· 22 ·

Brian was already rolling when the signal turned green.

He had to beat Stephen back to the station. The Tox-Away can in the boat had not been enough. Trychticholorate in this form was available to every fireman in the city.

The sky was clearing. The two inches of snow on the pavement had been churned by tires into riffles of dirty slush, and a low icy mist seemed to be drugging the pedestrians into stiff, crawling walks.

He flipped on the fire band radio, and the sqawk of mundane station traffic set his teeth on edge. No wonder Rimgale left it off most of the time. He listened for Stephen to come back on the air, to advise Central Dispatch that he was returning to the Seventeen.

Plumber's putty.

He would look for this one more corroborating element. And if he couldn't find any? Then he would give in to his gut feeling that Stephen had not been inside Swayzak's house last night, that he would never try to bash in someone's brains with a pry bar.

A dispatcher called a number.

She repeated it a few minutes later.

Brian finally realized that it was Rimgale's call sign. "Go ahead with your traffic," he said into the mike, raising his voice over the blowing defroster.

The dispatcher gave him a message consisting only of a telephone number.

He acknowledged, but would not return the call. No time. The number was to a private hospital in Highland Park, where Swayzak was recovering from a one-inch laceration above his right ear and a mild concussion. He no doubt wanted reassurance. With the election only days away, he had readily agreed with Brian's suggestion that the cause of the fire that gutted his Tudor castle be put out to the media as accidental, a faulty gas space heater.

Brian had not been worried about the alderman's election chances. Rimgale would have wanted a news blackout in any event. "Publishing the facts of the case in the *Tribune* is like sending your torch a Candy-Gram," he had said.

Brian already missed him. He wasn't sure he was up to what had to be done. The taste of bile kept coming back on him.

He parked in the alley behind the Seventeen and entered the station through the storage room door. He slipped a large screwdriver off the tool bench and walked up the stairs to the locker room. Walked, not rushed. No one was among the lockers, but he could hear water prattling against the tile floor in the shower enclosure.

"You feeling better today, Axe?" Nightengale's voice drifted out to him.

"Yeah," Adcox said with gruff good cheer, "it must've been just one of those twenty-four-hour things. Sorry I missed the union meeting. What finally got done?"

Brian was staring at Stephen's locker without seeing it. Eyes blazing in the crazy light of the socket last night. But then he threw off this memory fragment and jiggled the screwdriver blade into the crack near the combination lock. He pried, and the door gave with a groan.

Everything in a jumble. Once it would have been a

model of obsessive neatness. Socks rolled into tight balls. Toiletries in martial rows on the top shelf. No sign of putty. Brian even opened a jar of Noxema.

"Baby McCaffrey!"

Brian slowly turned.

Adcox was standing at the far end of the aisle, a towel wrapped around his waist. His grin faded when he saw the buckled locker door. Disappointment. "What're you doing?"

Brian kept silent.

Adcox approached, his bare feet slapping wet over the floor. He pinched his lips between his fingers as he inspected the damage. "This is no good," he finally said, dropping his hand. "He's your brother. We're all your brothers." He slammed the door, tried to iron out the buckled metal with a blow from his fist. Another slam. Harder. His towel slipped lower by a few inches, and Brian saw a small rectangular burn in the small of Adcox's back. Fresh. Still seeping.

Brian rocked as if Adcox had shoved him. "Oh, Axe."

Adcox glanced down, then snugged the towel higher again. "You don't know what it's about, Brian."

It felt like breathing with broken ribs. "Axe . . . Axe."

"You just don't know, son."

"I don't?" Brian pulled his coat and shirt collars away from his neck, exposing the purple lump left by the pry bar.

Adcox was whispering, almost wheezing. "I didn't know it was you guys until I ran out front. I saw Don's red car, and I thought I was going to die."

"There wasn't much chance of that." Brian's anger was rising. It was burning off the numbness.

"They killed Teddy," Adcox went on. "They cut stations. And that was just the same as putting a gun to his head." He tried to touch Brian, but he stepped back. "You met Lucy. His kid. Saw how hard it is for all of them. I did it for them too."

A wave of dizziness came over Brian. He fought it with

a deep breath. Adcox's warm, reasonable tone was doing it to him. Making him sick. "You've got to come in. You've got to talk to the cops."

"No cops. They're not family."

Yet, Brian thought he could detect a dim yearning to end all the madness. "Then let's go see Rimgale. He should be coming around by now. We can start with Don."

Adcox shook his head. The same lucent sadness in his eyes as when he had held Lucy in his arms at the kitchen window. "Do you know what would happen if this got public? What Swayzak would do to this department?" His rage suddenly kicked in. "The department! That's all I was ever thinking of!"

Test his sanity. Stretch it. See how he reacts. "You murdered three men. In cold blood."

But then Brian was cheated out of seeing, for the alarm Klaxon went off and Adcox pushed him aside in the rush to his locker.

Brian stared at him a moment longer, the man who had taken his brother and him into his home, who had sobbed at his father's death. He had a ragged, empty feeling. He wanted to sit down on the bench behind him. Instead, he slid down the pole onto the apparatus floor.

Stephen had arrived and was suiting up. A wrinkle appeared between his eyes, but he went on dressing. "I get the feeling you're shadowing me, little brother."

"It's Adcox," he said simply.

Stephen's fingers stopped on the last snap fastener. He started to say something, but Grindle passed between them, chewing insouciantly on a wooden match.

"He damn near got Rimgale and me last night," Brian went on, hushed. "He's killing people."

"I know."

Brian was stunned. "*How* did you know?"

"Bits and pieces. I was getting close. But it all came together when I saw you going through my chemicals this afternoon."

Santos whisked by. "Sounds like a major deal, L.T."

229

"Let's roll," Stephen said.

But Brian grabbed him by the sleeve. "What was the Tox-Away doing there?"

"It strips off old grease like nobody's business. And that's the goddamn truth. Okay?"

Brian followed him out to the engine. "What're you going to do about Adcox?"

"Sure as hell not throw him to the wolves."

"Nothing, you mean," Brian said bitterly.

"I'll handle it. I'm his L.T. He's my responsibility." Stephen climbed into the cab.

Brian felt a tall presence behind him. "It's over, Axe," he said without turning.

"It's over when I know my family's safe." Then he stepped into the riding compartment and sat facing Brian, his eyes no longer warm. They were icy.

Then the engine pulled out of the station. The ladder crew was slower getting their truck under way.

Stephen was wrong. He was trusting that Adcox would listen to him. The man was beyond listening; he was locked into a cycle of killing. And then more killing, if necessary, to cover up. He was no longer Uncle Axe. He was a fanatic, and he had to be stopped. Now.

Brian ran to the equipment racks and pulled a spare set of turnouts off the hooks. He fumbled into the gear, then jumped onto the back step of Truck Forty-six just as it swung out onto the apron.

The driver hurried through the gears.

The cold wind felt like sandpaper on Brian's cheeks. He flipped down his face shield. No night for riding the tailboard. Tim's old place. Guilt made him lower his head. He hadn't gone to that dim cubicle in Intensive Care in nearly a week. Tim had improved to the point of realizing how bad his injuries were, and then withdrawn into silent anger.

Brian crouched, trying to get out of the air stream.

The truck sped north along Ashland Avenue, out of the district. They were going to a multiple-alarm, then. He thought he could see a domed brightness over the south branch of the Chicago River. Near Mason's Canal, maybe. The driver veered off Ashland onto Cermak Road, kept hitting his horn to blat the cars of the curious out of the way, then rocked over the rail lines that flanked the canal.

The brightness was concentrated over a four-story industrial warehouse. Turn-of-the-century construction. Limestone mortar that would soon be weakened by the flames he could see shooting like rocket exhaust from the windows.

Engines were parked everywhere, with more arriving every minute. An entire task force.

He leaped off the tailboard before the driver had come to a complete stop and asked a battalion chief, "Where's the Seventeen?"

"On the roof."

Brian borrowed an air tank and a rubbish hook off a utility truck and ran to the nearest of two aerial ladders that were reaching up to opposite corners of the building. He climbed the rungs, his breath hot and noisy inside his mask.

Smoke soon enveloped him, and he had to climb blindly into the bucket. After a moment, he saw that it was poised over the parapet. He gingerly stepped down onto the roof.

The smoke scudded past, cleared briefly, then closed in around him again. He had seen several ventilation teams spread across the tar-paper flats, some of the men cutting holes with chain saws, others sounding the roof with hooks and axes. It was impossible to read the company logos on helmets in the chaotic light from the aerial spots. It was piercing the smoke in dim, broken shafts.

Brian began working his way toward the center. He didn't give in to the urge to cross diagonally. Instead he kept to the waffle pattern that revealed where the beams and rafters would support the combined weight of his gear and his body. Three hundred pounds. Plywood could burn off in layers, leaving a thin skin of tar paper that only looked solid.

"You seen this?" he asked a captain, pointing out the

flashing around a ventilation pipe. It was six inches higher than the level of the roof, which had sagged by that much.

"Yeah," the officer said, stepping lightly toward the ladder, "have fun."

"Thanks." Brian moved on.

Bayonets of flame suddenly stabbed up through the charred center of the roof, flickering jauntily. The seat of the fire. Most of the men were working right over it. Chain saw engines were killed, and the crews began backing off. The fire would soon ventilate itself—by collapsing the roof.

Yet, two men stayed near the patch of flames, oblivious to it as they faced each other. The number seventeen shone on both helmets.

Brian started toward them, but then stopped dead in his tracks.

The surface now felt spongy, vaguely alive, and here and there the tar paper was blistering. He punched downward with the rubbish hook. As hard as he could. A geyser of smoke fumed up. The whole of the roof was rotten. Honeycomb. "Stephen!" he hollered.

His brother didn't turn. He had pulled off his mask and was shouting something at Adcox.

Brian crept closer and heard Adcox rail, "I did it for you too, Stevie!"

"Did you do it for Tim!"

Brian forgot the roof for a second as his eyes fastened on Stephen, standing toe-to-toe with Adcox, his gloved hands in fists. Then he cried at the top of his lungs, "This mess is falling in!"

Adcox shook his axe for Brian to shut up. "Tim was an accident, Stevie." He was pleading now. "Surely, you see that. Your dad would see that."

"I just see a probie who's crippled for life. I haven't slept since, Axe. I can't sleep!"

"Why'd you have to go in there so early? Always got to be the big man, always got to do it harder than anybody else. Why didn't you listen to me!"

"Because you're crazy!"

Adcox was grinning, a strange distillation of rage and hurt and hopelessness. He was still blustering with his axe, but he suddenly threw a broad left with his free hand. A clumsy swing because of his bulky turnouts.

Stephen ducked, then lunged against Adcox's belly. He drove him all the way back to the parapet.

Brian moved to help Stephen pin the bigger man against the bubbling tar paper, but Adcox jumped up on his knees and butt-stroked Brian across the side of the head with the axe handle. The blow came through his helmet like an electric jolt. He folded over the parapet and waited for the lights below to stop dancing. They steadied into fuzzy blurs. A fireboat was churning around mid-channel, its fly bridge monitors heaving twin plumes of water against the side of the warehouse.

Brian reeled, drunkenly, clumsily, and looked for the two men.

They were clutching each other, rolling down the slope created by the sagging of the roof. Brian made for them, but then a loud crack stopped him. The crack faded into a slow rendering sound that made sense only when a tracery of black fissures began spreading outward from an emerging hole.

Stephen and Adcox let go of each other. They scrambled upright and started running in opposite directions.

The hole was widening, devouring the roof as it grew. A maelstrom that was sucking saws and roof ladders and pike poles into its vortex.

"Run!" Stephen shouted to Brian, then vanished into the smoke.

Brian made it to the parapet again and leaned his chest over it just as the first wave of flame broke against his back. He screamed in pain for a few seconds, then felt no sensation whatsoever. A breathless suspension in heat. Below he could see the foredeck of the fireboat with amazing clarity. Safety. He believed that he could jump and reach it. This is what people felt right before they leaped, he realized with a shock.

Then the roof dropped out from under his boots, and a

second burst of fire was pressing against his back. He clung to the parapet, screaming. A glimpse of iron railing below and to the left caught his eye.

He sidled along the parapet on his stomach, then swung his legs over and let go. Falling. Rising panic as his fall went unbroken. Delirium. He had only imagined a fire escape. He had been tricked. Too late for everything. Except. *Now and at the hour of our death.*

But then his legs slammed against a platform. He tumbled on his side; his helmet smacked against the railing. A ringing like chimes.

He didn't budge for a few seconds, afraid that he was badly hurt.

Finally, he stirred, frisked his dazed limbs for unnatural angles, for warm wetness, and then staggered to his feet.

Heat. Too much. He leaned over the railing and saw why: flame was gushing out of the windows directly below. No escape that way, even though the water streams from the fireboat were beginning to shift toward this new eruption.

The window behind him was locked.

He braced his arms against the sill and kicked, then hunkered tight and braved the shards to crawl inside.

A smoky corridor lay straight ahead, as dark as a catacomb, but to the right was a stainless steel door. He fumbled for a latch. There wasn't one.

He threw his shoulder into the door once, twice, and it staved in a few inches. Again. He got a running start, crashed against the steel with his full weight—and fell through.

His hands flew out to cushion his slam against the concrete landing he expected. But he went on falling through the blackness. Stairs. He expected to hit stairs and glance along them until he could grab something. He went on plummeting. Into a waterfall. Cascading down with him, around him in all its wet heaviness. And then a loud crinkle of bubbles filled his ears. He sank. Water as bitter as lye.

His helmet was already gone, but his air tank was dragging him down. He unhooked it, wrestled out of his coat. Slowly he began to rise. He breached, but when he opened his mouth for a desperate breath—falling water thundered against his face.

He went under again, flailing. His hand brushed something. A greasy cable. He seized it and pulled himself up, clinging to this lifeline as the torrent broke over his bent head.

He quit retching and started taking in air.

A latchless door. Cable. He had broken into a freight elevator shaft. Idiot. And the fireboat was somehow pouring tons of water into its upper end.

He had to slide his grip higher on the cable. The surface was rising, bearing him upward like a cork.

A vermilion sheen suddenly came to the plunging water, and the foam heaped around his shoulders looked like chrome ball bearings.

He squinted upward. The fire had invaded the shaft. He flinched. White-hot specks of plaster were raining down on him, sizzling as they plopped into the water. The specks quickly became fist-sized chunks, and then sheets of the flaming stuff were falling around him, adding billows of steam to the smoke.

He squirmed between the cable and the wall and, shielding his face with his forearm, tried to dodge the collapsing masonry.

Soon bricks would start falling. And that would be the end.

A clang echoed in the confines. He craned upward for a guarded look. A gas main had been struck. A deafening hiss, and then the pressure in the line split apart an elbow joint. Ignition came with a roar. A canopy of flame filled the top of the shaft, a huge broiler.

He had to cool his face in the water.

A door floated past, but he had nothing but his bare hands to wrench it open. He clawed. But no use. No leverage. It slipped away under the turbulent water.

Then he had to dunk his head for a few seconds. More chunks sputtered past. Better to drown, the child voice told him. Duck down and get it over with. A few frantic moments of suffocation, then unconsciousness. Another fifteen feet and the topmost layer of water might begin to boil. He would die with all the dignity of a lobster.

But, instead, he cried for help.

No answer.

He tried to activate his PAL, but the doused alarm refused to yelp.

Then the growing heat and a quick vision of Tim's ruined face made up his mind for him. *Pray for us sinners, now and at the hour of death.* He let go of the cable, let go of the air in his lungs, let go of everything, and was fading down into the depths when he realized that a flash-light beam was probing the water.

He scrambled for the surface again.

Stephen was leaning out of an open door the next floor up. "Can you hang on?" A daunting tone, even now.

Brian nodded.

Yet, three feet above him, the cable was red-hot. He could no longer grip it. An idle thought broke through his exhaustion—What happened to my gloves? He couldn't recall losing them. Maybe dying was like that. My body. Can't recall losing it.

He was treading water but knew he wouldn't be able to keep his mouth above it for long. Any moment he would have to start thrashing. He could feel it coming in his bones, like a racking chill.

"There!" Stephen said triumphantly.

His shout drew Brian's attention to a shut-off valve directly across the shaft from Stephen. A distance of twelve feet with nothing to land on once he got there.

"Not . . . not unless you're a hummingbird," Brian tried to joke, but his voice was lost in the tumult of the water.

Stephen stepped back out of sight.

Did he have a roof ladder with him? Not likely.

Then he burst into view again, leaping across the shaft without his tank and helmet. He slammed against the wall with a sickening thud, but managed to grab the valve lever and hang on until his own weight pulled him off.

But the valve was closed. The jet of flame whooshed out.

Stephen splashed into the water beside Brian. He surfaced, tried to get out of his coat. "Damn," he said, grimacing. "I think I broke my arm."

Brian reached to help him, even though he wasn't sure that he could keep himself from going under.

"Don't," Stephen said, freeing himself of his turnouts at last. "I can make it. Just a few seconds more."

"Don't have . . . few seconds."

"Sure you do."

The firelight was dim now. Brian groped for the cable but couldn't find it. He felt Stephen hold him with his good arm. His powerful legs were churning under the surface.

Then a ledge at the foot of the open door slid down into view. Brian hooked his elbow over it. Stephen's grip went from supporting Brian to clinging to him. His face was now clenched in agony.

Brian started to climb out, but Stephen said, "Just wait. We got half the Chicago River helping us."

He was right. Within seconds they were floating out onto a concrete floor, skidding along on their knees. Brian glommed onto a banister and then anchored Stephen before they were both swept down the cataract of a stairway.

Stephen was cradling his left arm. His look of pain vanished under a burst of anger. "What the hell are you doing here?"

"Adcox. We've got to deal with him tonight."

"No, we don't. He's regrouping. Believe me. He'll listen to me. He'll go easy if I handle him right." Stephen waded down the stairs to the next level. He felt a closed door with the back of his hand, then opened it.

Over Stephen's shoulder, Brian could see hundreds of metal drums. The fire was nibbling away at them one by one, cooking off the volatile chemicals within them. A barrel suddenly rocketed over the stack like a Roman candle, disintegrating into a shower of liquid fire that set off a stack of wooden pallets.

"Out of here—quick!" Stephen cried, pushing Brian along several turnings and then into a cavernous room filled with more drums. "Keep moving!" Still nursing his arm, he skidded around a corner, catching up just as an axe blade flashed out of the shadows.

· 23 ·

The blade missed Brian, but the handle didn't.

He was driven off his feet and landed on his tailbone, hard. His vision was like overexposed film, and his ears were ringing. But he could still breathe. And swallow. His left shoulder had taken the brunt of the blow. He squirmed around on the hot iron platform to make sense of what had happened. He only recalled a glint of red passing in front of his face.

Stephen was rushing forward to drag him away when something made him stumble and fall. He twisted around and looked at his boot, bewildered: the heel had been shaved off by an axe blow.

Adcox was looming over him, his eyes metallic.

"You stupid son of a bitch!" Stephen cried, scrambling to his feet.

Adcox readied the axe, but Stephen caught him on the back swing, tackling him, driving him against the platform railing.

Below the two men Brian could see a confusion of catwalks and palletized fifty-gallon drums, all wrapped in flames. He tried to rise and cross the platform to his brother's side, but his legs were dull and prickly, as if they had fallen asleep.

"Let it go!" Stephen was trying to wrench the axe out of Adcox's grasp with just one hand. His broken arm was limp at his side.

Brian struggled to his knees. "Axe, for chrissake—we're Dennis' kids . . .''

A hard ache pulled Adcox's eyes to the side, remembering maybe. He relaxed his grip on the handle a little, but didn't let go.

"Stephen and Brian. We're Dennis'—"

"I know your fucking names! Don't treat me like a mental case!" The sweaty face convulsed. Loud crumpling echoed up from below: the drums were bulging under pressure. "I could've made everything okay again. Safe. Happy. Brought all the stations back." The eyes were no longer metallic: they were moist, human, as he trained them on Stephen, and he kept blinking as if trying to erase something ugly behind them. Tim's ruined face—Brian was sure of it. "Lights in all the stations again." Adcox turned toward him, crying now under his words. "I just didn't check the cross-traffic, you know? And I got blindsided."

"Let go," Stephen said gently.

Adcox released the axe, and Stephen pitched it over the side. There followed an instant in which Brian believed that the two men were moving to clap their arms around each other, but the image of joining movement was blotted out by an explosion. Vivid orange boiled up and scorched his eyes.

He shielded his face with his forearm, knowing that several drums had gone up at once. The decking beneath his knees began listing, sloping off into the heat, but then stopped with a neck-jarring lurch.

He slowly lowered his arm. The platform had buckled. Beyond a screen of debris tumbling from the ceiling he could see a hand. It was gripping a bent railing strut. Stephen, hanging on. Losing his purchase.

Brian tried to duck through the falling embers, but was driven back. He shifted to the side and saw why Stephen could not hang on much longer: dangling at the end of his broken arm was Adcox. Towering shots of greasy flame had ignited his trouser legs.

Again, Brian tried to pass through the debris. But the bite of coals through his thin shirt made him retreat, shivering from the icy sensation of the small burns.

Stephen was looking down at Adcox. His lips moved. Brian thought he had said: *You go, I go.* Adcox nodded with a smile, even though the flames had crawled up the back of his turnout coat and were singeing his hair.

Then Stephen growled as if he detested himself, and his upper hand slipped off the strut.

Brian hurled himself through the debris to the railing. "Stephen!"

He and Adcox fell with a kind of heavy grace, neither man flailing, neither crying out. But Stephen's chest struck a narrow catwalk halfway to the floor. He quickly seized it, threw a leg over the lip and held fast.

Adcox went on into the flames, a billow of sparks marking where he had vanished.

In the time it took Brian to find a ladder leading down to the catwalk, Stephen's PAL started yelping. His brother hadn't stirred a muscle in over forty-five seconds.

Brian rolled him on his back and Stephen let out a sharp breath as if his lungs had turned to glass. On the grating was a metal shard from one of the shattered drums. He had landed on it, puncturing his side, splintering ribs that now lay exposed.

Brian whipped off his shirt, using it to apply direct pressure to the gaping hole. "Hang on . . . hang on."

"Turn off that fucking PAL," Stephen said, hyperventilating.

Brian flicked off the alarm.

Stephen tried a deep breath, but then froze in pain. His skin was already mottled from low blood pressure, and his pupils were dilated. No matter how firmly Brian pressed, he couldn't quite stanch the flow of bright red

241

arterial blood. He had to get his brother into an ambulance.

Stephen read his mind. "No fireman's carry."

"I've got to—"

"I'll go over . . . if you pack me out."

Across the warehouse a hose team charged through a door, their stream of water exploding into steam. Nightengale and Pengelly, Brian believed. He stood and waved. "Here! Over here!"

Pengelly nodded, and they started toward him. But then a drum went off like a bomb, flattening them. "Christ!" Brian cried. It had either dazed or killed them. All he could see was the hose snaking across the floor, sprinkling the large room without beating down the flames. He wanted to go for it, but Stephen was holding on to his sleeve. "Wait for another hose team. You don't have a chance in there."

"Yes, I do. You know I do." Then, quieter. "Got to shine sometime."

A dim smile that made Brian's heart catch.

Then he ran. Whip the fire so the paramedics could get in with a stretcher, hook him up to an IV as quickly as possible.

Much of the floor in the middle of the room had collapsed, exposing a skeleton of I-beams. His only way across. He could sense the hottest part of the fire lurking below, out of sight, ready to surge up. He chose the coolest-looking beam and stutter-stepped out onto it.

A tongue of flame shot up beside him, whirled in orange and blue skirts, then shrank again.

A signal that the worst was coming.

But the fire was not alive. It was not an enemy. It had not murdered his father. It had taken him, but not murdered him. An obstacle—that is all it was, and it could be overcome.

He stepped off the beam onto a floor that had begun to shudder. The fire was building below. He would not reach the hoseline in time.

He glanced round. A puny fire extinguisher was

242

mounted to a support pole. He ripped it down and tore out the cotter pin.

The flames howled up, bent smoothly like water over the jagged edge of the rent in the floor and cut him off from the hose.

He bashed the neck of the extinguisher against the pole, then heaved the whispering cannister into the heart of the fire. It ruptured into a cloud of powder through which he sprinted, feeling the heat on his face and bare chest as if it were dry ice. He tackled the squirming hose to the floor.

He found his feet at once, braced himself and aimed the stream along the path back to Stephen.

Pengelly stirred, shook himself to alertness, then staggered toward Stephen. Nightengale rose a moment later, and shouted into his radio handset for paramedics to come up.

Everything seemed a hundred yards away. Brian's grimy face tilted over him. The paramedics. The siren thumping on the roof of the ambulance. He was sinking away from this bright chaos.

Stephen squeezed his eyes shut for a few moments.

The sensation of sinking intensified. There was no question in his mind. All he wanted was a few more lucid moments. But it was almost impossible to breathe. The need for air kept shoving aside all other thoughts.

So much to say. Too much. Prioritize. You were always so good at prioritizing. "Brian . . ."

His brother glommed on to his hand. Stephen didn't like the sensation. It was like being pinioned. Restrained. "You . . . you were something else in there . . . you were great . . . the best . . . come home . . . the Seventeen . . . okay?"

Brian was sobbing. He always looked so ridiculous when he cried. Instant transformation back into a little boy. "Fuck the fire, man. Fuck the station."

"Fire never got me . . ." Stephen paused. He really had no idea what had gotten him. Whatever, it had tried to warn him for weeks. Whispered from the sad, dark places within him. Yet, for some reason, he had never quite gotten the message. He had not stumbled onto the thing that might have saved him. He had come close that night with Helen, but then she had asked him to go.

A sudden feeling that his windpipe was being shoved to the side of his neck. He knew at once. Spontaneous pneumo-thorax. Nothing like being too well informed. "Oh shit," one of the paramedics said, "give him some lidocaine *now*."

That meant an erratic reading on the monitor. EKG all over the screen.

Stephen took this in without fear. Too tired for fear. Just that vague urgency to get everything squared away. All the hose rolled. Trucks washed. Supper on the table. And an overpowering sense of loneliness like the sound of rain in the gutters along the station roof.

Sean.

Should he say something? Maybe not. Better left unsaid. It might seem less of a burden that way. More voluntary.

But would Sean grow up creeping around another man's house, trying to make himself invisible? Brian would see that coming. Sympathize. Do something to counter it.

Brian's face was slipping in and out of focus. "About my kid," Stephen said. Each breath stabbed him in the heart now.

"Don't worry . . . don't ever worry about that. I'll be there for him. I will always be there, goddammit."

Brian's grip was still making him uncomfortable, but now he squeezed back.

One more thing to handle. "Axe."

Brian leaned closer. "What?"

"Axe . . . it's over . . . everything." Then he squeezed Brian's hand again, more insistently. "Axe." So much more to it all. Seeing Dad die had done things to Brian. Wounded his spirit. Made him different. Well, Axe had seen him die, too. And then Ted. Damn near had to hospitalize him for depression after Ted. So much to explain. Forgiving and condoning weren't even close to being the

244

same. Don't you see, brother? "Axe . . . give him a place in the memorial case."

Brian didn't look convinced. "I don't know, Stephen."

"Yes, you do," Stephen pleaded. He could hear himself wheezing. "It's over. Nothing more to tell."

Then he felt an ambo bag being fitted over his face. No disappointment. Nothing more to say, really. Now everything was two hundred yards away. And fading still. He tried to hold Brian's eyes for a moment, his mother's eyes, but he couldn't find them. Somebody was shouting that it was time for some Adrenalin. Don't you die . . . don't you die on me, man. Brian's voice, full of anguished love. If only he could answer in the same tone. He had been seeking that tone for so many years. To offer Helen. Three hundred yards. Warmth coming on, all around now, enveloping him. Was it the boosted IV pouring into his veins?

Sean . . .

Far down Michigan Avenue Brian could see two aerial ladders jutting up through the dawn mist, crossing over the thoroughfare like swords. Closer, leading the procession, were the hearses, Stephen's ahead of Adcox's by virtue of rank. And then Engine Seventeen. Schmidt was driving, running the emergency lights but not the siren. The rest of the company, including Brian, walked behind. The street had been sanded after a few inches of snow had fallen during the night. Spit-polished shoes sparkled blackly against the gritty whiteness. No one had slipped, but all strode with care.

Brian's nose was running, but he didn't reach for his handkerchief. It might be misunderstood. He would not cry on this day for Stephen McCaffrey. He already sensed that he had filled a fresh void in the company, and crying would not help him settle into it.

Yet, surprisingly, Grindle was weeping. So had been Helen ever since Brian and the battalion chief broke the news to her. Guilt perhaps. Regret. Maybe that was it: he himself felt no guilt. For the moment, he could only remember his brother leaping across the top of the shaft, his coat spreading behind him like a cape.

He smiled in the dawn chill. With envy that might never fade, after all.

The few pedestrians on the street stopped, doffed their hats, crossed themselves, or just stared with solemn eyes. He was moved. On this, the morning he had expected to resent them, he was touched.

The procession turned west. For the first time, Brian glanced back at the cavalcade of twenty engines, the dark mass of men in blue uniforms, fire fighters from all over the Midwest. Officers even from New York and San Francisco. The brotherhood. He wished that Adcox could see. He would not begrudge him this sight.

At the cemetery, he held Sean against him. He couldn't concentrate on the prayers. Helen and Stephen had bought the two plots years before. She had now donated her plot for Adcox to lie in. Brian had felt betrayed that she, in the end, had made up her mind not to rest beside Stephen. Yet, his emotions of the past week were so jumbled, so contradictory, he kept his disappointment to himself.

Helen was here. She was visibly hurting. That was enough.

Rimgale had shown up against doctor's orders, his arm in a sling to isolate the punctured shoulder. He had insisted on taking a part in the farewell. After taps, he said in a voice slightly weakened by his injury, "In the Chicago Fire Department the alarm code three-three-five signifies that the company has returned home to quarters. We will now ring out that code to welcome home Stephen Dennis McCaffrey and John Charles Adcox . . ." With a small brass hammer he tapped out the code on an old fire bell.

After the last ring, he looked at Brian—questioningly.

Brian just stared back, and after a moment Rimgale melted into the mourners.

Helen was looking at the folded flag in her black gloves as if she didn't quite understand what it meant. She had begun the journey from shock to confusion. She said she was cold. Brian drove Sean and her home. He told Sean about the three Blackhawks tickets he had bought for the following weekend. The boy quietly agreed to go. Helen didn't. Brian kissed his nephew, let go, and then impulsively kissed him again before hugging Helen and leaving for Station Seventeen.

His request for transfer back to the engine company had been approved the day before. A new lieutenant was already dozing in Stephen's room. Dennis McCaffrey's encased helmet was gone. In storage, someone later explained. Brian let it slide. He remembered. That was enough.

He lay on his bunk and waited for the next alarm.

Two weeks later, on a frigid Kelly Days morning, he was at Willie's when Rimgale slid onto the stool beside him. "Give me a coffee, Willie," he said, chafing his hands together. "I need a clear head." Then he turned to Brian and said, without smiling, "How about you, probie? How's your head?"

"Getting better every day."

"Here's to Stevie and Axe." Rimgale hoisted his cup, then took a sip.

After a moment, Brian drank, too.

"You *know,*" Rimgale said accusingly, "you saw the last piece fit into the puzzle."

Brian kept staring into the dusty mirror behind the bar.

"Oh, I got it doped out," Rimgale continued. "Two firemen die in the line. Pass clean as a whistle into legend. Heroes. One of them was boozing it with Pengelly the same night my probie and I went up to Lake Forest. That's ironclad. The other begged off a union meeting because he was sick, but his neighbor saw him drive away from his apartment at nine that night. That's ironclad, too."

"What I saw is all in my report."

"And a doozie, too. You learned a lot from me about keeping the brass in the dark."

Brian swiveled on his stool toward him. "Is this supposed to be pressure?"

"Hell yes."

"Then take your best shot."

Rimgale nodded gravely. "Okay. Stevie died hard. The hardest way I can imagine." He paused. "Tell me it's all square with you."

"It's square." Then Brian buried his face in his glass of beer.

"Bullshit."

"Clear out, Don. I'm not in the mood."

Rimgale smiled. "You don't really know what this is about, do you?"

"Yes, I do. And I'm not budging."

"Take a drive with me?" Rimgale asked. Brian began to shake his head, but Rimgale growled, "Just take a goddamn five-minute drive with me, all right?"

Once they were in the sedan, Rimgale said, "You picked one helluva a time to dump me and go back to an engine."

"It's where I belong for now."

"I agree," Rimgale said, pulling out into traffic. "An arson dick has to ride those years on a tailboard if he wants to be worth a shit. And you got something else to figure out."

"Like what?"

"Like trusting that an old backdraft won't get you if there's nothing left to burn inside."

"You just lost me."

"I just *found* you. And thanks for leaving me short-handed." Rimgale paused. "But you're welcome back to Arson as soon as you get yourself squared away. You got the temperament for it. A little off-kilter, know what I mean? And you trust nobody." He smiled. "Not even me."

"You got that right." But then Brian faced forward and said quietly, "Thanks for opening the car door that day, Don."

"Biggest mistake of my life." Rimgale double-parked in front of city hall and took a large manila envelope from the backseat. "Come on . . . this is what makes it all worthwhile."

Brian followed him up to Martin Swayzak's offices. He looked for Jennifer, but her door was shut.

"Don Rimgale to see Swayzak," he said to the secretary.

"I'm sorry, the mayor-elect is in a press conference right now."

"Perfect." Rimgale did a quick end-run around her and barged into Swayzak's office, which was crowded with news people.

Brian stepped inside just as Swayzak shut up and looked at Rimgale in confusion. A faint pink line under his hair showed where the sutures had been. "Investigator?"

"Morning, Alderman."

The newsmen sensed something coming. Sharks and blood.

"Is there anything . . . ?" Swayzak cut himself off, turned irritable. "I'm a little busy right now."

"This'll only take a minute. This afternoon, two investigators from the attorney general's office will be flying up from Springfield to ask you about this—" He dumped the envelope on the desktop. The scorched FRAMER reports spilled out. "This is just a guess from an old smoke-eater, but I think they're going to want to know why you secretly paid Alan Seagrave, Donald Cosgrove, and Jeffrey Holcomb, your old fishing buddies, to come up with a bogus manpower report that closed seventeen percent of the firehouses in this city. At a time when fire incidents increased by twenty-nine percent."

Swayzak sank into his chair. A quick smattering of flashes, and the cameras had caught him looking old, small, exhausted.

Questions flew at him like stones.

Brian saw that the door to Jennifer's office was ajar. By stepping back he could see a slice of her inside, packing files into a cardboard box. All at once he had no urge to see Swayzak's world disintegrate; it seemed like voyeurism, gloating. He went through Jennifer's door.

She glanced up, her face blank, then began emptying her pencil drawer.

249

"This mean what I think it does?" he asked, gesturing at the boxes.

"Probably."

"I had you covered."

"I know. It wasn't that. My choice."

"You quit just when he made mayor?"

She smiled, but not happily. "Something a friend said got me thinking. Something about a city not being worth his soul."

Brian didn't know what to say. He felt both pleased and guilty. He hesitated, but then said, "I've got three tickets to the Blackhawks game Saturday night. I'm taking Sean. You want to come along?"

"I don't know." A quick, frustrated shake of her head. "I just don't know."

"Understood. You take care." Then he hurried out.

But her voice stopped him in the corridor. "Who're they playing?"

"What?" he asked, puzzled by her smile and wet eyes.

"Who are the Hawks playing?"

It finally happened in May. The klaxon bellowed in the middle of the night—when it was easy to believe that Stephen and Adcox were still in their bunks, and Dennis McCaffrey was flying between the balconies—and Brian came down the pole to find the new probie consumed by the excitement of his first tap-in, flushed with the majesty of the occasion, fumbling to buckle his turnouts and join the measured rush toward Engine Seventeen. The front of his coat was skewed. Brian reached over and gently unsnapped the fasteners. "You're doing it wrong."

"Sorry."

"*Nobody* gets it right the first time . . ." Then Brian laughed. With this sudden, hard-fisted burst of laughter the old dream withered, and his father reached the safety of the far balcony.

He could see it in the wide eyes. The probie thought he was out of his mind.